Born in London in 1962, only 17 years after the end of World War II, the author grew up against a backdrop of 60s and 70s London, from flower power to walking on the moon, punk rock to the IRA bombings, a canvass developed with a sharp eye for 'the human condition'.

'It is not that right and wrong, good and evil, are not considerations; it is only that they remain the purview of humankind alone in all the cosmos.'

To The Fantastic Four: My Legacy Soon Enough

David Jackman

WISE HERMIONE

AUSTIN MACAULEY PUBLISHERS™

LONDON • CAMBRIDGE • NEW YORK • SHARJAH

Copyright © David Jackman 2024

The right of David Jackman to be identified as author of this work has been asserted by the author in accordance with sections 77 and 78 of the Copyright, Designs and Patents Act 1988.

All rights reserved. No part of this publication may be reproduced, stored in a retrieval system, or transmitted in any form or by any means, electronic, mechanical, photocopying, recording, or otherwise, without the prior permission of the publishers.

Any person who commits any unauthorised act in relation to this publication may be liable to criminal prosecution and civil claims for damages.

This is a work of fiction. Names, characters, businesses, places, events, locales, and incidents are either the products of the author's imagination or used in a fictitious manner. Any resemblance to actual persons, living or dead, or actual events is purely coincidental.

A CIP catalogue record for this title is available from the British Library.

ISBN 9781035857005 (Paperback)
ISBN 9781035857029 (ePub e-book)
ISBN 9781035857012 (Audiobook)

www.austinmacauley.com

First Published 2024
Austin Macauley Publishers Ltd®
1 Canada Square
Canary Wharf
London
E14 5AA

1
A Brave Face on a Sorry Business

She awoke to the sound of a blaring horn. A delivery driver, if the coarse language was anything to go by, had opened his mouth and his vehicle's horn, both vying for attention just twenty feet from where she lay. She was curled up under a wealth of rags and blankets, magazines, and cards, all of which had been constructed five hours before to insulate against the biting cold that drifted around endlessly. The woman wiped bleariness from still-tired eyes, and as she did, she noticed a byline on an info paper that had slipped out from under her cardboard construct. 'Too young for your body…' she couldn't see any more of the piece from where she lay, but she harrumphed at it, nevertheless. She didn't have much track with reading these days; in her world, such prosaic pastimes proved of little value. But as she creaked her way up from the foetal position she had woken from, creating a brief storm of paper and weary, many-hued clothes, she wondered at what that lead line might preempt.

'Too young for your body, too tired to care' shot to mind, although, as she shook the night from herself and shuffled sideways over the top of an open drain in order to squat and urinate, she had to admit that she actually felt better than she had done in a while. It was indeed better than she had felt in, well, quite a time now that she came to think about it.

As her bladder performed its functions, she pulled back the grey coat that had obscured the anaemic polypaper data sheet and began to read.

"Too young for your body? Come and join us at Agetec. We are the people that will help you take on a new lease on your life's dreams." And then, a line further down, "Agetec, committed to making you young again."

She noticed that the company named was based in one of the twelve burbs, and that in turn itched at some distant faded memory, one that sat primly, just out of reach. She threw down the newspaper in renewed disgust and, half-rising, pushed out of her board and cloth palace, as ready as she would ever be to face the toil of another day.

It was indeed a delivery driver who had been making the din; his waggon was idling not two dozen feet from her, the driver now down from his loftier perch and arguing vehemently with an unseen character who, at least from her vantage point, had blocked him and his waggon into the same side access way that she currently occupied as home. She was about to lay into them both, pointing out with a few choice expletives that perhaps he might want to think a little about waking poor souls before the first bird had sung, but something inside made her stop short. Perhaps it was because there weren't any birds. Well, of course everyone knew that; perhaps it was just because she was feeling somewhat chipper. She couldn't really be certain, but whatever the reason, she opted instead to just pull down the flap across her cardboard home, in a kind of closing the house way and set off in the opposite direction.

Her name had been Hermione once, Hermione Zatapec, and then, for a time, Hermione Wise. But she hadn't been wise, had she? She thought to herself. Mind you, she considered that it had all been a terribly long time ago. These days she did not need to answer to names at all, because in the brave new world down below, well, the few people left in that world that might ever address her had little if any use for such a name. She considered. Soup kitchen attendants had tried occasionally, she thought; maybe the grunts in security had managed a dig or two once also; but it all seemed vague, all so long ago. Truth be told, Hermione had decided her world would run best if she just kept moving. If she really tried, then she remembered yesterday and the day before. Well, she thought that she did. The day before that? Well, it all became much of the same, and when you're battling to just keep moving forward, well, why bother? Cold, walking, and grabbing at sustenance when fate allowed, she was vague on much more than that. She felt herself vulnerable staying in any one place for too long, lost among the invisible folk who didn't see her around for enough time to make any badge as colourful as a name stick that was best.

She was indigent—the shuffling old lady who spoke agitatedly to herself when she became frightened. She was the woman who carried a large battered brown case, like its owner, one that had seen many better days.

The case was one of a kind, once popular with life teachers and specialist educators who brought the few young squadron brats through to adolescence back upstairs in the burbs. Her dark tan leather-battered case, whatever its origin, was nevertheless clutched tightly to her chest, and it never left her side. It bulged, packed, it seemed, to burst with items likely of use to no one, and it must have weighed five kilos or more.

Hermione wore what appeared, from a distance, to be a miasma of cloth, layer upon layer of clothes, garments of every conceivable type. Often, she would be seen in ill-matching shoes, and to any watcher, she would immediately have been categorised as 'tramp' or 'vagrant', and in truth she was both of these things. She believed her life had been in the cold of down below for many a year, although in truth, she had no clear idea of the passing of those years. She had no place to call home beyond the three little pigs' house of straw she was at that moment walking away from; had neither material means nor ID of any kind, excepting only one credit chip inscribed with the uninspiring words, 'Enter this way up'.

She walked her way across the length and breadth of the icy cold down below, treading a path that ran under the radar of almost all the other sixty thousand or so souls she shared the vast expanse of The Behemoth with.

But in truth, Hermione was not as straightforward to categorise as all that, had she known. Should you be brought close to her, perhaps by some curious twist of fate, you might notice that, despite being of advanced years, she still had a mouth filled with her own teeth—a singularly unusual occurrence amongst the truly indigent.

You might also note, whilst standing close to her, that the usual pungent odour associated with the great unwashed appeared to have passed her by. Remarkably, upon closer inspection, it would have been your assessment of the multiple layers that she wore. Old, certainly; faded, probably; but under the outermost coat and shawl, you might be surprised to find that Hermione Zatapec was personally clean, and her clothes were equally well laundered. Her nails, whilst broken in places, were clipped, not bitten.

Upon closer inspection, it might conceivably seep into your mind that perhaps this was a more resourceful person than you had first thought to encounter. And if you took the time and remained interested after that first engagement, perhaps you might begin to ask why such a person inhabited the world she most certainly did.

And if you kept on watching, you would perhaps reach the conclusion that a woman that resourceful, that diligent to their personal care and hygiene, that much of a survivor in the deep dark, where life's judgements were at their most harsh, was outside of the bosom of squadron society's loop.

Well, such a person had to have no small amount of determination and sit squarely alongside a damn good reason for being in that forbidding world. And most times in that type of situation, a good reason, well, that equated to one thing and one thing only. A secret…

2
Maybe and Somehow Won't Make Tomorrow Good

"Four hundred and forty million. Do you have any concept of how much resource that is?" The man speaking was tall, imposing in a more than physical way; he strode confidently around the twelve-by-twelve windowless office.

"I'll tell you how much it is, shall I?" he said, continuing without, it seemed, really expecting a reply.

"It's enough to get people killed. For Christ's sake, we're called Agetec; we've spent nearly half a billion resource credits on what? Twenty-thirty days, and what have we got to show for it, Lyle? No, well, I'll tell you; we've got squat, nothing, zilch, we've got a resource credit black hole you could lose a solar system in, and the project appears to be making no headway whatsoever. You do know that resources are finite?"

The room's other occupant was also a man, but very different; wiry, with unkempt russet-red hair and black taped spectacles over tired mid-fifties features, he was sitting behind an equally weary-looking desk. The man looked up.

"Well, we have completed the DNA mapping. A computer model with over twenty-two billion entry codes isn't chicken feed, Mister Symonds."

The smaller man looked expectantly at the other, who strode around the small space like some caged big cat. Sigmund Symonds was executive CEO at Agetec, which in pedestrian parlance equated to Behemoth's enforcer, the man who got things done…by whatever means. And so, as the other ceased to speak, the bigger man stopped moving and, glaring, suddenly shouted.

"Don't you get it? We have overseers watching us; we have shareholders waiting on us." He took a sharp breath. "My gods, we even have a damn dungeon godfather backing us with off-the-book credit. And d'you know what? We aren't in the business of mapping the fucking human gene. Agetec. Age technology;

get people feeling younger by making them younger, that's the promise. It never was 'give us half a billion in resources and we'll piss it up the wall, drawing a fucking map'." He paused. "Of people's insides," he continued incredulously. "A map, by the way, that team IV Salacious finished last month anyway. It's not gonna cut it, Lyle; you made me a padlock promise. You said you'd get this done."

The big man fairly throbbed with righteous indignation and glowered at the room's other occupant, who, despite all that, remained relatively sanguine, even under the enforcer's hostile attack.

"I understand what you're telling me, Mister Symonds, and I have said many times before that we will get there." His voice sounded scratchy and unconvincing.

"But this kind of science doesn't work to a time clock or to a budget. We were close, what, eight…ten thirties back, but we lost it; we seem to have turned down a cul-de-sac since…well, since, you know."

The small man in turn paused, seeming to choose his words carefully and his tone with a similar gentle wariness.

"We're playing God here," he smiled and then added, "And when you mess with the big man" he broke off and paused, "well, dead ends happen."

Then the red-headed man trailed off, and both men looked at one another for a long time without another word being spoken.

Eventually, after a few minutes had passed, the bigger man chimed in again, seemingly marginally calmer. "Lyle, I know all about what you say, but listen, what can I do? I've got to make this move, and it's a bit lively," he leaned forward onto the smaller man's desk. "The natives are restless, and I've got to give them something." He paused then, and a perfectly stage-managed wintry smile crossed his features. "And believe it or not, I don't want it to be in your head. So, give me something."

The smaller man stood and briskly walked around the worn desk. He was six, maybe even eight inches shorter than Symonds, and he carried his narrow shoulders and bony frame awkwardly. He knew that they were closer to a result than he had let on to the room's other occupant; in fact, they were exponentially closer to engineering an age-reversing gene compound than he had let on to anyone, barring Ellie and Joshua, his two closest aides, and even they knew some as opposed to all. But was he ready to give Symonds anything yet, even the tiniest chink of light?

He didn't think he was.

And though Lyle Cardington was first and foremost a scientist, pretty much since the day he was born, it was also an absolute that, like a good many of his companions on the never-ending road of intrepid discovery, he was a dreamer, too. He held on to a few images of personal glory, perhaps some small recognition from his peers. He understood that as he hoped to find that one thing—that science with which he might forever change the landscape of humankind—well, at least this little corner of humanity…and for his hopes to succeed, timing would be everything; he was certain of that.

Let others play the politico merry-go-round. Lyle Cardington preferred to avoid that particular shark pool.

Symonds spun on his heels and left the room, with the door swinging loudly shut behind him. He had delivered his message; he saw fear and doubt in the other's eyes. FOG, as he liked to remind himself: fear, obligation, and guilt; and so he moved away like a tiger shark in the shallows, off now searching for the day's next prey. Cardington understood that he and his team had it all to do if they were not to finish the next thirty down below, but at least he had managed to hold himself.

He understood, at an instinctive level, that if he had let his guard down and allowed Symonds even the tiniest insight into where the testing was really at, then at that moment his own project would effectively be over. They would have herded in like bull elephants, shoving and pushing him and his small team aside, to be forgotten in seconds; but worse than that, the project would have been taken over by achievement-driven egoists, and the science would go bad.

Science always went bad when the core values were timescale and cost; humanity had not reached for the stars in the twenty-first century by worrying about how long each step took and how much each step cost.

Necessity truly had been the mother of invention, and so whilst Lyle Cardington understood that sixty thousand people needed Agetec to come up with the goods to deliver on their loudly proclaimed promise, he also believed that only he and his small coterie might bring the result they needed.

"They must leave us be," he mumbled to himself, still gazing at the door he envisioned rattling in its frame.

He waited maybe a minute, then he, too, left the small twelve-by-twelve space through that same door; but before he did, he leaned over the grey rectangular furnishing, and as he twisted the auto-lock to secure the desk drawer, he caught momentary sight of the vial of turquoise blue tucked to the back of the single drawer, and so that had remained just outside of the other man's eye line as he had strode around, declaring his piece. Cardington smiled grimly and pushed the drawer closed, twisting the securing knob in one movement. The heat was most assuredly on, but whilst he had that vial hidden in his desk, he thought that they might be in with a shout. It had worked, hadn't it? They had done some bad things in the name of science him, Jojo, and Ellie, but the bigger picture was…well, bigger, really big, and sometimes pilots died testing planes, didn't they?

But it worked, he thought to himself, for a moment at least.

Lyle left the office and walked down myriad corridors, each one of them the same, a mixture of hard grey rock and vague off-white plastique lit unevenly like a miners' tunnel but with the tiniest 'twinge' of green within that gangrenous lighting. He hated that green: it got under your skin, and once it had hold of you, you remembered it, felt it, and were repulsed by it every single time you walked under the same limpid pale glow. No windows adorned the corridors, and each one of them had an exact replica pattern that consisted of three doors, uniform and uniformly cold, he thought. One exit door connecting to the next length of the corridor, one entry point, and one additional door equidistant from each of the others, each of these with a four-digit number sprayed onto the door's surface.

After maybe a dozen such corridors, all of which appeared to go nowhere in particular, Cardington stepped through a door the same as all that had gone before and arrived at a new space. A wider area than the previous corridors, this place was higher, longer, and darker. At first, it appeared that the new space was even less well lit, but after a few moments of acclimatisation, Lyle Cardington fixed his eyes on the windows, which were small and spherical, like the magnified base of old-time Coca-Cola bottles. Four of them were spaced evenly along the hallway's forty-foot length. Cardington smiled again, this time without the grimace attached to his earlier effort, and he began to walk directly towards the closest of the four windows.

As he walked, he reached into his pocket and pulled out a small packet from within. He grabbed at it and, after a second, extracted a three-inch cancer stick, stuck it between his teeth, and sparked a non-flaming match. Inhaling deeply, he arrived at the closest of the three-foot spherical windows, where he leaned onto the sill and looked out. The stars beyond were cold, stark, and yet deeply beautiful, a stunning panoply that lit the darkness of eternity with the promise of life. Cardington felt the full rush of fear and thrill mixed, and in that moment of ecstatic outlook, he understood with a razor-sharp focus that time had run away from him. He felt shame as he inhaled the cigarette—shame that he had not yet found the answer for his daughter. Hiding here, smoking, whilst she lay in the pall of the cancerous cells that leeched her young life from her.

Cardington wanted, more than anything, to find a way to take mutated cells and persuade them of normality. But he was honest with himself; he wanted to be the prime scientist, the great founder of a new scientific dawn, a dynasty, no less, but not for the power nor the glory that such might bring, nor for material reward, such as was left in this final cave of humankind, nor even fawning vanity.

He stood and looked out at the stars inching their way minutely across the inky black void, and truly he understood that without cracking the code that managed the process of ageing in those people on board, ultimately sixty thousand souls would perish in vain, having undertaken what might yet prove to be perhaps humanity's greatest folly, and his beautiful daughter Muriel would be simply amongst the first.

As he stood staring out, he felt released, albeit briefly, from the crushing responsibility that was pressing upon his narrow shoulders.

Floating on the still air of the high-ceilinged space came the sound of organ music. Lyle Cardington recognised the sound as being synonymous with the bowling alley. Old organ notes, deep and sonorous, tunes unnamed repeated in a loop, reminiscent of some ancient end-of-the-pier entertainment from a couple of hundred years before. He liked the tunes, although he could not have named even one of them. He came down here often at the end of his shift, especially when he felt the pressure building on him. He listened to the vague strains of computer-generated organ tunes, simple melodies interspersed with laughter, and the irregular clatter of heavy balls on skittles.

It appears a strange contradiction that you could walk a few hundred metres and be transported from hi-tech science to a bohemian indoor sports arena and have that all accompanied by twee keyboard lullabies. Lyle considered that the recent visit to his office from Sigmund Symonds (Cardington remembered how he always lost the final 's' somewhere in translation) was almost as filled with contradiction as the strange geography of this world he found himself inhabiting. He understood that Symonds had come specifically to apply pressure. Undoubtedly, one of The Eight had in turn applied pressure on Symonds, and

Lyle had no doubt that would not have been in any way pleasant; it had been ever thus in both the military and corporate worlds that most of the people around Cardington hailed from. But, he reflected, Sigmund Symonds, for all the bluster and menace that mixed up to make him such a successful achiever, was nevertheless intelligent enough to understand that this kind of esoteric *wish for* science could not be bullied to a successful conclusion.

During their tenure together, the two men had been party to a variety of misdeeds and misdemeanours that began with lying, moved through kidnapping, and covered many areas of moral turpitude along the way. He had been able to justify this all thus far on two fronts. Firstly because, of course, it was all in the name of science, and despite this being science on the hoof, it was no less necessary or profound for that. The second thing that had given him security, to that point at least, was the belief that Symonds had his back. The tacit understanding that they were in this together had seemed, at times, to have Lyle's approval enough.

So it was that the recently completed visit had been, to him at least, like the opening of a pair of curtains onto a long-since dark and musty room. Cardington now saw that his assumptions had been but a part of the clever deception that was at the heart of the 'getting it done' style of CEO Approver Sigmund Symonds. He suddenly understood that beneath the veil of a hand around the shoulders and nudge-nudge-wink, his co-conspirator was no longer his backstop and never really had been. He was glad now that he had kept his counsel when, six months before, he first thought that he might have broken the elusive code, when the reversion therapy appeared to have succeeded, at least for those few hours. It would have been the easiest thing in the world—completely natural, in fact—to have picked up the communicator and buzzed Symonds and asked him to come downstairs when the first instant of success appeared to beckon. He would have basked in his colleague's admiration, finally a morsel of acknowledgement of his budding genius.

Not in an egotistical way, just the shared joy of achieving the bar—a bar set at an exceptional height. And even later, when the genetic code appeared to have reverted to a dormant state, the astonishing leap forward would have guaranteed him—both of them, in fact—a place in the spotlight. But once more he acknowledged that he wasn't that kind of man; instead, he had sat and stared at the small vial of turquoise blue that harboured a reworked human and nematode genetic string in a balm of life-preserving gel. It did not work, did it? He understood quickly that the experiment really had been a failure. His results exhibited properties for a time that even resembled the act of multidirectional ageing, but a half-life of 2.77 cycles, about two and a half hours in old money, whilst mega-long in nuclear or indeed even atomic terms, in genetic terms, 2.77 was, quite frankly, a joke. He held onto the vial nonetheless, like the kid at school who makes a poor man's pencil case in woodwork class (the joke of the class, if truth be told), but his best effort was so treasured in spite of its failure to impress. The boy would hold onto the imperfect result without any certainty as to why at the time. Cardington had done the same, and by telling no one, he had made it his secret.

Declaring the result a complete negative, like all those that had gone before, he had told not even his laboratory colleagues. Now, as the pressure began to rise and threaten his placid procession through the avenues of gene research, he wondered whether even an ugly and poorly made pencil case might prove valuable, and the answer came to him that perhaps it would.

At least it would if a lot of pencils could find no other way to get to where they needed to go, he told himself.

3
The Morning Is Wiser Than the Evening

Hermione found herself an hour later in a diner. It was vaguely warmer than it had been in the communal area down below. She checked her hand and knew full well what she would see. The old lady had credit for noodles and water and nothing more besides. She could not be certain when the next opportunity for credit would come. She just seemed to have lost track when it came to such minor irritants as sustenance and survival; she guessed it was old age, but the lady felt certain credit wouldn't be arriving any time soon. A thought (well, more alike to a memory, really) of a different woman, manoeuvring tracts of wealth and power, a player of games that ensured she was given what she wanted, whether earned or not. In that moment in her mind, she saw herself, a different self, but her for certain, and yet, as is the way of the drifting mind, that self was also some other woman. Something corporeal, shifting, and dangerous existed in cold blood without, it seemed, compassion or empathy; to Hermione, that other seemed like nothing more than a vampire, a phantom of the night sent to prey on the weak. The old lady shuddered visibly.

Some moments passed, and Hermione came back to the present. It was just past shift changeover, and there were no more than half a dozen patrons sitting around the tired interior of the eatery. She looked about and carefully spotted the right place to park herself, and by right, of course, she meant safest, so the voice of her mind helpfully chimed in. She saw nobody who seemed especially threatening, but then, how could you tell? She thought darkly. The old lady then proceeded to pick a booth in the dimmest corner of that darkly lit place and sat heavily down on the creaking red vinyl of the bench. She had ended up somewhat across from a man and a boy, a father and son; she was short to learn. The weary, poorly dressed lady hitched her battered case up onto the table and keyed the digital menu. She was surprised to find it working and so quickly proceeded to order noodles and a litre of water; that was her limit, and it was also the cheapest combination. Part of the problem with feeling chipper, as she undoubtedly had upon waking earlier that cycle, was that she was damn hungry.

Worse still, she was thirstier than she remembered being at that age. One of the many issues with living on the *Leviathan* was that everything was rationed, and the likes of her did not appear on any ration list. The machine bleeped and burped and took the last of the credits on her chit in payment. Moments later, that same bleeping icon for ancient technology issued a three-digit code, closely followed by a ten-minute wait instruction, both appearing in flickering blue on a small plasma screen. Hermione turned away from the screen, and, as she did, she noted with distaste that it was dirt-encrusted and covered in dust. The ancient excrement of a thousand previous food orders crusted around the rim. "Fast food!" she exclaimed, shaking her head and mumbling quietly to herself. Hermione looked carefully round the room's interior, secure in her corner booth, but ever watchful.

Hermione Zatapec, sometime Wise, was no longer young, and whilst she had nothing of obvious value about her person, a predator generally didn't ask about your viability as a victim first, and her world had seemed full of predators. This was another lesson the old lady had learned along the way, though at that moment she couldn't quite remember where or when she had encountered that exact tender treasure. Some people lost their minds first and some of their bodies, she figured, then considered it damn frustrating that she appeared to be losing her grip on them both.

Hermione looked again at the man and boy, and a moment later she tuned in, satisfied that her passive radar was on the lookout for anything beyond the safe zone of her booth. The older man appeared to her to be perhaps sixty. "Well, that ain't so old, honey," her mind's voice spoke up. Although it was notoriously difficult to assess age in that environment, the ninety-one percent gravity, the recycled air, the lack of real sunlight, and a million other factors were either unaddressed or unthought of, or, worst of all, unable to be replicated. This had all led inexorably towards a kind of gentle physical slide for all the passengers on board that immense rocky liner. Rodin would have enjoyed sculpting their minds, certainly more than the physical prowess of even the most assiduous exerciser. And, of course, the vast majority of people who carried on the rock were now in their middling years.

They had been travelling towards their own old age pensioner's demise, contained for more than twenty years now, aboard *Leviathan*. Nonetheless, this particular individual, well, did not look in optimum health—a middle-aged man made old by something quite debilitating, Hermione thought. He was a big man, probably six feet and two inches or even six-three if he had been standing upright, and that, too, was unusual in Hermione's experience of that place. But as she looked again, only a little surreptitiously, she considered that he did look remarkably unwell. The man had grey, slightly receding fuzzy hair surrounding equally grey features; he appeared gaunt and unshaven for at least several days. A South American shade to his skin and the colour of his eyes, if she had to put a bet on it, but skin fading from grey towards a pale sickly yellow.

The man wore a Navy squadron shirt, and it, too, had seen better days and, furthermore, was buttoned improperly. And Hermione noticed, too, that this man was sweating copiously in spite of the chilly environment. The other occupant sat across from the sickly man in the same booth. He was an adolescent boy of no more than twelve or thirteen years. The boy looked like all the other grunts around the place: pale and skinny; short, yet in a slightly elongated way. It was like someone had taken a small boy, and instead of waiting and letting him grow naturally, they had chosen to stretch the boy out over his undernourished frame. Somehow, this was how everything grew in this place, plant, and mammals alike.

The child had a shock of unruly black hair sitting big over piercing blue eyes and was dressed in a vaguely brown overall, clean enough to be presentable but also that had seen better days. He was looking earnestly at the older man, who continued a tired-sounding monologue, all watched casually by the invisible old lady from her booth. She tuned in to what the man was saying, carefully keeping her eyes downcast, apparently preoccupied with the lock on the battered brown case that sat in her lap.

"And in case you don't, then you must remind the marshal of his promise to protect you. He is a great man, and he has many things to concern him, Remus, but he has given his word, and he won't let you down, all right?" the old man paused, and Hermione found herself listening more intently at the mention of the marshal. The squadron marshal was an individual with huge authority, she knew. It was rare that even a mention of such a revered person took place in down below.

The man continued, "You know that I love you, Remus. Whatever happens, you must keep your faith. I can't stay with you forever, you know that, but if you have faith, I'll be close by. I'll be watching out for you…" The man's words stumbled, and then, choking slightly, he quickly continued, "Watching over you."

The older man spoke quietly but with an earnestness, a tone that spoke to Hermione of meaning strung with the care of a loving parent, and his pain was etched into each of the words he uttered. She glanced upwards for just a moment and saw that the man's eyes were, in fact, wet with tears.

"Don't cry, dada," the boy suddenly blurted, offering instant confirmation as to the relationship between them both.

"Tell me you're not going away. I'm a good boy, aren't I? Promise you won't leave me in the barracks, dada?" the boy implored, wailing at his sick father.

"They won't like me there," the boy's voice hitched between his own tears, now freely flowing. "I am so small and unimportant, dada, and the marshal he hasn't got time for the likes of me." The boy stared imploringly, desperately, back at his father, who in turn just seemed to crumple further into himself under his son's desert-bright gaze. Sweat was beading above the older man's brow line, and his hair appeared lank with the damp heat of fever.

"Listen to me, son; I don't have the answers. I'm sorry. But you're going to have to stay in the barracks. I can't be certain, don't you see? I can't be certain of…" he paused, really struggling to push the words out, it seemed. "I can't be certain of myself anymore. Promise me you'll have faith, and I promise you that when I go, I'll wait for you…" Another pause. "When I get to the other side."

The boy looked confused. He was grasping at his father's words but had clearly not fully understood the meaning within them just yet.

Hermione understood. The older man was, in fact, trying to prepare his son for a life after dad. She wondered where or if there was a mother; a distant echo rang in her own mind, and she instantly pushed it back down with an utterly unstoppable NO.

Single-parented rants are rare, but not completely unusual—not even around down below. But it was much more common to find that a one-parent combination involved a mother rather than a father. She hoped the boy had a mother out there still, but yet, as she continued analysing the older man's words, she doubted that was the case. The digital interface at her table bleeped twice, and Hermione's thoughts and overhearing were interrupted by a quiet sound affirming that her order was ready. She rose a little awkwardly, and, looking all around the place once more, she moved as swiftly as she was able towards the galley counter. Once there, she picked up a salmon-pink plastic bowl of steaming anaemic-looking noodles and sat upon a numbered dispensing tray alongside a plastic carafe of clear cold water, an exact two-litre measure she was absolutely certain of. She looked around for chopsticks and spotted an additional dispensing counter a little further past the servery hatch. An opening that was closed but emitted quiet rhythmic thumps thoned off at offered some small clues as to the musical preferences of one of at least the kitchen's occupants completing the restaurant space. No napkins, Hermione thought to herself; there were never any napkins these days. She reflected a little moodily.

She trudged back to her booth, placing the noodles and water carefully on the clean but worn plastic tabletop. This, in turn, freed her arms and so allowed her to put the battered brown case she had carried with her even to the food servery down onto the bench. Hermione tucked it up tight into the corner between her and the wall, and, catching the grey man's eyes, she nodded briefly as she sat back down. The man nodded in response and smiled a little winsomely back at her, just for an instant. It was an inconsequential thing, but as if some small understanding had passed between them.

She guessed it must have been the food and water. She had left the food station an hour before, depositing a small Lutheran Bible on the table where the older man had been preparing his son for a life without him. Death, the old lady considered, must have been an increasingly common occurrence within the confines of their small and ageing community. She had listened without making it obvious, as the older member of the family had struggled and sputtered in an effort to say both 'sorry for leaving' and 'have faith'. She had seen in both of their eyes the pain of separation that was to come.

Then, after some moments, the boy stood suddenly and walked away from his father, his own terrible bright eyes full of the fear and blame that losing a parent brings to one so young. After another moment, the father stood and followed quickly after his son.

Hermione had not been certain at first whether they would one or both return; until that was, she had spied a watch sat upon the side of the table where the boy had been sitting. It was a man's watch, obviously, and she understood immediately that this had been something that would become a symbol—something passed over, something handed on from father to son as a bind, a tie across the utterly impossible chasm that was about to open between them. It was a Russian Squadron watch, and so it went some way towards offering insight as to the man's origins aboard the great craft.

The old lady could not help with 'sorry', nobody could help with that, but she thought that she might have something, some small thing, to help the boy find his faith as he took those first foal-like shaking steps towards his own manhood. Looking around quickly in order to ascertain that nobody was watching, Hermione opened the small locking clip on one side of her battered carry-all. She lifted the connected leather flap clear and opened the bag six inches or so in order to reach inside. Without apparently fishing around at all, and with a deft hand, she pulled out a small, deep, red leather-bound book.

Gold leaf adorned the page edges and the book, whilst no larger than the old woman's palm, waxed deep red softly in the room's dim lights. Snatching at the end of the noodles, Hermione rose quickly, and without, it seemed, additional movement, slid the book stealthily under the watch, still sat upon the table. She left immediately, quickly, attracting no attention from either the two security officers patrolling the thoroughfare outside or the single lonely soul wandering about, apparently aimlessly and somewhat worse for wear.

Hermione had hoped that perhaps her gift might be a good thing. She had no use for religion; it had played a singularly disappointing part in her own life, or at least that was the feeling that scratched at her. But the book had been imprinted on a fine gold leaf with a minute script that said, 'Old Testament', and, on one single line below, three words: 'Lutheran Holy Bible'. Hermione had no idea what a Lutheran was or was not. But she knew about the Holy Bible, and instinct told her that the boy would need something to hold on to in the darkest moments of the months, years even that stretched out now in front of him. Those Old-Testament tales—were they not simply the distilled wisdom of humanity, told, and told again, timelessly down the years? Till, in the end, whether Adam and Eve, Cain and Abel, Moses, or the Tower of Babel, each served simply as a teacher and taught, lessoned, and learned.

The boy would return to the table, at least in order to recover the watch his father had given him. And there he would find, by some unexplained twist of fate, a book. Not just any book, either, but one chock full of tub-thumping fables and faith by the bucket-load.

And the old lady that had left it there, a person all but invisible to those around her, well, she, it seemed, had understood that years before, when the book had come into her possession, its future worth to another was already written.

And though she had wondered much during her wandering about the altruism unlooked for and given unreciprocated, she hoped that at a universal level it was another grain on the scale of goodness. Like Moses's Ten Commandments scribed into tablets of stone, a guidebook for a boy writ in another time, perhaps by another kind of people than those that lived in these latter days. She laughed fleetingly at that as she stepped away from the food station, thinking again about how fine she felt.

It most certainly must have been the noodles, she thought to herself, once more heading deeper into the cold heart of down below. That was her place—the realm she called home. As she walked, she found herself wondering at the strange contradiction between her good feelings and the tragedy she had seen unravelling so near her, querying whether her gesture was an attempt at empathy or, conversely, the actions of her ego, still believing it knew better. She wandered away, thinking deeply about the conundrum of limitation.

4
All Cats Are Grey in the Dark

"Attack, attack! Why won't you damn well attack?" The voice crackled harshly and deeply, even when reproduced electronically, and the speaker sounded mighty pissed. The marines began to sidle forward, stepping from cover to cover, in truth without much apparent enthusiasm or energy. The terrain was highly colourful, with a cloudless purple sky almost luminescent in its brightness yet lit by no sun that was visible to any watcher. There were a variety of lines and angles that suggested a cluster of buildings sitting upon the dusty grey ground, but they were nothing like the concrete, brick, plaster, or terracotta structures that the watching marshal Major-General would have thought of as a town. Sixteen squaddies were spread out unevenly, for the most part hidden amongst the yellow- and red-hued shapes that were more akin to a kiddie's set of building blocks made gigantic than a huddle of more traditional structures. The marshal was about to bellow down at the marines again, but then he suddenly exhaled; he seemed to kind of deflate visibly as he wondered himself whether it was really all worth it.

He understood the reluctance of his men. Christ, they had been doing this same drill countless times, many of them for more than two decades, and what for? Even the marshal had to admit to himself that it was difficult to keep the motivation high; all this to police a few drunks and vagrants. To even the most disciplined of military men and women, it became all a little pointless and sterile, like a computer game you've played so often that you know the outcome. The training routines had been designed for another world, a place a thousand million miles from anything his men, or indeed, he had ever encountered.

All of a sudden, a giant weaving creature hove into view, resembling something from a cheap B-grade Hollywood horror flick. It was, to all appearances, akin to a giant slug, fifteen feet or more from bow to stern.

Somehow, this creature-made animate was both fitting and ever-so-real in a pseudo-multi-hued setting. Things had slid out of a crack in the terrain some distance beyond the yellow and red building blocks. And by its sheer size, the crack itself must, in fact, have been a rent a slash in the ground that would have run twenty feet from end to end and perhaps as much as ten feet at its widest point. The thing climbed quite unreasonably into the air, rising up maybe as much as ten feet, and then, a few seconds later, it hit the ground with a heavy thud. Astonishingly quickly, the slug started sliding across the dark grey, hard-packed ground, moving to the left and then to the right, and then back again, similar to the motion an ice skater might use.

It seemed menacing to the marshal, he supposed, and he knew that now was the time to take direct command of the sixteen grunts. But just as he was about to issue his attack instructions, with the monstrosity now no more than 100 feet from the top of the marines, like a well-oiled series of machine cogs, they all suddenly slipped into gear. The shout went out, "Slice and dice, boys, slice and dice!" The marshal stood upon his promontory and watched as each of the sixteen men proceeded to efficiently dispatch the strange, colourless giant slug. Searing luminous beams of green light shot out from a selection of short-range pulse rifles, and instantly the thing began to sizzle. This continued for only a second or two before the creature collapsed into itself, pooling quickly into a slag of steaming tissue and wet, spongy innards. The marines stepped out from their various cover positions, and the marshal was just in the throes of speaking once more when a door opened behind him, and for him, at least the illusion that he had at that point been immersed in was instantly dispelled.

A tall man stepped through the open door and looked with more than a little disdain at the back of the grizzled, uniformed man standing in front of him. In turn, the marshal had one handheld clenching a waist-high steel rail as he looked out over a three-dimensional reproduction on a sixty-foot plasma screen playing out behind a sizeable staging area. A production stage upon which, in various positions of repose, sixteen uniformed men.

"Marshal Stormbader, I've been looking for you. We need to speak," the visitor said equably enough. Stormbader knew about the intruder's arrival before the door had stirred in its frame. Nonetheless, years of practice in the art of subterfuge persuaded him to feign surprise as he turned and faced the enforcer, Sigmund Symonds. Both men were tall, and, at six feet three inches, Stormbader himself was one of the very tallest men among a population of nearly sixty thousand. Yet, despite this, Stormbader visited him by at least an inch, and Stormbader had to admit that to most folk, he probably appeared taller even than that. Symonds's presence was imposing. But Stormbader was made of sterner stuff than most; he had risen to the post of one of 'The Eight' exactly because he was entirely unlikely to be imposed upon by an arraptchik like Symonds.

He was major-general of the marine detachment, and he made it his business to know who within his radius was capable of what, as well as ensuring that no one (neither enemy nor friend) found themselves able to blindside Major-General Alexei Stormbader. Sigmund was a little grated at addressing him as marshal. Before his elevation as commander of the marine force, he had indeed spent many years as the land-based marshal of a number of divisions of crack troops; political machinations had prevented him from climbing higher, as men of little courage but much political capital had not liked the ilk of Alexei Stormbader. He had proven to be that most heinous of successes in a communist country: a poor man who had climbed the ranks sufficiently to cast a shadow across the lawmakers, those men and women who were generally also the chief lawbreakers.

And so it was that Stormbader held back. It was recognised that he was a commander of men without peers, both uncompromising and yet commanding of such a level of fierce loyalty that men would fall to their deaths for him without even asking why. Such a breed was rare in a country where a good many of those men had soldiered on for barest rations, often without pay for months at a time.

And so, Alexei Stormbader was therefore a conundrum for the powers that governed the Motherland. In a nation that, in its prime, spread across thousands of square miles and more time zones than any other place or people on Earth, here was the governor of mean and desperate men. Here was a man who was in equal measure a necessity in that governance and yet always held the possibility of a threat to the nation's powerbrokers. So it was that Stormbader was held back and forced to remain marshal when so many lesser men had been pushed forward for greater honours. He had never regretted those times, and he had worn (indeed, did still, as far as his men were concerned) the rank of marshal with dignity. Nonetheless, when Symonds addressed him, there had been just enough of a tone in his carefully articulated greeting to suggest that an insult was gently nudging behind the deliberately incorrect invocation, and Stormbader had not forgotten those times long past, either. There was a time, in years dusty and ancient, when

Alexei would have risen to that other's feeble challenge, snarled in anger like some baited brown bear.

That, though, was before the Black Days. He wondered where men like him and Symonds might now find themselves had the final conflict never occurred. In the last thirty years before the Endgame, most of the data community, as the western world had become known, had increasingly been proven to have been arbitered by a small sector of society. That sector was shown to be one that created addiction via negative emotional absorption; many later wrote the history of that time as a world run by psychopaths. It was often stated in the grandest of terms that humanity had allowed the lunatics to run the asylum.

Twitsnapfaceogram, the sinister global online self-promotion phenomenon, had been engineered to be addictive by drawing on the repetition of subscribers' negative emotions. It had spread like a virus in a world of nine billion. Some five billion jacked up viewers at their peak, whose chief problem on a daily basis, in the absence of the particular need to hunt down safety or sustenance, had become visibility. *Twitsnapfaceogram* had, in less than forty years, devoured its competition and then gone on to create a new fantasy world. A new world is segregated not by geography, not by religious sectarianism, not by class or even wealth. Instead, the online embodiment of viral infection had addicted people to the pursuit of notoriety, watching constantly and infectiously how those few that succeeded arrived at the Halcyon Nirvana. Thus, it was that ninety-nine-point nine percent of those people, who by then made up more than half the world's population, became twisted, filled with a rising tide of bile and bitterest envy. Terrified at the loss of individuality, but like a lottery, each living with ever greater odds of a failed outcome.

Stormbader, to his eternal good fortune, had lived a life outside that circle. He had read books, watched documentaries, and remembered, like many others, story of the first live online suicide. This is ultimately a futile attempt at notoriety and self-promotion. Stormbader was a teenager and clearly recollected the last group suicide. The day when two thousand people chose death over life. Nobody would ever know whether they all truly went to their death freely; already, they were so diluted by their number that even death was no longer an online card worth playing. He had, in fact, become a soldier only a few months after the worldwide online shutdown in 2066. He remembered how that had been hailed as the true moment that humanity created an egalitarian garden in which to live and to love. A new direction for human history, prompted as it was by the sons and daughters of the founders of the web monsters. They had paid too little heed to the millions upon millions of disaffected and invisible citizens of planet Earth who had instantly had the needle taken out and were forced to go cold turkey, the marshal thought, remembering what came after.

Stormbader, with his myopic view of the rest of the world, identified the likes of Symonds as being at the very heart of that poisoned legend. Marshal had watched from afar the evolution of both narcissists and co-dependents, recognising their character and the macabre balance between inhibition and ambition. He looked on and favoured neither one nor the other. He was a soldier, and though he would not have sought out the terms, at an instinctual level he watched the change first in his own nation, and then, from the cold snows of deepest Siberia, stared at the evolution of these behaviour patterns at a macro level, on a global stage. Marshals felt certain that insects like Sigmund Symonds would have only become even more bloated with their own importance had the long peacetime continued unbroken. That, of course, was part of the strange contradiction that these administrators were.

People seemed to spend their whole time agitating against one theme or another, pulling at the stitching of civilisation in pursuit of some vague personal goal. Each one is masked in well-articulated moral high ground. Yet so often they were at the very core of that which undermined, that which leeched the nourishment of nations, stabbed most deeply at so many different groups of people. Until, in the end, one side or another felt compelled to act with aggression, and then, well, then they all disappeared. These peacetime aggressors were invariably the first to hide at the back of the cave whilst other men took up the fight. The general, of course, had no idea whether, in fact, this scenario had been the case at all so many years before, but he imagined with distaste that it was certainly likely. What he did know, though, with absolute certainty was that ultimately somebody had been prompted to action.

One faction or another had taken it upon themselves to change the future irrevocably, and, as a result, twenty-seven nuclear warheads had been detonated upon Mother Earth before the poison could be bled enough to make them stop. His home planet, the only home planet any of humankind had ever known, had been ruined beyond repair. And in the same period of madness, brief, in fact, even amongst the brevity of all human history, lasting just seventeen hours, nonetheless, humanity had been equally ruined, and to all appearances, beyond redemption. Nobody had ever found out who had sparked the conflict.

In the days that followed those twenty-seven atomic eruptions, some of the doomsday scenarios suggested by various scientists, journalists, authors, and other professional commentators had indeed come to pass, and yet some others had not. Some fears foreseen had proven unwarranted, and yet other issues unanticipated had ensured that mankind had begun to slip, like a large globule of syrup dripping from a spoon, slowly but inexorably towards extinction. Whilst many millions, perhaps even as many as a billion, or around one in nine of the planet's human populace at that time, had died in that initial pitter-patter of explosions in the days immediately after.

The government had, in fact, stayed far more in control in most regions of the world than had ever been envisaged. Despite all the warnings of the doommongers, the remains of the military eased into a position of control behind the seat of legitimate government, and the vast mass of the population, in fact, accepted this and looked to their leaders to offer them a route through the horror scenario that they had watched, heard, and read about for nearly one hundred years. Little did that majority understand that they had not, in fact, escaped lightly by surviving the initial nuclear conflict. In reality, they were sitting in the eye of a tornado of destruction, a fact to which they only awoke slowly in the coming months.

Four of the world's continents had indeed avoided any direct initial impact: Australia, Russia, and, perhaps not surprisingly, the two poles. This had initially given hope to all the free peoples of the world; the possibility of safe zones was a real allure to the dispirited masses, who, in the days and weeks after, had to deal with spade-loads of death and destruction. One might have suspected that the landmasses that had avoided initial destruction might have been at the root, even suggesting the conflict. After lasting less than a whole day, nobody had the temerity to call it a war. Had it been precipitated by economic gain rather than religious or political zeal? Nobody ever knew for certain. Alexei had to admit to himself, at least, that his own nation had slipped some way down the league of economic superpowers somewhere back in the mists of the second half of the twentieth century.

Australia, the other mainstream populated landmass, had never been a contender, either militarily or economically. In the days after the twenty-seven impacts, it seemed this had proven a boon to the populations of both. In addition to Europe and North America, there had been massive economic growth in India, the Chinese Federation, and the Middle Eastern nations early in the twenty-first century. Later, the African continent discovered sizeable oil and gas reserves, and, once its deeply tribal peoples had stopped killing one another, the continent had quickly become much of the world's raw material reserve at the dawn of the third millennium. South America continued in a smaller but similar role for its North American neighbours and was the world's medicinal dispenser to boot, both legal and illegal.

And so, a balance existed that was, of course, imperfect. Continuing disparities existed throughout the world, but until the very end, the delicate balance appeared to be enduring. The trouble with tactical balancing is that you cannot take your eyes off the prize, even for a moment. And so, of course, to those that read history and understood the downfall of the Romans at the hands of the Visigoths, or Alexander the Great, or even Gandhi holding the fate of India and Pakistan in his small hands. As such, it always appeared obvious that these cultural and economic differences would eventually precipitate a catastrophe, very much like the seventeen-hour solution.

Others argued that economics were controlled by mainstream government, though no record ever surfaced that any one of these major nation governments in fact 'pushed the button'. Unfortunately, as the guilty first-strike party had never owned up, it was most likely dead, according to a majority of commentators, perhaps killed by a return missile or, at the very least, during the aftermath, when so many met their end, maybe even by their own hand. Who might wish to survive till the day after Armageddon and then face the wrath of a mortally wounded planet? Who would wish to watch the pulsing of blood and the cries of death in all that carnage? Whatever the truth, no one ever stepped forward, and so speculation was all people had.

Alexei Stormbader had been based at the time of the conflict deep in the frozen heart of Siberia, and that had been good, he had supposed. He and around twelve thousand troops were billeted in temperatures approaching thirty degrees below zero. He and those troops had food, they had weapons, and, after a fashion, through the coldest of winters approaching the end of the twenty-first century, they would survive the end of the world. Not because they were strong in numbers, nor because Alexei Stormbader was a remarkable leader of men, though both of those statements were true. But instead, because Siberia was a place where, in those latter days, even the prevailing weather chose not to go.

The movements of the world's major weather fronts in the years that followed the twenty-seven nuclear strikes became the single pivotal factor in deciding who lived and who died. The fate of communities and even nations, and certainly the billions or so that died in the first days of the strikes, more than doubled as those fateful clouds of death wandered their unstoppable way around the globe's temperate regions.

And it was by accident (fate, if you will) that the four continents that had avoided any of those initial bursts of atomic warfare were indeed also the four places where the world's weather seemed least interested in blowing either of the two great post-atomic death clouds that steadily grew high in the planet's stratosphere. Death had come, of course, in so many ways in the years that followed. But humankind was without neither the resources nor intelligence to oppose some of the worst of doom's harbingers, as many might have believed.

Melting ice from polar caps, mountaintops, and much of eastern Russia has proven a viable alternative to irradiated water supplies. Nuclear power, surprisingly, quickly won the survivors' hearts as a provider of warmth and light against the vagaries of a post-holocaust atomic winter. And though millions and millions continue to die, the world's infrastructure hung on. Indeed, after thirty-six months, some watchers began to predict that, despite all the odds, a sizeable fraction of the human race might yet survive, maybe even eventually prosper. They are learning their harshest lesson at the very brink of destruction.

But the mega-clouds continued to form, and in spite of the best scientists worldwide devoting their energies to finding a way to dissipate them, no answer would be found. And so they blew, inching slowly back and forth across the planet, death and deprivation running before them.

It was months before Marshal Alexei Stormbader was called back to his nation's seat of government. Leadership, such as it was, still sat in Moscow at that time. That leadership would eventually migrate to Murmansk, in the country's extreme northwest, as the military took increasing control and the remaining politicos sought refuge from the ever-present nuclear death clouds.

But during those early months, the various surviving factions still vied for control over the remaining populace and, more importantly, the country's poor, dwindling resources.

The heart of both the United States and mainland Europe had been decimated by fourteen of the twenty-seven exploded warheads, split eight and six between the two landmasses, and whilst a full picture was not readily available of the global picture, the Soviet Union came quite quickly to the knowledge that, in fact, they were no longer a bankrupt nation, rich as they were in raw materials such as gas, oil, and steel. All of this was once again enhanced by the wheel of fate. It appears that the vast majority of these raw materials can only be found in the country's most ice-locked regions, places that just happened, in fact, to escape the more temperate weather fronts that circled like carrion fowl in the more southerly latitudes.

At the very beginning, Mother Russia was fearful of invasion, most especially from their Chinese neighbours. After all, the western world's policeman, America, was pretty much out for the count, and the Russians' Asiatic neighbours had been devastated by the two biggest warheads to be detonated. One of these bombs tragically exploded six hundred metres above Beijing, killing an estimated ten million people in the first three minutes and perhaps as many as thirty million more in the next thirty-six hours. At that time, nobody quite understood the impact on the world's psyche of that long-feared atomic event. And so, the prospect of the world's largest standing army marching across the border into the former Soviet Union seemed, to the good of many of the surviving leaders, a very real threat.

So it was that Alexei Stormbader and his twelve thousand underfed, underpaid, but loyal 'crack' troops were called back from Siberia and placed at the heart of the remaining nations' raw materials defence force.

No invasion ever materialised; whatever stomach humankind once had for war had been crushed by the deaths of one in every six people across the planet. Whilst the will no doubt still existed to take from one's neighbour in such desperate times, many parts of the world found themselves in a direr plight than since records began. In fact, little more than the smallest of conflicts ever broke out. Indeed, after the brief period that changed the world forever and until the time of final choices came about, the spirit of helping fellow men, perhaps surprisingly, rose to its highest point. Perhaps had this alone been presented at the table of humanity's judgement day, then the race would maybe have been blessed in God's eye.

So, Alexei held his men together for twenty crucial months, and during that time, the geopolitical map of the world changed irrevocably. In Russia, the military once again gained the ascendancy, in part because of the strong leadership provided by men like Alexei Stormbader. Elsewhere, the world slipped slowly downwards from the lofty pinnacles of humanity's greatest achievements, and in many places, communities tried desperately to find a new, if lesser, plateau upon which they might settle.

So it was that when the marshal was summoned to travel to the new government headquarters that had only recently been set up in Murmansk, he did so not just against a backdrop of tragedy but during a time of the greatest change humankind had ever been faced with. Once there, he found himself quickly promoted to Major-General, in part as recognition for his achievement in such a trying time but also because, in the face of such enormous uncertainty about the future, strong, single-minded men who were able to sidestep the most precarious pitfalls that befell one and all were an increasingly rare breed.

In the fullness of time, he also realised that the promotion, such as it was, had been pushed through in order to impart to him at least some measure of the seriousness of all that followed the initial devastation outside of the small area of Siberia in which he had, until that time, been. Russia's population before the event had been a relatively steady two hundred and ninety million. By the time Stormbader pinned General's stripes onto his uniform, nearly forty percent of those people were dead. And despite the best efforts of the leaders of the time, no end to the dying had appeared on the horizon, and so some, seeing the inevitability of it all, were beginning to examine more radical solutions to their survival.

At first, Alexei had been shocked, whilst nobody had spoken of anything else since the event; nonetheless, he had generally been a solitary man, a situation much enhanced deep in the snowy white of wintering Siberia. As such, having lost nobody that he was especially close to, he had not entered into debate about the rights and wrongs of what had taken place; in truth, he had avoided asking too many questions of anyone, preferring instead to push the dread and the reality of such distant events behind the needs of the here and now. It therefore shook him to his very core when dawning understanding hit him that more than one hundred million of his Russian compatriots were now dead, let alone what might be happening beyond his nation's borders out in the wider world.

But the men and women that had promoted him finally beyond the rank of marshal, that rank that had so long bound him, nodded to one another with increasing certainty when they saw how quickly he was able to digest even a shock as great as the destruction that he now saw wrought. He swiftly took on board his new responsibilities, and with a relish for life that only a very few had after so much. And whilst like everyone in those latter days, he lived every day with a mixture of fear and depravation, of a kind that had been much removed from the world during the previous two centuries, he still attacked each of those days with poise and a cast-iron will.

"Symonds, what do you want? You can see that I am busy, no?" he asked, coming back to the present with a mental jolt. "And for the record, Mister Sigmund Symonds, I am to be addressed as Major-General. I grant that I may allow my men to call me marshal; let us call it a small courtesy to their unending efforts to this point. But I am quite certain I have earned the rank, and as such, if some such should seek and address me in my place of work, then in the future it would behove the seeker to address me properly. Do we understand one another?" Stormbader stopped speaking.

He knew he was being mercilessly small-minded and petty, but he also understood that he was pushing his visitor onto the back foot, at least for a moment. Even as a pointless exercise, this brought him some small satisfaction. Sigmund Symonds looked back equably enough at the other and drew in a slow breath before replying, "Of course, Major-General. I apologise; I meant no offence. I have been pressed by a number of somewhat trying issues these past few days, and, of course, whilst this in no way excuses my tardy disregard for your full rank and title, I did in fact mean any such slip in only the most complimentary fashion. Your many years in Mother Russia as the marshal walked in front of you for so long a time, as bright as the brightest lamplighter's torch."

Alexei looked suspiciously at each other. The compliment was fulsome enough, and yet the man's tone suggested even then that his words were, well, duplicitous. He shook his head.

"Forget it, Mister Symonds; you and I shall start over. Now, what is it that you wish so desperately to say to me that it cannot wait until after the exercise?"

"0940," Symonds answered, looking at his watch. "Why do you waste your time with these drills? My god, these men are old enough to know better! Anyway, what was that thing, that worm they were butchering?"

Stormbader recognised that this was Symonds making an effort at being amiable, but he was happy to play along, at least for the time being. "Actually, what you see there is a Tyrolean sand snake; the system just maxed it up; that one was about a thousand times its usual dimension. But in answer to your question, I can only say this. One day we will get to where we are going, and when we do, who knows what we may find? If our new home is empty, then so be it; you will have every man under my command fit, well-exercised, and ready for the undertaking that is ahead. But if not, well, if not, then maybe even such as you will prove thankful that such as I kept those under my command ready and able for action, whatever action that may prove to be. There are many proverbs in my country that are used and some that are misused, but I will say this: Poor men seek meat for their stomach. Rich men seek stomach for their meat. We are the hunters for those men, and whether they be rich or poor, none will say that their stomachs were empty because of a failure of diligence from those in my command.' The marshal recognised he had begun to sermonise towards the end, but he was Russian; he enjoyed standing on the box and speaking his mind. 'Now stop looking at your damn watch and tell me what you want, man."

The other looked back insolently and replied after a few long moments, "I…I don't want anything; I'm here for her. She wants to see everyone at 10.30. She's convening The Eight."

5
Trust in God but Steer Away from the Rocks

I feel great, Hermione thought, smiling gently to herself as she walked along one of the wider promenades of down below. She couldn't get over how good she was feeling. Whatever was in those noodles was worth every credit, she told herself. She noticed a clock on the wall of a small manufacturing unit; it said the time was 11.04 am. She was up and out for around five hours. Time was not generally relevant in her life, yet she got an inkling that perhaps this time the ticking clock was important. The old lady didn't understand why, but something was gnawing away at the deepest recess of her mind, right down the bottom of the well where amygdala looked up and myopically kept guard.

She felt the smallest shiver of anxiety, smiled once more, and walked on. A bowling alley up ahead was emitting a curious electronic organ version of that ancient standard by The Beatles, 'A Hard Day's Night'. She recognised the tune despite its tremendous age and thought about the song, a genuinely classic piece of music when judged in comparison to much of the electronic invocations that people now refer to as music. It was strange, she reflected, how so many parts of the human jigsaw had developed at a pace whilst music had appeared to stall. Jammed in the works of the machine. Somewhere along the way, Beethoven and Tchaikovsky had become Elvis Presley and The Beatles, and for many years in between, things had been fine. Yet it was true, was it not? Hermione thought to herself that of all the tunes that might have rung out of the venue she now walked into, they were playing the simplest thing by four young boys jamming and having a good time, from a band more than a hundred years ago. She sighed.

Hermione knew of no anthems that were current at the time of The Behemoth's launch, and even less of any tune that grabbed at her in the long years since. It seemed they had lost the art of making songs, she decided, looking up at the neon sign above the door that boldly proclaimed she was entering 'The Strike It Lucky Bowling Pleasure Palace'. She ruminated for a few more moments and wondered about how humanity had lost hold of that simplest and most driving passion: to simply be creative, to make something in this life that had not been made before, or even if it had to make it your way, however raucous and incomplete that might seem. The old lady believed that only from there could truly birth those moments of genius that they had sometimes touched in so brief a history.

Inside the emporium, she came sharply back to herself. The place was dimly lit, aside from the bowling alleys themselves, and appeared sparsely populated. She looked around quickly, and spotting the restroom sign, a bright neon counterpoint to the place's dim demeanour, she strode purposefully towards it. It was good, she considered, that venues such as Strike It Lucky were completely automated; were that not the case, she felt certain that entry to the restroom, let alone the bowling alleys themselves, would long since have proven off limits to indigents such as her. Inside the place, the music was somewhat louder, and although it was not the best rendition she had heard of a Beatles tune, it was nonetheless not unpleasant, and it certainly added to her feeling of general well-being. A hubbub of voices drifted towards her just as she passed behind the partition that separated the washroom area from the main floor.

A scratchy laugh with an evil-sounding undertone made her briefly uncomfortable but was soon lost and forgotten as soon as the urge to urinate drove her into the toilet block directly ahead of her. The trouble with getting old, she thought to herself, was that the urge to pee became almost constant. Hermione Zatapec placed her battered case on the floor of the trap, furthest from the washroom's entrance. Ensuring first that the grimy plastic composite tiles were at least predominantly dry, she then parked herself on the toilet properly. Proceeding to urinate vigorously, she thought about the day to come. Generally, she was confident to live only within the confines of the day in which she found herself: time is just a window, and death is not a doorway.

This was a phrase she often fell back upon when trying to explain to herself why it was that she had moved so far from ambition. Beyond the here and now, even down to where she might look to find herself. She thought hard about this once more as she straightened her clothes, wondering why things were so damn vague. She couldn't even remember where such strange words as those had come to her from. If she squinted mentally, she caught sight of some other woman, a different her, it seemed, driven by ambitious self-aggrandisement, and that was not a clear image but rather a kind of twisted nest of feelings and visuals, mental sounds, and smells that sat just beyond the lady's grasp. Yet somehow, she knew this other her was her, too, without a moment's doubt, a creature of little or no empathy, fractured from herself in such a way as to leave her exposed the moment she was not striving to win.

And the sight of that other made her shudder, and as each moment passed, like a steam train approaching, she felt that distant Hermione draw closer; and so, in fraction, though the greater part of her psyche craved the recollections she lacked, a significant voice spoke up and, in fearful tones, reminded her that what she did not know might well prove to be good for her.

An image of a man eased through her mind, warm and gentle, reaching out and holding her hand in his; and then, puff, in a second, it was all gone again. Back in the mundane, she thought, I need a wash and brush before stepping out on show. She prompted herself with a forced mental grin. She figured that the washroom at the rear of an empty bowling alley was as good a venue as she was likely to find. The place was almost empty, she reminded herself, thinking momentarily about the raucous laughter she had heard as she stepped through the washroom door.

Convincing herself that the laugher would undoubtedly be more occupied by their own world than the ablutions of a grey-haired old woman, Hermione stepped from her private booth out to a communal area that consisted of six nylon plastic basins, each deeply scored and worn. Under her feet was a grubby, plastic-coated tiled floor and surrounding her on all sides were wall tiles interspersed with random chunks of asteroid rock. The rocks were all grey and brown, and the walls and floor were all of some neutral salmon-pink colour. Above the sinks were six equally uninspiring mirrors, also made of some nyloned plastic that appeared to have lost a good part of its mirroring capabilities down their long reflective years of use.

Hermione Zatapec shuffled over to the sink furthest from the door, carefully placed her battered case on the vanity surface to the side, allowing it to lean up against the wall tiles nearest the sink surround, and then proceeded to take a look at herself. After squinting for a moment, she noticed that, in fact, she did not need to squint. Slightly perplexed, she relaxed the muscles around her eyes and, despite the slightly milky quality of the mirror, found that she could see herself quite clearly. She ran water into the bowl, aware of the one-litre limit, and resisted the urge to drink it, remembering that this was only reconstituted wastewater and was best left outside the body. She stopped at about two-thirds in order to ensure that she might have some small reserve with which to clean her teeth; well, just a splash, her mind spoke up. Looking still at her reflection, it slowly dawned on her what it was that so long had held her gaze with such curiosity. Golly, she thought to herself, is that a patch of brown hair? It was just at that exact moment, just as that thought was taking hold, that the door to the washroom swung wildly open, banging loudly on its hinges.

Hermione looked up quickly and watched carefully as two women entered, one loud and with that slightly discomforting squawking laugh that Hermione now remembered from earlier. Anxiously, she looked back down, hoping impulsively that she might somehow blend into the background. But Hermione Zatapec's instincts were sharp, honed by a whole forever of surviving in the gantries of down below, and she admitted to herself that she had let herself get cornered. She understood that these two women were trouble—most likely riggers, she figured. In an off-shift, a few hours layover from working in the deep vacuum of space repairing the inner skin, or maybe even the hull. Hyped on pills and/or booze, most likely, and although it was unusual to come across such party animals so far from the social activity epicentre, the haunts of gangsters and whores, she knew that she ought to have spotted the signs when she came in.

And so now here she found herself directly in their path, with no way to go but forward. The old lady felt butterflies in her stomach but also knew that they would likely enjoy watching her panic. It would do her no good, and so she forcefully butted those expressions of her terror aside and proceeded to dip her hands into the half-full bowl of tepid and vaguely discoloured water, staring at the mirror still in front of her. Hermione tried to remain casual with any onlooker for as long as was possible. The two women continued their loud banter for long seconds, apparently oblivious to the room's other occupant, and some other anxious person in that situation might just convince themselves that such fears as Hermione's would prove unfounded, and such a person might smile to themselves with relief, and that smile would drift across their features in just the exact moment that the large laughing bullock of a woman would first spy on you. And she's now even worse for wear, and you have a naïve, dumb-ass grin spread across your face.

As it proved, the buffalo-sized woman did indeed spot the other washroom visitor, and immediately was driven to silence, the laughter cut off from both women in an instant. Of course, Hermione was not grinning, wise old sage that she was, but as it turned out, this was a mistake.

"Can ya tell me why yer got game face on oozy bitch skillin?" the big woman suddenly screamed, nudging her companion heavily and lurching a couple of steps closer. "Finking yaw might face me down, hop so?" she continued questioningly. "Oozy frag wipe dat serious from yaw bitch." This last was said particularly aggressively. The big woman stood straighter; her smaller companion, who had as yet not spoken, stared hard at the old woman.

For Hermione, everything seemed to slow down the instant the other two women entered the washroom. Inside her mind, she knew immediately that she was in big trouble; street speak of the sort the big, aggressive one had been spouting held half a meaning to the older lady from the words themselves. But she garnered much more from the tone in which they were uttered and almost as much from the very language itself. Speakeasy, as her kind of slang-cum-rap chatter was generally referred to, was a crème de la crème language within the private province of the 'heavy water' and 'cold black' engineering teams. Hermione, like most people on board the great craft, felt instinctively that she ought to hold these men and women in no small amount of awe, for were they not the folk who, by their work both inside and outside of the *Leviathan*'s hull, kept the great craft alive and in good health for the benefit of all, patching and repairing as need arose, and it frequently did.

They were in some ways regarded with almost hero status by most of the sixty thousand on board, but equally the high-risk lifestyle that they led, the iron nature within each one of them that this generated, and the addiction to high-octane drugs and alcohol that inevitably were needed to bring them back to some semblance of reality between so many hyper-tense life or death shifts meant that they were effectively ostracised from the rest of the population. Heroes but marginalised into a prehistoric testosterone-fuelled world all of their own, a micro-community within *Leviathan's micro-humanity*. These were rough-edged and utterly derisible people within what passed as a mainstream society. In many cases, obnoxious and deliberately vocal, bellicose, and aggressive. Years ago, they had devolved downwards, separating from the main body of the ship's militarily governed crew.

They, around six hundred in total, had wound up in down below, the only place where a blind eye might more easily be turned towards the inevitable excesses, the brutal and simplistic prioritising of survival, and, of course, the highest death and serious injury rate on board a craft where harsh was a daily diet for everyone. And now one of them, large and bristling with indignant muscle and gristle, with her sidekick at her shoulder, was staring the old lady, Hermione Zatapec, down. The older woman was certain that the excesses that so many others avoided were imminently going to be visited upon her. Hermione stared back unblinking; she was more than a little afraid, but she was well aware that any expression of that fear would gain her nothing in the confrontation that was likely to come. So she just gazed back, squinting very slightly against the bright neon lights overhead.

The big woman closed the distance between them in about a second and a half. Hermione noticed that the other woman held back, remaining within the closed vicinity of the door, perhaps as a lookout, perhaps as an unofficial bouncer, and most certainly as an enthused cheerleader. Up close, the older woman noted the wine-like alcoholic reek on the big woman's breath, mixing with undisguised body odour, and what she was reasonably sure was the stink of toilet underlying the other smells. 'Cannas fuck wimi bitchin,' the big woman boomed, and the reek suddenly ramped up, spit splashing onto Hermione's cheek and chin. She reached up and carefully wiped the wetness away with the cuff of the worn cardigan she wore, her eyes not breaking contact with the others even close to her. She had placed herself between the battered brown case and the washroom's two other occupants. She would have liked to take a step backwards in order to cover the case from sight more effectively, but a step back now would be a mistake, so she simply held her ground, and finally, as both women just stared at her malevolently, Hermione decided that it was time for her to speak

"Whistlin in tha down below int right for de big bitches likin you is it."

She was rusty, but the brief but unmistakeable widening of the other woman's eyes told Hermione that whilst she quite obviously did not belong to that other's fraternity, nonetheless she knew at least some small fraction of the general down below slang; she was stating in the only way that she could that she was more alike to the room's two other occupants than they might think. She noticed that the big woman's skin was terribly pock-marked and that around the edges of the eyes were burn scars, which suggested at least one nasty deep-space incident in that other's past. She suddenly felt a rumbling growl and felt more than heard in those first fractions of a second. She did not believe her senses to be truthful in so far as her hearing was not so great; it had deteriorated badly over the past four or five years.

And so she felt, and then she heard the growl that emanated from the other woman's throat, which turned quickly into a rage-filled guttural shriek aimed squarely at this old woman. Some ancient bitch from the upper decks, who had gone and gotten herself lost, washed up in this scum-sucking venue deep in the down below, and then an old bitch who had dared to wipe her face down dared to respond in their private pigeon slang. High on alcohol and amphetamine concentrations, the big woman bunched her well-honed muscles as her poorly regulated internal emotions exploded, and in that moment, she lashed out violently. Hermione closed her eyes and allowed her arms to drop loosely on either side of her. Flowing like water, her mind spoke up. And once again, she had no idea from where inside of her these words came from.

But they helped, and at the speed of thought, she was instantly focused on relaxing all the muscles in her body, denying the instinct that suggested she tense up and clench every part of her, in anticipation of what was to come. And so it was that when the first heavy crunching blow arrived, slamming into the side of her head with the impact of a sledgehammer, the other found that, instead of smashing into a stiff yet fragile old lady and bringing pleasure by crunching through old bitch bones and sinew, she found herself hitting a body that seemed more to resemble the stem of a flower, that just loosely fell away and allowed gravity to drop her to the grubby washroom floor.

Hermione went down, but she kind of flowed down, bowed easily like that stem pushed suddenly by a sharp puff of wind. Much of the weight behind the heavier woman's blow was lost, not transferred to the other on impact, as might have been expected. This, of course, aggravated the attacker even more, and so, fuelled by the drug/alcohol-induced state of mind, her anger heightened, and she began to rain blows down onto the older woman's prone form. That older woman rolled loosely into a ball, and her mind squawked at her, thinking that this was ideal if she was being mauled by a bear. So, the big woman became a bear in her mind's eye, and her kicks and roundhouse punches were merely the pawings of some great Russian brown bear. It hurts, and yet somehow it hurts so much less than it ought to. As the seconds passed, Hermione Zatapec still managed to keep herself as loose as possible; she had taken beatings before.

Whilst a small part of her understood that at her age she would do well to come out of this at all, let alone intact, nonetheless much of the force of the other woman's fury would be lost if she was able to stay loose, physically, and mentally, as it turned out. Her eyes, which she kept tightly shut, and her hearing, better than they had been in an age, seemed preternaturally sharp in the echo-filled washroom. She heard the big woman grunting as she levered her bulk into a position where she was more able to heap punishment on the other. Hermione was surprised that she had neither heard nor felt anything from the room's third occupant. Despite the punishment she was taking, the older woman's mind still appeared to be operating in a pretty clear-sighted manner; she was surprised at the other woman's absence from events, and it was this fact that persuaded her an instant later to open one of her eyes and take a swift and momentary peek.

And so, it was at the exact moment her vision locked onto the other woman that the siren began to scream, its own earnest tone immediately drowning out the panting grunts of Hermione's attacker. Another smaller woman was staring at the attack victim on the tiled floor with an icy, vicious indifference. As the sound began, she instantly started to glide across the intervening space, neither quick nor slow. This took her about a second, and in that time the big woman had slowed considerably, as both her fading rage and the pure physical exertion had jointly taken their toll. Hermione tracked the nasty-eyed woman's movement and, at that time, actually felt nothing at all of the physical assault she had suffered. Instead, she watched as another prodded her bigger companion to the shoulder once, and then a second time with a much sharper jab when she obtained no response.

"Heh Jelly Jo we be missin and we need be gone, tha's the breach alarm. Leave that dried up old meat ya tendering and get yourself together."

Hermione saw a small smile play across the smaller woman's lips as she said her piece. She was not a hull engineer, that was for certain. She spoke clearly, and though she drawled the odd slang here and there, she could not wholly disguise her speech. More eloquent were her words, yet delivered without inflection of any kind: no slang, no swearing, and an intelligent and educated woman, despite the where and who that would be apparent to any onlooker, and the more dangerous for all that. Earlier, she had appeared to Hermione to be the sidekick, the lesser of the two characters who had barged into the room in what was still, in fact, only a couple of minutes previously. The big woman grunted, happy, it seemed, to cease her beating at the other's suggestion, and sufficiently multilingual, it seemed, to grasp meaning in her words.

Mind you, Hermione reminded herself, though they might work and live in down below, it was a fool that supposed the likes of 'Jelly Jo' were stupid: multilingual was no great feat. As she went down, the older lady had managed to dislodge her battered case with one of her loosely hanging arms, which swung freely after the first blow. The case landed first, and she had fallen atop it, effectively covering it from view. Albeit that it was certainly no more comfortable than the floor she found herself laid out on. She groaned involuntarily, but neither of the two retreating women looked back, and she watched Jelly Jo recede, her massive shoulders heaving as she sucked in huge lungfuls of air and sought to slow her thudding heart.

The older lady lay prone for long moments, attempting to assess the damage to her body without shifting unduly. She was alive, and she supposed she had to be grateful for that. The last time that she had found herself in quite such a vulnerable position, she had awoken with a black hole in her mind. On that occasion, her head had been aching terribly and her anus had hurt like god knew what; she had bled softly from a dozen small insertion wounds, and she had absolutely no idea where, what, why, or how any of that had been visited upon her. Though she knew then, as she knew now with absolute certainty, that something very serious had stepped in front of her path.

Upon that distant, dark waking, the bruises on her arms and legs suggested a beating similar to the one that had just been administered, though as she lay there comparing, Hermione recognised that she hadn't thought so at the time. She had been frightened at her inability to remember how she had gotten herself into that state. Nonetheless, in a puddle of water and heavy diesel mix, she was grateful that she was alive and still had hold of her battered briefcase, whatever might have passed. The case had seemed important enough for her to clutch on for dear life in that distant past, and so it was still, to this moment, inscribed on the lock with the letters JDW.

As she climbed gingerly to her feet, feeling deep aches across her body, Hermione caught sight of herself in the mirror; not surprisingly, she was a bit of a mess: clothes dishevelled, a trickle of blood running down the left side of her face, bruised around her left eye and the cheek underneath. But this was the thing that astonished her, her attacker (a much bigger and younger specimen than she herself) had to have struck her more than twenty times, and yet, as she gathered herself together, dishevelled as she had been, beyond the cut and the bruising, she felt remarkably well.

"But not wise, eh, Hermione?" her mind spoke up. "Leave me be," she mumbled to herself, dabbing at the blood and squinting in the fading reflective glass. Once again, she considered how well she had felt that day; this, she supposed, was passing strange when you considered she had just been beaten up.

She moved towards the exit, her bag once more clutched tightly across her chest, and she noted that the alarm had ceased; furthermore, she could hear raised voices from the other side of the door. The old lady contemplated waiting for a few moments more before exiting but understood that it would be fatal if she allowed herself to be caught in here once more, should her previous antagonists have a mind to.

Hermione pulled open the door and stepped from the brighter interior to the darker main area.

She spied a sign that said, "Come watch the big game. Friday night, The Sultans of Swing v Bad Intentions."

This distracted her momentarily, and in that instant, she was out in the open before realising that the raised voices were, in fact, the very two protagonists she had most recently been engaged by. It turned out the alarm, whilst timely, had not ultimately lasted quite long enough to warrant continued concern once they had exited the lavatory. Hermione understood that the actions of the big woman were likely stim invigorated and that she had little premeditated idea what she was doing. And similarly, the woman would have no recollection of any of it after a few hours' sleep. The other one was a different proposition. Not wishing for a repeat of the previous incident and noting with concern that there were now no other patrons in the bowling alley, Hermione clicked open her bag and walked over to the two women, who seemed to spot her simultaneously. Hermione, without waiting for either woman to speak or saying anything herself, pulled her hand from deep inside the brown bag, and in it she held a flower, which she now brought forth with a magician's flourish.

Upon a single stem, the palest of rose pinks and yet not a rose, more akin to a pansy or the like, no more than four or five petals, the flower was perhaps five inches from top to bottom, made of the finest silk, and was completely incongruous within the surroundings in which the three people now found themselves. Hermione held out her hand and said in a steady and authoritative voice, "Please take this; it is my small way of saying thank you," and then, after a brief pause, "For all that you do for us," and then, after a longer moment, "Both of you."

The one called Jelly Jo looked long at the flower in that older woman's hands, and then, all of a sudden, she just kind of crumbled. A huge smile lit up her features, and she reached out ever so gently, considering her monumental bulk and the earlier assault. She took the flower into one of her huge fists. The other, smaller woman looked on with an unreadable expression. Hermione Zatapec closed her case carefully, pulled it close to her chest once more, looked for a moment at each woman, smiled, then, looking steadily at the bigger lady, the flower clutched still in her mighty hand, she turned on her heel and left the room without looking back.

6
Economy Makes a Good Servant, but a Poor Master

Lyle Cardington lay in the dark, wide-awake, deep, sonorous belly of midnight. He felt the warmth of his partner. Susannah was not his wife, but a significant other nonetheless. She was still, and by her breathing, he knew that she lay deep in her own slumber next to him. He wondered briefly at the now-old and much-debated decision to retain a day/night cycle on board the ship. Lyle reasoned that it seemed even now passing strange that each cycle had been decimalised to a twenty-five-hour day, alongside so many other 'adjustments' that had subsequently and quite easily become second nature. And yet The Eight had sat and debated for three days upon the question of night-time, or, as he considered more precisely, daytime. Because it was nothing if not perpetual night aboard the *Leviathan*, that most ancient lump of rock that carried them, all sixty thousand souls, minutely inching across the infinity of stars in a cold black universe.

Somehow, that eight-strong top table had come, by overwhelming majority, if reports were to be believed, to the conclusion that humanity, desperately seeking an escape from a dying Earth, would be better served in a new sanitised world by a lights up/lights down night and day cycle: thirteen hours for day, and twelve for the night. Cardington had often cynically guessed that small leaning towards lights up was to ensure the support of the economists: an hour a day multiplied by the work ethic of so many thousand souls, well, bugger, he was certain they had done the math. And over the twenty-three intervening years, had they not been proven right? By God, even the night staff, of which there were, of course, many, wore the badge of their out-of-hours service with pride, relishing the kudos such might impart, most especially in a world where so much else had been eroded and shrunk to the mundane.

Lyle Cardington, though, knew something that all those mundane souls did not—something that would do more to erode the enthusiasm of the masses than any single piece of information had done in nearly a quarter of a century. In fact, more than all of the cumulative gossip and knowledge together had gained since climbing aboard, as he saw things. And that knowledge was giving him one hell of a sleepless night. He turned from laying on his back and slipped noisily onto his side, facing away from his sleeping partner, who appeared unaware of his sleeplessness. He found that even as he turned and stirred restlessly, he was still willing himself not to open his eyes, understanding that this was the final barrier between his mind and full wakefulness.

In a little over twenty-four hours' time, a majority of the thousands of people on board were due to find out the final countdown details to the end of the most monumental journey humankind had yet undertaken. This was information that all had anticipated for so long, but that would not prove to be quite as palatable as had been hoped. It was a bit like Christmas, he supposed; well, at least for those that still celebrated the bizarre Christian pagan holiday hotchpotch, as he remembered, or contrived to remember, from the movies he had watched in his formative years. Each individual anticipating the coming day, uniquely and yet joined, and each with a clear idea of what that day would entail, excited little Santa Claus true believers.

But what Lyle Cardington knew, that almost nobody else knew, that not even one amongst those elevated people that made up the council of Eight knew, barring Ariel, of course, and her oaf enforcer Symonds, the man who had made the chore of sharing that knowledge with him, as he latterly realised, only to apply pressure. But despite all that, what he now knew was that in reality, through one monumental scientific flaw in the original calculations, or what might more simply be called a cock-up, the *Leviathan* was, in fact, not eighteen months out from taking up orbit around a new home, a destination five light years from Mother Earth. In fact, they were somewhere between fifty and one hundred years out from their descent into that star's gravity well.

So maybe as much as one hundred years out from an untried solar braking exercise that would, if successful, put them in low orbit around the fourth planet of five, grappled to a single 'yellow sun' star, known as 1344XVX29078655, or to most aboard and those of a more prosaic disposition, Tinkerbell. And so, like that unlikely name, chosen by a now-long-dead star-spotter in memory of his equally deceased cat, this was just another cosmic joke. Another deposition into the almighty of the frail and deeply flawed character of humanity. With a decent nitrogen-oxygen mix and, more importantly, an 81.7 percent surface water area, the fourth planet seemed like a boon, discovered as it was by black-light telegraphy late in 2039. It was deemed attainable by the technology that those desperate pioneers were able to cobble together in that post-apocalyptic winter. And yet, as had so often been proven to be the case, on the cusp of great achievement, humanity had once again found its own destruction.

Many issues had lain between that group of desperate men and women, and, indeed, it was understood that even upon crossing that greatest and most harsh of divides, humanity's science had proven to them all to be far less credible than they might have hoped. This was all before they left the bosom, the protecting umbrella of their dying home world. All aboard knew clearly that life in another world was a thing of vicarious opportunity at best, and for those that prayed to their many and various gods, piety drove them on rigorously to seek deliverance for one and for all. Nevertheless, up until that coming day, for the majority, an extra century of travel had not been one of the issues that threatened their mind's-eye view of chance and success.

Dying, along the way, of nothing more intrusive than old age whilst on the longest coach trip in history was bad—very bad, in fact. Dying of old age is when a population of sixty thousand, with a tally of three percent already having passed on, manages to cultivate only three hundred and forty-three children in twenty-three years between them all. Well, that was catastrophic—a mission doomed to long, slow failure without landfall—and soon.

And so surely, once the news is out, this could only become a mission that increasing numbers of already middle-aged folk would just sign off on. Lyle Cardington had carried that knowledge inside of him for long months as he worked, nibbled, and pushed at the problem of extending humanity's lifespan, his mind and his temper swinging between altruistic care for the race and the more real and specific wish to save his daughter Muriel. Increasingly, he had begun to wonder what he might save her from and why, if only to presage the catastrophe of their group's demise.

Tears touched the corners of his eyes, but he knew he must open them in order to blink, and so he did not, allowing them instead to gum his eyes closed. The scientist visualised the vial of bright turquoise and again wondered at it, fingering at the formulae in his most advanced of scientific minds. After some time, he stopped and drifted back into an uneasy sleep. A sleep filled with dreams of dark and light. The dark shadows hiding the crimes he had committed in the name of science, whilst the light, as had increasingly been the case in his fractured sleep, filled with images of his daughter.

Muriel was his very own member of the three hundred and forty-three club, and in his mind, he saw her running and playing, laughing as she called out to him to come and join in with the fun that was her adolescence. But in his dreams, he always remained seated on his laboratory bench, looking on, never, it seemed, being able to quite pull himself away from the science, his science, for just long enough to go join in. Strangely, his dreaming mind taunted him with the judgement of Muriel's mother, a good and decent woman who had died quietly and without barely a protest in birthing their only child. Harsh were the words in his dreaming mind—that secret place where only he could reflect on her wish to leave him and bring up their daughter apart. A separation that would have been divisive for his daughter's well-being, but unconsciously he still recognised how it played a part in his 'how to parent' manual.

"Oh, tragedy is the foolish parent who sits and twiddles at childhood's end; for time never did lie, and only the old find moments to sigh."

He heard this irreverent accusation in his mind's ear as vividly as he had lived it within the dreams he dreamt, and perhaps, as well, that made him cry, too.

Cardington awoke at 05.45 to the tiny recourse of shipboard news on a small, embedded screen that was ever rehashing the same banal drama. Everything was the same: he shook the night fears and the night tears from his waking features. As he did so, it seemed to him to be something he was doing increasingly often. Muriel's father rose lethargically, as had also become usual in recent weeks. The small-framed man proceeded to grunt quite indiscreetly, grumbling audibly that his general disposition was his partner Susannah's damn fault for snoring. It was that which caused him to be both tired and tetchy.

Within just thirty minutes of waking, the scientist was once again tramping noisily down the stark utilitarian corridors towards the Agetec corporate and laboratory suite that took up a sizeable portion of deck forty-three.

He had come to think of *Leviathan* in the context of a cruise liner. Lyle remembered as a much younger man, an intern, being on a beautiful American vessel as it had ferried scientists and dignitaries of seemingly great importance around the Baltic Sea. He had been so impressed by the fifteen decks and 140,000 tonnes of engineering splendour, and with no thought to his own very modest quartering, he had decided there and then that it was not the scientists that deserved humankind's accolades.

But, moreover, it was the engineers, the craftsmen, that managed, in spite of burgeoning technology, to mould and build craft of such immensity and beauty as the SS *Dixie Queen* had been. Of course, the *Leviathan* was at a different level as a feat of engineering from that other ocean-going liner. Indeed, as that liner might have been to a Viking longboat, he guessed that *Dixie Queen*, were she still in existence in some alternate universe, would be to the *Leviathan*. Lyle Cardington understood that as well as any man. A 4.2-mile-long, 50 million-tonne piece of rock, iron ore, and nano-myte silicon plastic infill powered up spin wards to recreate 91% full earth gravity on its outermost inward surfaces, the absolute best the scientists have been able to achieve. Driven by a raft of nuclear fission propulsion technology based on the very stuff that had pretty much consigned humankind's home world to the dustbin.

The 'space rock' had more than one hundred decks, more than three hundred businesses operating on board, twenty-six religious' denominations, nine parks, a zero-gravity core, and a six-mile running track around the inner surface of the outer core. It was the biggest moving object ever made by the hands of man, but the scientist figured it was not going to be big enough for the news that was about to break.

And worse than that, Lyle considered, for more than twenty-three years he had ridden aboard this particular liner, and yet she had never once managed to evoke that romantic pleasure that he had found sitting in a six-by-eight cabin on deck zero, below the water line, listening to the rumble of the engines so many years ago.

As he had left earlier, he had spied his daughter and sat quietly in her room atop her bunk, gazing at some far-off place that only her mind could see. It had crushed and yet lifted her father, for he also realised that to gaze and to consider, as his daughter had been in that instant, in fact you had to have a soul. And so, he was glad to affirm that his beautiful and perfect daughter, born in space with no world beyond that spinning hunk of rock, nevertheless she had a soul. Muriel had more love at a single glance than he knew how to deal with, and she seemed well this morning, and that, too, was a boon and enough for him, and so he quickly scuttled on.

So far as he could tell, *Leviathan* had no soul, and he figured that unless that changed really quick, then that was all she wrote for him, his daughter, and about fifty-nine thousand others that rode in the belly of the whale.

7
The One Who Dies with Most Toys Still Dies

"It's past four o'clock, Ariel. I, too, have appointments that are pressing; can you not just say what you have brought me here to say?" the general waved his arms around him in sincere frustration.

"It's been more than four hours since your secretive bloody mouthpiece dragged me from my day," Alexei Stormbader spoke through pinched features. All present could see that he was unhappy at being detained, most especially at the whim of Ariel MP. Whilst speaking, he was pointing and staring quite malevolently at Sigmund Symonds, who appeared to him to be standing at his mistress's side, belligerent and preening, like a contented cat. If he had taken to pawing and licking at himself, the old soldier would not have been surprised. Others present included Zsiobhan Sildar of The Eight, Overseer of Sociology and Human Resources, who sat alongside Grafton Shevnetski, also of The Eight, Governor of Engineering and leader of the unofficial union that effectively ran down below and that was known only as 'VSYO PAD KONTROLEM' (Everything is under control).

He was a cryptic and, and on occasion, dangerous group that, in twenty-three years, Alexei had been able to learn only a little of. All of those present were Ariel's people; there were a couple of others, arraptchiks scurrying back and forth with data pads and various charts and refreshments. Five in total, plus Ariel MP herself, and then there was him, Alexei Stormbader, and he was definitely not one of the lady's puppets. Nonetheless, despite all that, he did not leave the room. Whether it was curiosity or perhaps that he had a care not to cross his mysterious long-time co-member of the governing elite, even he was not certain.

This was a lady who had grown in stature for much of their quarter century of shared incarceration—how much, none could tell, for few understood the real

Machiavellian manipulation of the arch-narcissist. Ariel was predator supreme; born of the terror of an infancy, she ran from full steam; she had cornered the market in stage-managed personae. And in that enclosed space, that new world, where the boundaries were so clear for all to see, she had slowly and surely drawn the *Leviathan* and all its many inhabitants into her web. That most on board had very little idea of the machinations she orchestrated was ultimately just a further testament to her success in usurping all other bases of power in favour of the whim of her rule.

As Stormbader reached for a fresh carafe of water, peering across at a visit-screen showing the daily diet of 'non-news', the double doors, deeply embedded into the rock face of the meeting chamber, whispered silently open, and four more people entered a huddle. All of them spoke animatedly and seemed almost oblivious to those already present. Alexei looked up and watched as the four remaining members of the eight-strong group that had effectively governed *Leviathan*'s community without election or challenge for twenty-three years entered. As one, they noted the group was whole once more and sat themselves variously around the chamber. A tiny smile played around the edge of Ariel's face, and Stormbader swore to himself. He at least understood that she was enjoying having them all at her beck and call.

It was a curious twist of fate that created The Eight. In the final run-up to *Leviathan*'s launch, a time when Mother Russia had begun to feel the worst of the depredations of a world ravaged by the aftermath of the nuclear holocaust, devastation had hit.

This was in the form of an appalling assassination attempt on the project chief at the time, the brilliant Spanish Muscovite Sergio Radzinski. Radzinski had returned to the former Soviet Union with a nuclear storm chasing behind him. The man had quickly co-opted the 'gravity tractor' programme, which had been semi-mothballed by a bankrupt nation twenty years earlier. It is said that luck is a more fortuitous bedfellow than brains or brawn, and as luck would have it, the Spaniard quickly rediscovered his Russian roots. He also discovered a sizeable rock that he managed to bring into a decent, if risky, Earth orbit in a miraculous two years and two months. Ten months later, and although the gas attack did not ultimately kill Radzinski, it had killed the three people present in his private chambers at the time of the capsule's timed release. Indeed, he had not been present; held up at a press briefing, he was thirty minutes behind schedule. His diary, it seemed, was something the assassins did not have access to.

One of those present had been the chief project scientist, a fifty-two-year-old reclusive Russian-Belgian immigrant, and the man who had drawn together scientific disciplines from across the globe to blend nanotechnology alongside robotics, further mixed with American specialties in biosciences to add to his own atomic energy team. Leonard Svenetski lost in the assassination bid, alongside two of the three remaining farsighted people who had kick off this particularly desperate attempt to escape a slow atomic death. Radzinski, who was already struggling too much with the politics of depriving a nation of scarce resources whilst providing passage for only the most privileged few, had fallen on his own sword. He was unutterably devastated, and he saw no way out. Reports later suggested he had begun to understand a little too clearly the plight of the many millions who he was in effect asking to lay down their lives in order to give a tiny minority the chance to find a new life beyond the sky.

He found in the days immediately following the attack that he was unable to carry the burden without his long-time friend and, more secretly, lover, Svnetski. And so, in the quiet of a rain-lashed and sub-zero night, whilst thousands rioted in the streets outside the launch compound at Baikonur in Kazakhstan, the brilliant scientist who had been the absolute pivot to that point took four cyanide tablets and so died ignobly. And that despite being seen as a man who ultimately gave humanity, or at least a few, a fighting chance.

In the ruins of the days that followed, there was much infighting and power-brokering amongst the many factions that operated the different disciplines that were bringing that great adventure, or perhaps folly, to fruition. Critically, as history later viewed those events, bickering and infighting were throughout kept inside the fences at Baikonur. And so, it did not descend into the kind of political farce that has littered Russian history. A prominent female Australian chemist, outspoken but heard because of her incredible achievements in micro-fuel management just the previous month, had brought things back towards some kind of consensus. She did this first by brokering the recall of Stormbader, when so many Russian decision-makers found themselves hampered by their subjective view of the world now gone. He came along with a regiment consisting of two battalions of the marshal's best troops, and they marched and drove their heavy armour all the way from Murmansk.

This move, at least history suggests, was in order to manage the growing civil unrest alongside the internal policing of the newly named Leviathan Camp, but, undeniably, it also very efficiently backed a new regime with some serious legitimate muscle. At the same time, the Australian woman had proposed a young woman, previously unknown to either management or to the massed ranks of working men and women. This person was specifically proffered to broker a route through the difficult days that lay ahead. That person had been the twenty-three-year-old Ariel MP. Such had proven to be that woman's ability to master the roiling human turmoil in the aftermath of the previous few weeks' events that, in less than two more weeks, she had promoted seven people to what were effectively positions of absolute power.

Alongside, but critically not above, herself. Ariel worked, and she seemed to do nothing wild, nothing that woke the stirring tiger of that mortally wounded nation. And yet time and again she brokered a solution, one that always flattered those that got the job done. So it was that, in the darkest days, the job of preparing a million-year-old space rock captured and redirected from a shallow orbit between Mars and Jupiter finally got done. Sixty thousand people found hope on the darkest of nights, and each was quietly thankful to the newly born Tsaritsa.

Each of the people Ariel spotted and promoted were specialists in a discipline crucial to taking the previously failing mission from plan to fruition. These eight had together calmed the tides of desperate discontent and made dreams a reality. Ultimately, these individuals quickly and efficiently usurped all others and filled the power vacuum before it became irredeemably damaged. Later, it was the same eight people who took their first berths aboard the newly completed *Leviathan*. Rocketing into a stormy night sky aboard a returnable Soyuz of a design both ancient and yet never surpassed in nearly one hundred years of space rocketry.

This had apparently all been in order to reassure the space migrants that were to follow the safety of their forthcoming home. Perhaps, but it had certainly ensured places for those eight individuals aboard the mighty ship. Though symbolic, this ultimately became a surety of their dominion in the time to come. And though no one had seen it clearly then, this had all been orchestrated quietly and efficiently by Ariel MP, a twenty-something beauty with a sweet voice who appeared to know just who to prompt to say the right words. Just who to ask to take the right action at the right time. Those times were chaotic beyond all others, and in the shadow of what appeared to be humanity's last stand, few would ever understand how close to complete collapse the project came on a daily, indeed hourly, basis, and so the manipulations of Ariel were, when noticed at all, valued as little short of a miracle.

It might be noted that the Australian lady who brought Ariel forward into the light from whatever obscurity she had come, whose name has been lost in the fractured history, seems to have never made the final cut. Some commentators have suggested that perhaps she knew too much, and Ariel MP would never answer anything relating to the woman. Nonetheless, so was born The Eight, and though no mandate ever gave them rights or power over the other sixty thousand aboard *Leviathan*, it was the case that a considerable majority of those persons, as the days drew to weeks and then months, accepted that their fate had been lit by the efforts of each of the chosen ones. At the very least, it seemed that they had won by endeavouring and crafting the right to govern.

In spite of the multi-cultural nature of those aboard, for centuries this had been the Russian way: they were a nation of immigrants, and so, in the shadow of death and humanity's likely final doom, Ariel had begun to weave her many webs.

Twenty-three years and seven months and thirty days since the hollowed-out four-mile long chunk of space rock had been pushed out of a polar Earth orbit, all eight at least heading into healthy middle age, all having survived the intervening years to one extent or another, living a life none could have anticipated in their infancy, here they were, Alexei considered, sat together once more.

Politics being such as it was, and Russians being just about the most insecure people on the planet, this kind of meeting of minds had become an increasingly rare occurrence during the intervening years. Each, to all appearances, had steadily retreated into their own domains, their own comfort zones, in an effort to hold, or, in the case of Ariel herself at least, enhance, the position that they each had risen to. The kind of torpor appeared to have afflicted each of the other seven, and it had certainly allowed Ariel, with help from the irrepressible Sigmund Symonds, to weave and wind her magic.

Ariel spoke. "Thank you all for coming at such short notice," gazing briefly but pointedly at Alexei, she then said, "I know that you are all very busy people, and I trust you understand that I would not be calling us all together on a whim. I have an announcement to make…" she paused. "And an explanation, I suppose, to give," she stared around the room and, raising a dainty left hand, briefly looked towards Symonds, who immediately ushered the various assistants and attendants from the chamber. Within moments, there were just The Eight and Sigmund Symonds himself left in the room. This appeared to pass relatively unnoticed to all those present, other than Stormbader, who considered how subtly Ariel had managed to usurp eight and turn it to nine. She continued to speak as the doors whispered shut.

"It may sound a strange thing to say after twenty-three years together, but time runs short, and I have kept from you all a problem that I have been aware of for some time now," she paused again, and so bated the breath of everyone present. "I don't know if you will understand my reasons why, but I took the decision that I believed was correct when I first became aware, and, furthermore, I have taken what I hoped would be the right action in the time intervening."

Alexei was fast edging towards purple and looked like he wanted to tell Ariel to get on with it, but he, like the other six leaders, sat silent and looked on. The room darkened, and a backlit screen appeared on one plastocrete wall. An arc of their flight path around the Earth, around Mars, then exiting the solar system after circumnavigating the sun to pick up the 'super' gravity push, and then heading out towards their new home, appeared on the screen.

This particular mapping image was something that all eight had seen on many occasions; indeed, since the project's infancy, the curves were even in daily use as the logo of Oxy-gen, *Leviathan*'s resident chemists.

"You all recognise this, I trust?" Ariel continued, her voice floating gently, almost childlike, from the darkness. The question seemed more like an assertion of fact. "When we came to the fore all those years ago, in simple terms, we understood that this was the plotted course to our new home, both the shortest route in terms of AU as well as in terms of subjective and real time." She spoke slowly now, yet still just swiftly enough to ensure nobody interrupted her flow. "And you would remember, I hope, that this information came to us from downloads that we obtained, well, salvaged from the offices of Leonard Svnetski after his death?" One or two nodded in the room's darkness; one or two others were paying more attention than they had been.

Leonard Svnetski, IQ recorded at one hundred and ninety-one, chess grandmaster at eleven, PhD in physics and chemistry in the same year, was his sixteenth and the cleverest man of his age. The route, the twenty-five-year journey—this was, well, basically, it was latter-day folklore. Ariel would not bring the most powerful individuals in the *Leviathan* together just to recap on things such as this. And the meeting was so close to the final gravity—announcement, the last push, and the final approach to their new home. The mood changed; hitherto distracted individuals recognised this had to be something big. In an instant, everybody was suddenly terribly attentive.

Several long moments passed...

"Someone made a mistake," Ariel said simply, and then, "Comrades, we are not two years out from Tinkerbell," she paused, and this time most definitely not for effect; what she was about to say was monumental, and she had held it inside of herself for a very long time. Everyone in the room heard a small inflection in Ariel MP's voice, and seven people grew a fraction more nervous. "Ladies and gentlemen, we are, in fact, as a best guess, sixty-three years away from orbit around the fourth planet of 1344XVX29078655, and furthermore..."

Ariel MP didn't get to finish; as the words sank in, suddenly the atmosphere changed, and the room went up like a tinderbox. It flared into an uproar. Everyone began to speak at once; the decibel level rose quickly as each of The Eight tried to speak at once, each leader trying to impose their view, questions, demands, fears, and truth on each of those other long-polluted egos. Much, of course, of the vociferation was directed at Ariel herself, and she had expected exactly that and long planned a stage-managed calm in the face of such a storm. None of those present were shrinking violets. Each were powerful leaders of men and women, persons of purpose and extremely high intellect, and each was used to being both listened to and heard when they spoke.

Symonds made some attempts to restore order, but even his bass shouts were swiftly lost in the melee. After perhaps five minutes or so, Symonds stepped off the dais and raised the room's ambient light once more. Ariel waited; she had more to say, and the lady was an expert in the nature of humans, and these humans in particular. She understood that at times like this, you needed to wait for the storm to abate. Equally, as she looked around the room, she was shrewdly gauging the reactions of each of those present. Ensuring that alliances were still in place, she purposed in her own mind where new ones might be wrought in the aftershocks that would follow.

Ariel spied that, underneath the obvious shock to all present, the one who had most quickly recovered his poise was Stormbader. She had begun to think in recent years that if anyone could, he might actually become the chief antagonist to the realisation of her ambitions. At first, when circumstances and needs had driven her to push these other seven to the fore, she had been the mistress of decision-making in desperate times. Stormbader had seemed to her like something of a buffoon. He had, without doubt, military competence, and his men followed him with devout loyalty, but he was a serious traditional Russian man, single of mind and purpose. Ariel knew that the marshal was neither co-dependent nor malleable to her webs; but, also, neither was he self-aggrandising nor achievement-driven.

It had seemed to her from the off that Alexei Stormbader, who did not operate in the parameters of the majority of that era, was, to her eyes, not given to, and therefore not capable of, highly innovative thinking. This simple, arrogant interpretation had allowed her to remain confident that she would have his measure through the years to come, and for many years that had appeared to be the case. He retained mastery over his men and their soldiering, and in turn, this gave him a measure of power within the new world on board *Leviathan*. This, it seemed to any onlookers interested enough to pay heed, appeared to have appeased any wish for advancement that the man, or indeed, the soldier, might have had. Ariel saw that he was not a political protagonist, and so, after boxing him in and isolating him from the other six main players, something had not proven difficult. And then, for her part, she accepted his abrasive and undiluted nature, and so she ignored him and moved on.

More recently, though, a modicum of seemingly inevitable paranoia had revisited Tsaritsa, and slowly, as the pressure of deceit and secrecy rose, she had begun to wonder whether perhaps ignoring the old soldier had been a mistake. He had become entrenched, surrounded by his own small entourage of warriors and wannabees, and he had settled like concrete into the hierarchy. And hitherto, marshal's entrenchment seemed to Ariel MP diametrically opposed to her own position and to her own plans. The man was a thorn—a hard thorn to pull—mindful of the military that had his back. Stormbader, for his part, saw no need for a political alliance, as he had no aspirations to lead or to be political. And so, the old soldier was a maverick, unconcerned about currying favour or remaining popular. It might be a problem for him, and that was something that Ariel MP was determined to resolve in the coming uncertain times.

Tsaritsa, as the ultimate player in the political game, understood that people would look to someone to rally to in the wake of the announcement that was inevitably going to need to be made. And she, or at least the paranoid voice in her mind, told her that Major-General Alexei Stormbader, a 'real man' standing at the gate of that closed-loop society, might inadvertently become a flag to rally to. The old soldier might prove an adaptive alternative just because he was not her. She was determined that the people would have eyes for only one comrade leader in the weeks that followed. If not she, then at least one is chosen by her and who would, of course, ultimately deliver on her grand plan.

The lady inclined her head slightly, a sign that she was thinking deeply. She also understood that policing the ship's population would be of great importance in the aftershock of any such announcement; she needed a plan for Alexei Stormbader before it became too late. There was room for only one sheriff.

As she thought, the room had calmed somewhat. Stormbader stared at Ariel. He was shaken, of course, but he understood that her crime, if the crime it proved to be, had been in not telling those present, perhaps even the whole ship's complement, that which she knew. The old soldier understood sheriffs and understood bullies, too. And so, he was not even certain that he thought of any of Ariel's actions as a crime. He was a military man, and as such, he had spent a lifetime operating on a need-to-know basis. He also understood that most of the other people in the room were, in fact, shocked at the appalling news itself and at their own position of entitlement. By each of them, little thought was likely given to what Ariel's role in it all might have been, except to Ariel herself, who seemed to be like a naughty child admitting to 'the lie'.

Stormbader also understood that if her statement was indeed proven to be true and he doubted that it was jest, in spite of his Russian heritage, then almost without doubt it was not a thing over which Ariel had any control, and it was not a thing that she had purposely desired or created. No, there was only one person aboard *Leviathan* who despised being there more than he himself, and that person was without a doubt Ariel MP. The old warrior knew that without even the smallest doubt. The thing that angered the marshal was quite simply the smug Cheshire cat grin that adorned the face of Sigmund Symonds. He had no right to be in that room; he knew it, and Stormbader knew it, too. He had known of this thing long before the other seven visitors, and he was nothing but the lady's bedpan and scratching post. Marshal despised that man, and so, as he sat there, he decided at that very moment that the two men would come to a reckoning, and soon, if he had his way. Ariel stood up daintily and raised both of her arms into the air. The room quieted, and in barely raised tones, she continued.

"There's more, but first let me explain, if you will. At the twelve-year-four and one-third thirty-day mark, we came out of our circumnavigation of the sun. Exiting its own gravitational pull to remain on target, we needed to be travelling at a significant fraction of light speed," she barked a small laugh and continued, "I won't get technical, and you all know that's not my strength."

A single echoing laugh from Symonds in response to this small attempt at levity died on the man's lips. This was serious business.

"In simple terms, we came out of that turn, and our rate of accelerated exit was less than it needed to be. I was aware of this early," she raised her left hand.

"And I took the decision to place my own people in positions sensitive to this information to ensure that it did not get out," she held the room still, just, and so the lady continued, "Whilst ensuring no single technician got to see the whole picture. I haven't been idle in the intervening years."

At this, the room looked towards her, and seven at least wondered, and in answer to the unasked question, she spoke again. "It seems that perhaps all of us took the information and endeavours of Radzinski and his people a little too easily, a little too at face value. I'm not sure we have either the time or, indeed, the technical expertise to do otherwise. Nonetheless, the calculations, or at least their execution, were wrong," she paused for breath, but no one spoke.

"In the first few years, I divided various research teams into small groups, each looking at something different, broken down into simple component units. How might we gain momentum? How might we amend our route? How might we even find a new location? It quickly became evident that there was no mileage in any of these, or indeed, the many other ideas that have been tried and discarded. All this in spite of the segmented nature of years of research—something, you understand, I felt obliged to do in order to ensure that there was no information bleed. Indeed, even a rumour would have been incendiary. So anyway, within a pretty short time of leaving our sun, I guess by which time we were far past the inner planets, I took the decision that it was time to start thinking outside the box. I brought Mr Symonds here into the loop, and after ensuring his credentials, I explained to him the situation as much as I have to you."

She did not even glance at the man sitting leaning back next to her.

"In the simplest of terms, even the best of us have not enough years left in them to see this journey through to its end. You all understand that the limits of much of the technology of our craft are untested. And whilst we certainly have untapped reserves of minerals and energy on board that may see us far beyond the original journey estimates that we calculate around, nevertheless, as the philosophers say, the future is the undiscovered country. Those of you who do not deal in economics will have to trust me on this. We can in all likelihood live on this damn rock a whole lifetime if we are prepared to be frugal and, of course, if we are lucky. That isn't the question," Ariel paused. "The question was then, and is now, do you want to live a lifetime on this ball of dirt and then die, having got nowhere?" Still, no one present had a word to say. "I brought Sigmund Symonds in because, in my opinion, he is the number one get-it-done man we have on board, and, once I had purposed on a plan, I needed someone in place that would get me access…" she slowed, "to the right resources, whilst doing exactly that, getting it done," she was in full flow, and the room was rapt. "You see, this has all been about our future."

Ariel stopped and took a couple of sharp breaths. Her words had been carefully chosen, and she had said only what she wished. If she was surprised at the absence of challenge or question from those present, it didn't show, and so, after a few seconds more, she continued, "I decided that our best chance lay now in changing ourselves. If we were neither able to shorten the journey by any significant measure nor go elsewhere that would bring us to some benign Earth sooner than a significant fraction of a century hence, then it needed, as I said earlier, thinking outside of the box. We…" and she turned and validated Symonds's presence in the room with her next words and a small nod. "We felt we had a shot at lengthening the time we all might have in order that we might get to where we were going. And yet, still arrive there, able to spend some significant years looking up at the sun."

Grafton Shevnetski spoke then; shaking his head and clenching his hands in front of him, he spoke in gruff tones and, interrupting the lady's flow, said, "I assume, Madam Tsaritsa, that you are speaking of cryogenics. I must say that, having spent three years at the Vladivostok Research Centre, you asked me if I might have saved you these many years of time and trouble," he paused and sucked down a lungful of breath before herding onwards, "The Americans chased it first, dear Lady Tsaritsa; it was always the Americans back then. Chasing that old dream of sleep and waking, refreshed and at your destination, the ultimate first-class billet," he continued with a barked laugh, "If only they had figured out where they wanted to go before, they figured out it just wouldn't work." The old politico seemed almost pleased as he raised himself up and stated with finality, "The engineering degradation is beyond our measure, and if memory serves, there was a similar rate of genetic degradation even at temperatures as close to absolute zero as they could get." Shevnetski was a man who enjoyed the sound of his own voice. A skilled orator, he had a reputation as a man who knew what he was talking about when he did get going. Ariel had smiled at the other man's outburst; still, it appeared outwardly patient in the extreme, but she jumped in quickly as soon as Shevnetski stopped speaking.

"No, Shev, we weren't looking at cryogenics; well, essentially, we were not. It is quite, quite true, I suppose; we did look at that alongside all the other options on the wish list, but that was many years ago now. It was a very short wish list, and, of course, I bow to your far greater expertise, Grafton. Indeed, such things we needed to achieve could not be done through cryogenic sleep."

Ariel moved now from behind the small dais she had until that point placed between her and her comrades, signalling with perfectly stage-managed aplomb that the final curtain was now to fall away.

"No, we were looking at something else, something a bit more radical; well, actually…a lot more radical. I am going to ask Mr Symonds to explain. Sigmund, if you would," she said, smiling.

Symonds stood effortlessly, having quietly sat down at some point during the previous minutes, and with a slightly pained expression, he then began to address all present.

"Thank you, Ariel. Yes, ladies and gentlemen, what we ultimately decided was, well, in fact, not to go down those routes that had been previously heavily travelled, some might say trampled," he smiled winsomely. "But instead, we chose to investigate a new scientific branch. Do you know the tale of the human mammal? The most incapable infant born of any mammal thrown out of the womb, it would seem, long before gestation would suggest it is capable of looking out for itself even in some basic sense. Think of a baby horse, or elephant, or tiger, or chimp. Of course, they all would have needed the care of the mother, but they all had some tools from the moment they were born to assist their survival, da?"

There were a couple of nods and some interesting faces.

"Now, we human babies, we are born incapable of standing, of communicating, of any self-care whatsoever, and do you know why?" Symonds did not wait for an answer. "It is because we changed the life cycle; humanity at some point in our genetic past, scholars have suggested, when we began to eat meat, well, we grew a brain so large that the head needed to encase it had to be born earlier or could not be born at all. We changed the life cycle by accident, it would seem, so why not by design? You see, we believed—we believe, in fact—

that with genetic re-sequencing, it is entirely possible to restructure the healthy lifespan of a human being. Well, to grow it exponentially, if the truth be told."

Gasps escaped the lips of several people in the room, and a low voice was clearly heard to say. "Agetec. I knew there wasn't something right with that bloody outfit."

Symonds was momentarily taken aback and uncertain who had spoken, but he quickly jumped on board. "Agetec, that's right, we used Agetec to front our research into gene re-sequencing. If we could keep this generation alive longer, then we might still make landfall with some years in front of us."

All of a sudden, Alexei Stormbader's voice boomed across the room, his frustration finally, it seemed, having got the better of him. "How long? How long are you going to give us, Symonds?" he sounded angry, and his voice boomed like thunder. Truly, he was the first person in the room to understand that Ariel was only now allowing her puppet to tell them all any of this because, of course, it must have all proven to be folly.

"Marshal, I am sorry if I anger you," Symonds responded, his tone still as smooth as silk and suggesting that he was about as far from sorry as any man might get.

"You don't anger me; you jumped up, bloody puppet!" Stormbader roared. "I just don't understand how the hell you think you can stand there as if you are, well…" he stumbled for a moment, trying to express his frustration at the other usurping a place of power, yet without the tacit admission that the eight others present were indeed the ultimate arbiters of all that took place on board *Leviathan*.

He changed tacks, got himself under control, recognised his own bullish ego, pushed through the undergrowth, and re-focused on the real business at hand. "OK, Symonds, you've got our attention; now will you answer my question? How long are you going to give us?" he stared unblinkingly at the other man.

"It isn't as straightforward as that; you must understand," Sigmund Symonds responded finally, beginning to sound ragged under the sheer weight of the other man's rage. "Things haven't gone quite as well as…as we hoped, but I believe, well, I am told, we are on the verge."

"On the verge?" The marshal fairly exploded.

Symonds's reply was almost panicky. "Yes…of a massive step forward," Ariel MP, almost imperceptibly, raised one eyebrow at this statement. "I am advised by my technical people that we are a few months, perhaps even only a few weeks away from an announcement that will blow today's bad news away like a spring fog in the morning over Moscow."

"Can you not just one-time answer a straight question with a straight answer?" The old soldier boomed, sounding, if it were possible, even more exasperated than he had before; this time, though, there were supporting rumblings from two or three others of those present in the room.

It was obvious that the disaffection with Symonds was growing swiftly, and so, ever watchful of the ramifications of a wrong move, Ariel stepped in immediately, shushing Symonds and waving him sharply back into his seat. This time she did not herself stand, but, sitting forward in her seat, which, of course, was just slightly raised above those of the others in the room, she nonetheless took back control.

"I believe that if you want it in purely numerical terms, we are talking about as much as ninety, maybe a hundred years of healthy core adulthood."

Using her brilliant instinctual timing, she paused before easing past. "As opposed to the thirty or forty years of healthy adulthood we presently hope to enjoy. Alongside this healthy improvement, there maybe as much as one hundred- and fifty-years' lifespan for a healthy individual." Ariel smiled almost coquettishly. "That's a full lifespan, with much of the additional time encapsulated in a dramatically slower easement towards old age."

The room watched her with an intensity that made all that had gone before seem like little more than a Russian children's game of pass the (hot) potato. "Once we get this right, effective childhood and adolescence will remain much the same…the biology of growth is too intrinsic to who we each are."

Ariel had skilfully avoided the trap of commenting either way upon the fact that what she had said was in no way a reality at that moment; she was happy, it seemed, to leave her assistant's earlier lie in place, for the time being, unchecked.

Ariel MP, Madam Tsaritsa's words were met with gasps of astonishment, and for a time the meeting descended into a good old Mother Russian 'Zsyo boodet harasho' (Everything's gonna be all right). Events wound to a close after an hour of further debate, and Ariel appeared happy that the majority at least appeared to have taken the bitterest of pills in a shared mouthful with the weakest of placebos possible. Everyone had agreed that the time was not yet right for a public digest or greater pontification than was already the case. And so, a short-term plan built around the lies hidden within the general truth of ongoing technical inefficiencies would be hard to dispute for at least a day or two.

In the hours that followed, this was put into play, a small sidestep to acknowledge that the masses still awaited final planetfall information whilst giving those same people none. It was also agreed that they would all meet again in forty-eight hours in order to bring together their separate conclusions and find the best way forward. It was, after all, a hell of a thing, and it seemed to each that their own ability to acknowledge and accommodate this brave new world would help immensely with the coming needs of many.

Alexei Stormbader had, though, quieted quite suddenly in the instant after Ariel's revelatory comments, asking sagely and terribly carefully only when they might see the results for themselves. This had been said mildly, almost like a whisper when compared to his earlier venting. Stormbader was becalmed, and this bothered Ariel. She had nailed her colours to a forty-eight-hour flag of convenience, and she knew that unless she was to end up falling very suddenly from her lofty perch, then they would need to pull a real rabbit from a quickly shrinking hat in less than two days' time. Ariel also knew that Alexei Stormbader was not one to fall for parlour magic, and that would need dealing with before The Eight were to meet again.

As he closed the door, Alexei let slip a long-held breath. He looked down at his hands and saw, for the first time in many years, that they were shaking. He examined the inside of himself with the careful precision of a lifetime in the military, and he found in a short time that he was afraid. Marshal had watched as that slightest of women had expertly played her small audience, and inside he felt certain that she had done so with nothing in her hands more than guile.

He didn't doubt that for everyone in that craft, as much as for everything he had left to hold dear, Ariel MP now played the deadliest of games. That there was no brave new world around the corner had, of course, been a shock to him, as much as all of those present, but he also felt a nagging certainty that she had lied about the other too, compounding all of those years of deception in an attempt to what? Muddy the waters, hide even greater bad news? Bolster her position? What, he wondered? Her powerbase, her alliances? He didn't have anywhere near enough of the facts, and that, too, only added to his growing anxiety.

Marshal guessed that she had no master plan, no solution, and that she, too, saw only a slow death for each one of them. A slow end, as some sixty thousand souls faded to a pointless and tragic death, and particularly harsh with no life thereafter.

And worst of all, as the old soldier saw things that slow the procession to death, carefully managed by the ministrations of Ariel Paver Mne and her prosecutor. For him, Alexei Stormbader, and perhaps only he, knew the truth about her mysteriously abbreviated twin-lettered surname for an MP to look in the reflecting glass, because the lady was the ultimate narcissist, and so mirrors were her special friend.

In that reflection, you would find PM, and for PM, understanding the games the lady played, you might walk straight down the path to Paver Mne (believe me), and there you were, another small mystery unravelled, another tiny game from the queen of game-playing, and a light into the mind of their great and wondrous benefactor.

The marshal understood the terrible sword that she hung above them all. Ariel MP had been critical in shaping their survival to this point. Her self-regard, her deeply disguised and yet complete lack of empathy, or indeed anything resembling genuine human feelings, had allowed Ariel to harvest the best and trim and order that best to a top table.

No one else could have pretended so much, and yet they only wanted to walk over the skulls of the dying millions that had been left behind. Stormbader could acknowledge how much they needed Ariel to get to this point and how terrifying it was now that they were here to have that future sitting squarely in her completely inhuman hands. She, it seemed, had long since placed herself as the arch-hunter; forget female-male; she was the Alpha, and Alexei understood that he had wandered out of the brush and today maybe became her newest prey.

He looked at his watch and saw that it was ten minutes after the second hour after thirteen; he still didn't get on with twenty-five-hour days.

He'd hated those arrogant British back in his days on Earth, but now he felt some sympathy as he thought back to the generations that had fought against the metric system, unwilling to be bullied out of the imperial measures that, during their empire, they had grown so accustomed to. It was all a bugger, he thought, as he walked away, shaking his head. He felt certain that even this small thing was some scheme by her highness to keep everybody just a bit off balance. He knew that his hand was weak, so he left to try now and find an ace of his own before it was too late.

8
You Cannot Write with a Pitchfork on Flowing Water

The day was drawing to a close. In the world of *Leviathan*, the social niceties of Russian tradition—daytime turning to evening, the masses returning home from good toil, had quietly been subsumed in years gone by in accordance with the needs of the great craft. Cyclical shift patterns through the thirteen-hour day, or 'lights up', as it was commonly known, accounted for about seventy percent of the total on-board activity, and it was the same pattern every day. Effectively, Monday was the same as Sunday, and Tuesday was the same as Friday. And despite the protestations of representatives of each of the Abrahamic religious branches, pragmatic need, or, as some said, the wishes of Ariel MP, won out once more. After a series of brief and bitter struggles, this new pattern was set. Lights down, the twelve-hour dark period, was perceived as night to the vast majority. But this was only because for those twelve hours, the nuclear sunlight used to manage the various hydroponic feed projects was in low mode.

The remaining thirty percent of activity that took place during those twelve hours was not, as one might expect, predominantly social in nature. Rather, this was really just an extension of the ongoing work-oriented function. The vast majority of ships' personnel interacted socially, in fact, on a pretty infrequent basis, beyond partners, some small neighbourliness, and, most commonly, work colleagues. This had been, so it seemed, an inevitable consequence of the trauma that everyone aboard had lived through; a certain detached grandiosity, it seemed, had developed as some kind of protection measure for the majority. This was a strange craft and a strange community. There was no pilot, there was no bridge, and they were not split into crew and passengers; this was a reworking of the structure of a community.

In the last century on Earth, communities had increasingly atomised and become separate and compartmentalised, and this had not proven difficult, whether by accident or design, to replicate aboard *Leviathan*. Sixty thousand was not an inconsiderable number of people, but they had all been squeezed into a four-point-two-three-mile by two-point-nine-mile irregular lump of quartz, iron ore, and carbon for nearly a quarter of a century now. And whilst the malaise that had so impacted on-board reproduction rates might be accounted for by science and scientists, no such alternate explanation could be found for this breakdown in dynamic social interaction.

A few, publicly verbose, had spoken up about the inactive, disconnected nature of the majority, but it seemed likely that the simple truth was that an unedifying diet of soft medicines and alcohol, alongside screened repeats of the same human parables told with dramatic and associated effects over and over, could not cure the global scale post-traumatic stress that to one degree or another had impacted everyone aboard. This was the new human paradigm. It may also be true that the steady calming of the massed ranks suited the on-board management; similarly, security considerations and logistics had certainly helped to manage resource consumption rates.

This, then, was really no change from the similarly dispiriting latter years of the twentieth and twenty-first centuries back on Earth, and so was simply the trauma response most consistent with the generation that had survived. A similar edict once explained how German survivors of the Great War from 1914 to 1918 had been so abused by the treaties that then arose; that, in defeat and abuse, they were birthed, even welcomed, by the Nazis—who in turn abused the Jews, who atomised, segregated, and in turn abused their Arab neighbours, and on and on. Each abuse is generating an ever more hostile model of narcissism, heading towards psychopathy.

At each turn, the abused nation behaved like an abused individual, a macro-level version of denying responsibility and so blaming what had gone before as the reason for their own poor behaviour. Some saw a clearer truth. Some began to say that the rhetoric of victimicity could only lead to further abuse, but they were too few and too small in a world swallowed up by such an overwhelming and self-defeating majority. In such a situation, it may have been inevitable that in order to survive, a stoical society with a traditional Russian mode of withdrawal, tradition, and distance in respect was the only way left for humanity to inch forward once more.

It was true that as the lights went down throughout much of *Leviathan* at what was quaintly nicknamed 'teatime', the general levels of movement around the craft began to dip towards a low point at about the eighteenth hour each day since lights up.

Hermione knew that it was around that time of the day. Her body clock instincts have been honed by many years of skulking around in down below. Years before, she had gained a habit of catastrophising, building nightmares into every dark corner. This had taught her some things well, such as avoiding contact with the larger working groups as they returned to their own and one another's quarters at the end of their various shifts. The old lady had grown accustomed to finding refuge and rest through these, the quietest and yet, in contradiction, seemingly most dangerous hours. Sleeping rough was a strange concept within the confines of that piece of space flotsam the remnants of humanity had taken refuge in, but Hermione Zatapec was by no means alone in that particular habit. And like the small but still significant number of vagrants floating unseemly around down below, she followed her own well-practised patterns when securing herself as safe a space as she might to while away the 'lights down' hours.

The trouble was, she thought to herself as she looked around for a suitable place to construct the four pieces of discarded polyboard she had managed to accumulate into a shelter of sorts. The trouble was, the thought repeated, that something wasn't right. She ought to be tired; she always got tired by this time of the day. In fact, more and more she was completely exhausted, and the simple challenge was to get safe, get warm, if that was ever possible in the belly of the whale, and get out of consciousness. Her mind spied on how, over the past few months, she had oftentimes struggled to keep going. Even to the point of occasionally allowing sleep to take her before she had really been certain of her coming night's welfare.

In a small, dark corner of her mind, a voice whispered. "Perhaps that's how they came on you. Were you tired and fell into the deep and dreamless sleep of the stone gargoyle, dear? We wonder?" She felt rather than heard the voice smirk. "How easy to take you, Hermione." And if that was the truth of it, then how easy indeed!

Hermione frowned, not quite understanding the thought at all, and yet feeling some faint itch, some vague eerie recognition. The tiniest tug suggested that perhaps once again she was missing something. She shook her head once minutely and then again more vigorously, refocusing her mind on what was presently wrong. Then she corrected herself, realising that wrong wasn't really the correct word. Things weren't wrong, by God, no. Things were, in fact, quite exceptionally right. Hermione felt twenty years younger than, well, twenty years younger than she had done when she awoke that morning. And not just felt; this was more; this was something truly amazing in the biblical sense.

She had progressively become dynamic and energised in a way she felt quite clearly, quite naturally, and yet perceived as completely unfathomable. Had she peered into a looking glass, she might have seen how much younger she was beginning to appear, and, armed with that clear knowledge so early in the piece, perhaps things would have gone differently. As she walked and considered, the lady happened upon a tight alleyway. Nothing more, really, than an access point, a path into various ducting and internal cabling, a space maybe four feet high by three feet wide that appeared dusty and unvisited for a long time. It ran two floors under and maybe as much as three hundred feet along the rear of an accommodation block sporting perhaps twenty or thirty residential units. Each of the housing units had a floor open onto a public walkway two decks above, sleeping quarters on a lower-unwindowed deck, and then a power and waste plant for each on the deck lowest of all; in fact, where she now stood, at the upper reaches of what was colloquially known as down below.

Hermione did not usually climb so high, and certainly not in the past few years. She had learned to complain about her legs bitterly, and so she rarely had the physical strength to drag herself too far from what she considered the main drag. But after the incident at the back of the bowling alley earlier that day, Hermione had found that, indeed, instead of suffering as a consequence of the woman's attack in the washroom, she had, in fact, found herself energised by those events, invigorated. Hoisting the brown case high in her arms, she strode away from the place with purpose, albeit with nowhere to go. In time, climbing and walking, she found herself where she now stood. The not-so-old elderly lady did not understand why, but she was not tired; indeed, she was not even especially out of puff, having stood for a minute or two breathing quietly.

She had to admit to herself that she felt damn wonderful. Hermione had read it once many years ago (in fact, she thought she might not have read it); perhaps she watched it on a newscast or overheard it whilst idling beside a carafe of water in one of the eateries. But she reminded herself, getting back to the point, she had read, seen, or heard somewhere that often people who were in a terminal condition had a brief period of wandering in wonderment. A kind of final clarity of thought and health reminiscent of glorious former days, and this just moments before the end. And as she stood at the entrance to that long-disused access path, four pieces of polyboard held under one arm and a battered brown satchel case clamped under the other, that was exactly what she found herself thinking.

It was just then that the young girl, who had been standing in the shadows watching the older lady with interest, chose to step out of the black into the dim night-time luminescence and speak. "Hello. What are you doing?"

Hermione Zatapec fairly jumped out of her skin, and a small yelp escaped her lips. So surprised was she at the young girl's sudden words. "Who are you? What are you doing here?" she replied, flustered and caught more than a little off-guard. Her words came out garbled, chasing one another like a pair of autumn squirrels.

"I could ask you the same question," the other replied, "but you seem OK, I guess. Actually, you look kinda nice in a scruffy sort of way," she continued, quite relaxed, it appeared, in comparison to the nervous older woman. Hermione looked the other up and down, her eyes focusing remarkably quickly on the dim light; she noted this internally with a small momentary furrowing of her brow. The girl was quite small, pale, and very slim, and she looked at the older woman like she might be quite frail. This child was not one to toss around playing tag or whatever games the children might now play, Hermione considered.

The girl's complexion was exquisitely pale, and she was dressed in a simple light blue one-piece cotton-effect frock and wore a thick cardigan and hat with fur flaps against the evening's biting cold. When she had spoken, her voice, whilst very pretty, tinkling in an almost elfin way, had been little more than a whisper. In the dim electric glow of night-time in down below, she might have been a ghost. If Hermione had believed in such things, then that might have explained her shock and momentary, ill-at-ease reaction. But this had all ceased the instant the young girl had walked forward and gently taken a hold of the older lady's free hand.

Hermione Zatapec was surprised, but not so much as to withdraw her hand; instead, letting the polyboard drop silently to the rocky floor, she had closed her larger hand around the girl's much smaller hand in response. And so, in the simplest of manners, a friendship was born.

Time passed, and the two had taken to sitting in the small access way; there they began to talk, speaking long and easily. They spoke of many things, all very random. Comparing their day, their journey to that alcove, their love of *Wind in the Willows,* and their respective lives. An amazing quality appeared to envelop both of them, in that once they had each overcome the initial contact, in their different ways, they instantly became perfectly at ease with one another. To an onlooker, both would have seemed nothing more than old friends catching up and comfortable in the extreme. Hermione had asked almost immediately what the young girl (Muriel Anastasia Cardington was her name, as it turned out) was doing in a place as grubby as where they had both now washed up.

Muriel, or 'Mac' as she preferred, and having persuaded her many doctors to call her, replied that she often 'mooched around' hereabouts. Her home was, in fact, to be found in one of the blocks set immediately above where they both now sat, huddled together like two giggling girls but also like a pair of escaped convicts. Hermione saw no lie in the girl's features, and during the next two hours, she learned much more about the reasons why such a frail, pretty young thing might find herself wandering aimlessly about in Hermione's neck of the woods. In turn, and later, Hermione could find no reason why, she had talked freely about her own travails, the tender balance between survival and not, and the small regard that she had lately come to for her own life. The older lady spoke willingly about how she saw her place in the scheme of things, and all the time she clutched the battered leather case close to her chest.

It was whilst referring to the incidents of the previous few days that Hermione Zatapec found herself looking into her own mind, and maybe for the first time, seeing and beginning the war of confrontation with the great blank darkness that sat squarely in its centre. How strange, that mind considered, that she was verbalising those thoughts in the presence of this tiny elfin young thing? Later, when they had parted, she convinced herself that she had not, but without much certainty. "What had she done?" Or, more precisely, she wondered what had been done to her; she felt certain she had been in the presence of magic, and only much later was she to truly understand how magical a child's powers are!

Time had a robust but limited meaning in Hermione's day-to-day existence, but now, she had opened herself up to it, there undoubtedly appeared to be a yawning chasm between the bitter separation she had begun in those hours to remember and the events of the past few days. Her mind and memory were clearing like stormy seas abated; she spied years before—maybe as many as a decade—a younger Hermione had chosen a path that now began to reveal itself. That younger version of her had wished only to climb, and in that climbing, had broken much and parted with force from her husband, her lover, and her friend

Jacob. She remembered now a little too well how at that time she had found herself in a place where, driven by all her own fears, shame, and a need for achievement, by some foggy imposed programming from her earliest years, she had lost sight of the simple goals of love and harmony. In spite of that fact—that blindness to the things she might, she ought to have valued most—it had been a tough choice.

Looking back now, she saw that even as soon as a day after the steady, shrill tone of her man's owl-like slow hooting had faded from her life, Hermione at that hour began to see glimpses of how, at some root level, she had made the most grievous error. It was a feeling, and even ten years later, deep in her amygdala, where there is no time, it was terrible and ominous. The lady was aware she had hurt a good man. But as she remembered then, she looked back and saw her arrogance and her self-aggrandisement. Even armed with her own pain and that clear understanding, she had put off any thoughts of attempting a reconciliation. How she had preferred wallowing in the reward that shame itself gave her; always vaguely certain she could change things at a whim.

Hermione's memory played tricks as she sat there, mixing images and metaphors. Nevertheless, she began to recognise, in part, that she had done something bad, something she was uncertain whether Jacob could have forgiven.

Remembering, in that calm and quiet place with the equally calm and pale Muriel, she was reminded how it diametrically opposed the very ambitions that had driven that other Hermione. Driven her onward and away from Jacob Wise. She did not clearly recollect it all then. How, in equal counterpoint, fate had presented her at the very moment of their separation with the exact hope for advancement she had been working for and fervently wishing for.

The universe, it is said, has no perception of good or evil. These are human-made precepts. Nonetheless, the universe is abundant, and so it will give you whatever you think you deserve, whatever it is that exists in your secret heart. And thus, it proved when, eleven days after their separation, Jacob Desire Wise had died screaming, tragically killed in a malfunctioning decompression hatch between inner and outer hulls. Hermione did not yet recollect this fully, nor did she remind herself yet that they had not spoken again, never a single word since those of their bitter parting. And so, she did not yet completely understand what had followed—how she had never gotten to tell the man of her life quite how much she loved him.

Later, the inquest traced a faulty motor sequencer as the cause of the tragic accident; no one, it seemed, had ever wanted to ask the question quite what was a senior bio-science doctor, a man of no small esteem, even doing in a decompression chamber? She remembered, as she sat there, chilly in a darkening space, small fragments of those tortured days, days that ran on and on. Each day, a separate island on an archipelago is filled with endless pain. It ebbed into weeks and months, each moment filled to the brim with self-recrimination and pity. Russians like to say that guilt is when we each know of our sin, when it sits next to our hearts and awaits the hard work of redemption.

But shame is a different beast. Shame is when everyone knows of your sin, and shame strips the soul bare. Hermione had been filled with that shame, and so, slowly, inevitably, she had slipped under the table and out of that life, the life she had sought. Running away as fast as she might, and as fast as she ever had, from the burden of responsibility that sat upon her shoulders. And now here she was, sitting there for the first time, finally beginning to understand why her mind had chosen to dwell in a garden of forgetfulness.

Hermione Zatapec had once been wise, but she hadn't been wise, had she? She had wandered long and aimless, itself an achievement in the deep dark and cold of endless space, aboard a godless hunk of timeless rock. Each day was the same, as she wandered and wondered and worried about who she might hold accountable. Twisting and changing the facts into something more palatable throughout those drawn-out years. Forcing forgetfulness upon herself and yet, for the longest time, scratching endlessly at all of her own unfulfilled promises. In the end, it had all just been words. And so, she completed a psychological collapse and so became her own version of Nemo (nobody), or perhaps more aptly, Siddhartha, Herman Hesse's wanderer.

She had become like the Brahmin's son, who had let go of everything and had stood naked facing the blast furnace of his own failed life in an attempt to recognise Atman in himself. Had Hermione known of Siddhartha in those dark days, she knew something, but the light as yet did not shine so far down. Hermione would certainly have scoffed and pointed out that she had not been searching for any higher purpose, simply that she had been dumb. That stupid is as stupid as it is, and so she had been brought low by her own ego and her own pride. Indeed, had she read the tale of Siddhartha, then she would have seen how she paralleled his path. She was once Hermione Wise. But truly, she began to spy; she hadn't been wise at all.

The older lady sat with the younger girl and drifted for a while, sailing slowly down the tributaries of vague, sad, and ancient memories. In some corner of her mind, she felt certain that the young girl would grow bored, or at the very least become frustrated at the older woman's silence. And so, in less time than she expected, and yet still far beyond the passing of many years within her mind, she spoke again. And though those countless years had been run up and down like fingers across piano keys, thought is a swift thing, and the girl took up the reins of renewed conversation as if there had been nothing but a moment of silence between them.

As they spoke, on and into the peace of that strange underworld, so it was that, in part at least, fragments of Hermione's memories began to return. They seemed to her the same as the drifting tendrils of icy cold mist, some floating gently on a current all their own, others sat still in her mind's gaze, and more still just on the edge of that sight, tantalisingly out of reach. The passion for loss, even after so long a time, drove lesser memories in front, like herded cattle pressed into winter pasture, beasts brought down from the high ground, it seemed, with nary a moment to spare. And yet, somewhat like those cattle, the memories seemed fragmented. Each was poorly fed, tired, and worn from the journey, seeming ill-fitting to her in that moment, somehow uncomfortable in the new, simple surroundings in which she and they found themselves.

So, whilst that was, in fact, the first moment in many long years when she might have begun to put together the strange dilemma that had become her life, instead she once again turned away. As she had done so many times, avoiding the pain and burden of responsibility. Instead, Hermione Zatapec turned and questioned gently the sanguine child, who, it seemed, to appear at least, was so much more in control of who she was than her older companion.

Eventually, a time came when the younger girl and Hermione parted ways. The older lady had reached into her battered brown case; her hands touched upon a small brass compass, a guide by which they might one day find one another again. But Muriel smiled and shook her head.

"We have what we are," she had said simply, and gently refused any gift as unnecessary. For them, a bond of friendship had already grown and swiftly become undeniable. So, it was then that they both made promises to meet again soon, in anticipation of the bond they shared, drawing a pleasant joint excitement from the two even in parting.

The girl left their dark place first, and Hermione watched her skipping away, slowly and yet with a purpose and youth, even in her frailty, that she could not fail to envy. She toyed with staying in the dark, dry place for a longer time, yet something in her mind nagged at her to move on, to save that place for another time. Her mind was in turmoil then, with memories and visions vying to demand her attention.

9
The Rules of God and the Laws of Men

Ariel was back in her quarters, a place of relative opulence in comparison to most of the mined and prefabricated spaces people retreated to in *Leviathan*. Her space accommodated both offices and an apartment of sorts, though back in the Motherland, the aristocracy would have viewed such a space as little more than a bedsit. But in her home amongst the homes, her trove of treasures, Ariel had built a private lair, which, had they known, would have been the envy of many aboard *Leviathan*. Amongst those treasures, she possessed her own coffee machine, despite coffee not appearing anywhere on either the frozen goods manifest or the hydroponic growth list. This small thing was a prize for her greater than the czars of old's greatest gifts of avarice.

Tsaritsa harboured a long-since dwindling supply against the prospect of caffeine withdrawal and entered into many a dark bargain to ensure she had whatever beans might be found among the more miscreant in order to put off the day the coffee died. Despite that care and harbouring, though, today all bets were off, and so Ariel mooned over a large cup of black liquid, sniffing at the indelicate bitter aroma of now steaming coffee, born of beans frozen at close to absolute zero. She stood absolutely still and gazed out of a tiny, deeply embedded porthole, a three-inch by three-inch windows to the stars (albeit with a little help from a dozen carefully placed refracting mirrors); this, too, was another treasure beyond reckoning that the lady had captured one of only three private rooms with a window to the stars on that whole barren spinning rock.

One issue that has never been of concern on a great long journey had been the capacity to freeze and freeze for the long term. They were, after all, two nuclear reactors and one hunk of rock away from minus two hundred and seventy-three degrees Celsius. Their shared life aboard *Leviathan* was, at least in part, both governed by and a result of enthalpy. There were no absolute closed-loop ecologies available to humanity, though they did a decent job of harvesting water and reintroducing nutrients. Indeed, splitting water and allowing hydrogen to fuel their warmth and voyage, oxygen to feed their atmosphere, and, in turn, carbon dioxide to feed the greenery, have all proven attainable. This all, indeed, had kept the rock and its occupants alive for nearly a quarter of a century. An onlooker from another time, any other time, would quite possibly have viewed that thing as humanity's greatest feat of engineering.

Enthalpy is the equation that says total heat is a result of energy within, plus pressure, plus volume. *Leviathan* was a cold place; mists of vapour drifted endlessly around down below and seemed as aimless as the souls that washed up down there, each slipping silently into many cracks and corners. The nuclear plants gave them what they had, but there were millions upon millions of micro-fissures and 'ways out'. Despite the plastocrete filling, the simple truth was that this 'small asteroid' which had been estimated at more than six million years old, had fissures and pathways at a microscopic level beyond the ability of these latter-day men to spy. And, moreover, as that rock spans its way across the void, more and more are being made as quickly as others were being filled.

Both of these facts ensured that the loop was never closed; absolute zero sat resolutely just outside the door, and so that cold got in; it always found a way. The daylight hours are better, and the heat of Psvedo Solntse (Pseudo-sun) would for some areas bring dryness and even a gently baking heat. But it was always short-lived: that man-made sun brought only the briefest respite from the cold, a brief and strangely surreal relief that was physical but could not dispel the aching, inching icy chill that clawed at the population's heart, and that lived oft times in those same people's dreams. That cold found a corner in each man and woman's soul as the weeks and months of their snail's-pace journey turned to years.

For Ariel, as for all aboard, another day had drawn towards its chilly close, whilst little more than a mile away, a young girl and a young lady cemented a friendship that might bring an end, or a beginning, to everything. In her quarters, Ariel blew on her quickly cooling coffee, and the words of a great thinker from her past ambled quietly across her mind.

"As far as we can discern whether God or eternity, the sole purpose of human existence is to kindle a light in the darkness of mere being." Ariel did not profess to be a deep metaphysical thinker; she preferred to line up her toys and ensure they were all facing forward and ready to step to her tune. Nevertheless, she considered and wondered whether she and the sixty thousand aboard the whale, in fact, now shielded the last guttering candle, the last tottering light against a universe that would run on to eternity uncaring, should that light be snuffed out. A light watched by none, explored, and discovered by none, cared for and admired by none. It did not seem credible to Tsaritsa when she framed it like that, but, as far as she and probably anyone that had ever lived was concerned, humanity was the only beings ever to have been blessed, or perhaps cursed, with the gift of…well, of being the witness. Carl Jung seemed to have fidgeted with the stitches of his sanity a century or two ago. Humanity had come only recently, and the universe, it seemed, cared not for watching one way or another.

The thought seemed momentarily to defeat Ariel, and she remembered the words of her father, long unthought and buried deep in her past.

"Remember, child, men make rules, but only God makes the law. You break the rules when you open the door of an aircraft. When you hit the ground a minute or two later…mmm, God's law. Most rules are there simply to stop stupid people from opening those doors and dying, but they are rules; they are the rules of men and women, and so they can be broken. The laws are God's property, daughter; they are made by the Father, and they are unbreakable, by yours or my hand. And that is the difference," his long-dead voice echoed down the decades as she considered the predicament.

Indeed, they had broken lots of rules in the past few months in an effort to conceal and deal with the dire change they had recently discovered in their situation. Ariel considered that she was the author, but she was right, wasn't she? But then she considered how changing the span of a human life—those were the laws of God, weren't they? She considered all that then and felt the anxiety of her most deeply held low self-esteem. Maybe there was no more messing; perhaps her father had been right so many years before. The reverie of her thoughts was broken as she heard the sound of dogs barking in the distance. Her dystopian doubt was immediately dispelled as she homed in on the guttural sound of those barks.

Her organising mind went immediately to work and quantified, visualised, hounds catching spiteful little shipboard rats, a simple part of the new delicate eco-balance that supported them all in that place. And so, she returned to safer ground, understood, and categorised the noise, and, as quickly as it had come, she put it aside. That was how Ariel MP was, and how she dealt with most things that were put before her.

At that exact moment, her doors chimed. Anatoli, who was her own and particularly Dvoretski (*sic*: butler), was absent, probably playing cards in down below, probably losing, Ariel considered. She sighed and winced inwardly at the thought of that stupid man giving up more than he had once more, considering the round-and-round nature of human beings and how predictable they all generally were. A low-level portion of her programming was already working on the additional leverage her butler's new losses would allow her. She would lecture him as she always did, and he would remonstrate briefly about his freedom to go to the devil in his own way.

But in the end, he, like so many others, hoovered up even the tiniest crumbs of Ariel's attention, taking even her harshest criticism as a kind of well-meant bullying affection. Anatoli had long since surrendered to the wiles of Ariel MP, and though he was well aware that she would cover his mark with the card master, the price he would be asked to pay would be exponentially high. Absolute devotion, absolute service, and no questions asked. And so, the circle closed: he would perform her bidding, and he would loathe himself for doing so. He would try and break free, and the gambling was really just a symptom of that; and then, when he had broken himself and filled himself with fear, he would come crawling back, a slug dragging itself across broken glass to do her bidding one more time.

Ariel, of course, did not recognise this cycle in the same terms as Anatoli, simply that she was hungry, and in some small way, the small, greying, grizzled old butler was another momentary distraction, a morsel to be grabbed at when other better morsels were not available. But tonight, knowing who was calling upon her, Tsaritsa was happy to leave the butler to his chosen sin, and so she drained the remainder of her coffee and went herself to receive her guests. Upon opening a pair of deep oak doors, she found two priests standing before her in full Russian Orthodox regalia. Both were men, both with similar lengthening grey beards, black headpieces, and flowing, though upon closer inspection, tired-coloured robes. They entered Ariel's ante room with a flourish of greetings, as if old friends were once again re-joined. Ariel MP played along; this was, for her, a far more traditional Russian game: pretend nice, play dirty. This was territory the Tsaritsa felt right at home in, and she had, she thought, the measure of both before they had stepped through her doors.

"Greetings to you, Alexei Smorzgard, and to you, Nicolai Shevchenko. I was, I must say, surprised to see you on my appointment pad for today," Ariel paused. "But pleased, of course, to have your company and to welcome you for the first time in all these years to my humble space here." She looked beyond both men at the screen lit behind them. A series of numbers scrolled across the bottom, providing technical updates about the many aspects of the great craft. Ariel absorbed the numbers and said simply minus three. She was referring to the ambient temperature that was anticipated that night on her particular deck of *Leviathan*. She shuddered at the thought, although whether that was at her own distress in the chilly evening air or was a thought for those poor souls in down below, it was not clear. Three degrees below on Ariel's deck would replicate somewhere pretty close to eight below in down below.

Smorzgard was the taller of the two by a couple of inches and heavier in girth. He bowed slightly and inclined his head just a touch to the left so he might keep an eye on the lady whilst greeting her. He smiled and replied, "Dear Ariel MP, my, my, I must wonder if this old bucket we fly in does not nurture for you a beauty like the Mother of Christ herself. Does she not seem more radiant than even that, Brother Nicolai?"

Brother Nicolai looked significantly uncomfortable at this effusive all-embracing retort but managed to smile, nod, and add himself, "My lady, thank you for seeing us; you do look well."

Over the pleasantries, both men accepted the offer of seats placed in front of a work desk covered in data sheets and small screen data pads, a desk that Ariel retreated from behind. And as she did so, she placed herself, though scant inches, just a little higher than her guests. Ariel was presciently aware that the strongly Russian contingent on-board *Leviathan*, though a fairly faithless and potentially ruthless mix of cultures and classes, nonetheless had a heritage of 'trusting in God'. Most of Russia's strong leaders throughout history had fallen in the end because they made the simple mistake of not allowing that their deeds be met, and so done, in God's name.

Ariel understood that, had the likes of the Czars, Stalin, Lenin, or latterly Putin and Chekov been able to stand down their own egos long enough to be seen to ask for the hand of a greater power, then it is likely that the Gulag Archipelago might have stood for many centuries as testimony to the cruelty of Russia the Fatherland. This as generations gave themselves up on the harshest conditions and toughest life imaginable in the name of God and their perception that Mother Russia embraced them, whatever leader had construed to enable that worship. Such was the curse, and such was also the indomitable power of Mother and Father Russia. Many aboard believed that worship and service were still the routes to salvation, despite their generally piratical nature.

The Tsaritsa understood this, and so she cultivated nationalism, though never sectarianism. lady considered herself tolerant of each of the main branches of the Abrahamic and Islamic faiths, deliberately designing and allowing small victories for each here and there. Non-denominational and smaller sects were given a voice, though never a platform, and all this whilst never nailing her own colours to any single mast. Such was the merry-go-round game the unofficial leader of sixty thousand souls played. The woman who lived deepest in Ariel's deeply narcissistic soul understood she could not overcome these traditions, these men of history, but she was forged and trained in the art of 'influence'. Tsaritsa's instincts won the day when, by force of arms, she might never do. Consciously, Ariel MP would not sway the masses with her wiles and beguiles, and so she wreathed her magic.

To any onlooker, Tsaritsa absolutely believed in herself, that she had an inviolate right to be who she was and to dictate the direction of the many because she really did know better. Through all those inner debates, though, the whisper at the back of her mind was smart enough to keep that direction so subtle. Most often, the pawn felt like the player, and she was merely an enthusiastic aide, one that seemed less. She often portrayed herself as the self-limiting equivalent of conscience; this is from a woman who lived in the absence of empathy. This was deep and clever stuff, a dangerous game, but one that had brought the lady her life when so many had died and power when so many had crumbled. Ariel MP was nothing if not a winner.

She offered sparkling water, waving vaguely at a sealed carafe on a small side table decorated with three small, coloured glasses sat around it in various states of repose. Such sparkling water was, in fact, a rare gift on board *Leviathan*, and setting out in such a manner was just another small accord to the sway this lady held. Both guests refused with a tiny shake of the head now bereft of headgear, and each man spoke no words. The two preachers watched the lady closely, though neither consciously noticed that they now sat with an eyeline some inches below their host. Nevertheless, both seemed to sense at some level that the lady had subtly taken control of the room. Ariel smiled and spoke up.

"And so, my esteemed brethren of the Russian Orthodoxy, how is it that you hope that I may help you today?" For Ariel, avoiding absolutes in her statements whenever possible, preferring to hint, gently opine, suggest, and wonder, left so much more wiggle room and so much less 'master talk'.

Alexei looked at Nicolai, who was, in truth, the more senior minister, but it was Alexei who was the talker, the pulpit basher, the singular preacher that would stand at the Gates of Hades and claim the expulsion of the Demon Lord in the name of our Lord God. And so, he looked at the lady, looked fractionally upwards into her unflinching gaze, and, after a few moments, asked simply, "Why are The Eight lying to us?"

When Ariel was surprised at the question, or even the abrasive nature of those words, she made no sign. The preacher continued, seemingly responding to the merest of nods. "The verse of St Nicholas tells us, my lady, that a lie is the destruction of love, and a false oath is the denial of God."

Ariel watched carefully and hid not so deep the predator in her. Wondering what these two men had or thought they had, she corrected herself. She wondered what, in fact, they wanted; the lady was nothing if not an optimising machine. She inclined her head once again, this time with a questioning look, but still, she did not speak. So it was that the preacher, of less constitution than she, was obliged to either look back and hold that silence, like a battleground awaiting the bugle call of the enemy, or instead to continue.

After a short time, the more verbose preacher Alexei continued, "My lady, it was agreed years ago, now more than ten, I am certain, that we would before this day closed have a final and clear signal of our new home. That which the almighty has chosen for his blessed few children." he waved his arms vaguely around the room and leaned forward, perspiring even in the late-day chill, sensing, it seemed, some malignant change in the room's atmosphere. "And yet here we sit in your…" he looked around and waved his arms "Kvartira," he spluttered. "Like children asking at the table for scraps, when it should be that these answers are ours by rights."

He summoned himself, hitched up his chest, and then said in a loud and shaking voice, "I demand," yet, looking at the diminutive lady, he immediately stalled, simply unable to complete the demand. The preacher looked sidelong at Nicolai and adjusted. "No, my lady, we request, on behalf of everyone aboard the whale" (for long since that rock devolved to become the whale of *Moby-Dick*'s famous telling). "To know how we progress and what we may now hope as the days draw long."

Ariel smiled back at both visitors, as if, indeed, they were simply sharing pleasantries and discussing the turn of the day's weather. That thought prompted her secondary hearing, and outside her quarters, she heard a steady patter of hydroponic rain. This was strangely reassuring. Each time the pumps poured out that remineralised and hydrated water, many abotord relaxed. They allowed a rest for a few heartbeats as they understood that *Leviathan*'s great engines continued to function, and in this case, Ariel was no different. It had been said that to grow old in Russia required an affinity with rain, and so it seemed to be even upon this far outpost of the old Soviet Motherland. The lady's smile did not falter, but she spoke now with gentle reassurance, like a mother both admonishing and encouraging a pair of small children in her care.

"Harsh words, Alexei. And does he speak for you too, Nicolai, in this?" She turned her head fractionally but did not wait for an answer. "You wonder, and that is no wonder, why we have not convened a council, yes? Why have we not proceeded to announce what will one day be the most momentous of all human days? A day that will dwarf even the day we came on board, and for us few, the day even our world was brought to its knees. That day, when our people," she paused for effect, "when your people, those you have shepherded across the widest of seas, will first know their home upon another world."

At that moment, she had become impassioned, and none of the three would have been surprised if one or all of the presents had gasped.

"I ask you both, do we know if that was part of our Lord's majesty? Did his plan ask for the fish not just to leap from the salmon pools but then to find a home on the furthest of distant mountains and then to stay? No…his plan would ask for more. The Lord's plan would, in fact, require us to flourish, no?" The Tsaritsa had herself sermonised. She was cultivating the hope that lived in all on board's hearts, and God's sake made it no less so for the two men sitting now in her ante room.

"You ask why we have not spoken forth. We live, dear fathers, in momentous times, and if the care and courage of some amongst us prefer to err on the side of caution, who might I be to stand affronted at that care?" She stood then, easing up like a well-oiled cat. She moved smoothly around the table that had stood between them and planted herself, almost coquettishly, on the corner of that same wood edifice. The Tsaritsa was now in the vicinity, deliberately, immediately, and suggestively close to the preacher, Alexei.

"It transpires that time is not yet quite ripe, dear Fathers. We are close, and I and those amongst us that are given the care of this mission, on behalf of all, and most of all, our dearest Lord, care deeply that we do nothing to jeopardise that very honour. Back home, did wise men not say that a fool's tongue runs before his feet?" She finished.

Alexei had reddened. Nicolai, the more senior of the two preachers, had thus far watched it all carefully and kept his own counsel. But now, as matters had so quickly reached their heads, he deemed it was time to speak. Nicolai did not see his brother as a buffoon. He was a real man of the people; his sermons and emotional delivery drew people to the pulpit, and that was sorely needed in these dark, cold days. But they found themselves now in the lair of a different creature entirely: they were sitting in the web of Ariel MP, the Tsaritsa and leader of The Eight. Pulpit-bashing would not help them here and, in fact, might well earn the lady's ire. Nicolai understood their peril and spoke now with more tact than his colleague, though his will was iron, and if she could read the man, then she would know his words meant deadly peril for the lady.

"Dear Tsaritsa, my brother means no offence. He speaks for everyone in our Lord's compass when he entreats to hear the words of the wise finally extolling the details of the future, of all of our futures."

As he spoke, Ariel moved silently; almost in perfect reverse, she returned to her side of the desk, to her elevated seat. In the merest seconds, the lady had placed a shield, as it were, between her two visitors and herself. Nicolai Shevchenko was subliminally aware, but he was not as hasty as his religious brother. Though the lady's actions might appear like a retreat, the preacher was not to be drawn until he was entirely ready. "It is not only the silence of The Eight that has brought us here today. There are other matters, for which," he paused and smiled before continuing, "for which we both hope, Ariel, you may be able to offer some guidance."

The preacher's pause was filled with meaning. The silence that then followed stretched and was filled only with the hum and popping of the on-board systems. That and the distant patter of rain. This time the man who held his part in the silence was not intent on speaking, and he seemed to be holding his comrade in silent thrall simply by force of will. Ariel, unblinking, looked long at him, glanced briefly at the room's other guest, and then, after long moments, in a voice that could no longer disguise her irritation, asked the question that sat in the air between them all, "And so must I ask" she spat shortly, with barely hidden rage,

"What are these other matters that you wish my," and after a small gap of her own, she finished angrily, "guidance on?"

"My lady, please allow us not to be hasty." Nicolai stood now and moved across to the side table. There he lifted the carafe and proceeded to pour himself a generous measure of water. He turned, took the four or five steps back to his seat and sat once again. All the while, he was gazing raptly at the red glass filled with that most precious gift and subtly demonstrating to all three presents that no tremble afflicted his hand. To a casual onlooker, it would surely have seemed that the religious man's greatest care at that point was nothing more than the tiny ripples that moved across the water's surface and made spin-ward from the great craft's motion. Each ripple settled into tiny concentric rings as they headed towards the edge of that glass of water held in his hand. Ariel was guarded; she was managing the fury at the temerity of these preachers. Nonetheless, what came next was a bomb that exploded in the midst of her flowers.

"Tsaritsa Ariel MP, you are by all accords the head of The Eight, and so by proxy at least the lady upon whom we all pay favour." Ariel lifted her hand to wave this away, but Nicolai was not yet to be thwarted. Long, indeed, had this one honed his own skills in the heat of debate, and few now were those that would challenge his flow, let alone his inviolated and deeply researched rightness. No, not righteousness, this was a man who spoke when it was right to do so, and when to do so ensured that he was right. He was perhaps not as overt as the lady, but few could doubt the arrogant certainty of the man. And so, he continued, "Indeed, my lady, it is not to you that we would seek to ask or to pay favour, for in the most part we defer, as we must, for such busy people, to those that administer and dispense for both the holy church and for the affairs of The Eight."

Ariel was bemused, though this did not appear on her face, although she had little choice but to wait until the man completed his meandering and got to the point. In fact, she had just about convinced herself that this was much ado about nothing when, of a sudden, he said, "So, dear Tsaritsa, please understand that for us to come to you directly is a measure of our concern. Our concern, my lady, is this…There are people who have gone missing. In this craft, Ariel MP, your ship, is in a place where going missing is not an option. And your man, Sigmund Symonds, seems to be up to his neck in it."

It took most of Tsaritsa's many years of political cuts and thrusts to hold her features through that first. But then, like waves following one another in squally weather, the preacher continued to poke and stab. He pointed to Alexei and said, "We have spoken earlier today to Marshal Stormbader and asked for the help of the squadron in finding those sheep that have been lost to our congregation." Nikolai waved towards Alexei, whose features were now carefully impassive. "He was most concerned. The marshal called me less than two hours ago, suggesting I raise this matter with you directly. It was he who reminded me how Mr Symonds works closely with your office, with you, my lady." Nikolai stopped and eyed the woman, whose features remained even.

If he recognised the effort of will such impassivity required, he did nothing to show this. And so, the two sat across from one another like the last remaining players at a table of Texas Hold 'Em. Or perhaps more alike to a pair of chess grandmasters, each plotting several moves ahead. The preacher was uncertain what response he might have expected; the lady was rarely caught without a sly word, a rejoinder to put her opponents on the back foot, for he had become her enemy the moment he spoke, of that he was certain. What he was not so certain of were the depths to which she might go. He understood that he had 'required' some kind of response from her. That indirectly, and yet directly, he had suggested accusations and links between the disappearances and the silence concerning landfall. Yet despite that leap, that logic jenga, in one crucial area he was even so completely out of a limb.

For though it was true that some amongst the congregation had reported a few souls who seemed to have slipped below the waterline, well, what of that? On board *Leviathan*, was this no longer such a rare thing? Father Nicolai did not think so. In fact, across the long years of the journey, it was true enough that many dozens of souls had been lost. Some had even found their way to the awful, screaming, empty, godless void beyond the boundaries of the cavernous craft. The only significant difference, it seemed to Nikolai, was a vague assertion by a pair of hearty yet not without flaws individuals who had reported seeing Sigmund Symonds moving around the upper reaches of down below with a pair of associates. On a number of occasions, that group had been seen with a poor, bedraggled soul gathered; indeed, it had been described as being dragged between the imposing trio.

Nikolai had held on to that information for many days, had worked it round inside his mind, but ultimately, he was a good man, and so he had asked his conscience, and the voice inside of him had said: These people may indeed just have slid below the surface, or they may be in dire need, but what of it? And the voice inside of him answered: You are a man of God, and in the Father's name, you know what you must do. It is not your place to decide who has needs; only if you might bring succour and help when that call goes forth, then that is your burden.

And so, he recruited Alexei, and from that brother, he had heard more dark stories and rumours about goings-on at the Lifegivers Laboratory at Agetec. People were found wandering near that place, aimless and lost. People whose senses have been popped and shot. Sad people that were there one moment, mad like ticking time-bombs, only to disappear into the maw of down below the very next, and then to be lost beyond finding.

Nicolai had approached the marshal. Here was a stern and gruff man who had no time for God and less time than that even for the acolytes of the Russian Orthodox Faith. Nevertheless, he was a simple, strong man, and he had listened to their concerns and nodded vaguely at the tales of Agetec. At the mention of the name Symonds, the old soldier seemed to visibly perk up. He had promised a pair of officers to begin sweeping down below. He had recommended they approach Ariel and had finally asked that he be kept fully informed. The old marshal had also taken Nikolai aside and whispered to him urgently that should he do this thing, then he would place both preachers in danger. Stormbader also shared in that moment his belief that in these latter days they all now faced a mortal peril beyond even the deadly void.

The preacher watched as Stormbader neatly sidestepped the question of landfall with prosaic ignorance, though not quite the same balletic grace as Ariel. But the marshal listened now with increased intensity to the strange tales of folks wandering lost, then found, and then lost again. I listened and nodded slowly at the description of the quiet tension that has underlayed everything aboard the craft in recent weeks. When all was said and done, Nikolai simply felt something was afoot—something was deeply wrong. He did not know what, but he listened to his instincts, and his gut told him it stank. He did think Symonds was the key, and to get to Symonds, you had to go through Ariel. And it was the mention of that man's name that broke the reverie of the preacher's thoughts and, in the same instant, brought a reply from the lady.

"You speak to me about the actions of an apparatchik," she spat. "I am, you say, your lady of grace. It is my honour to receive many people, great and small, but, Nikolai Shevchenko, I am also a lady of many responsibilities, and so I do not appreciate losing time to discuss…" She seemed to struggle for the right words for long moments, and the atmosphere hung icy; indeed, much changed in a heartbeat. "I absolutely will not discuss vague assertions about Mr Symonds or about Agetec; nor, indeed, would I speculate on why you think this connects in any way with the careful preparations so many are now deeply embedded in. I'm not the board director of that company, nor is Mister Symonds in my employ."

But upon this occasion, Nicolai was prepared, and Ariel had been ruffled, which in truth made him more fearful that there was some dangerous secret nestled in this loose scrabbling bag of facts than the facts themselves. Indeed, as his next words rang around that small space, Stormbader's warning that he was now in danger rang eerily around his mind.

"Nonetheless, my lady, in God's name, and for all those on board, you are recognised as our leader, our driving force. And so, it is up to you to direct these questions. What is Symonds doing? Where are these people going? And why?" After a breath, "Something has changed, my lady Ariel. I am Russian, too, and as we used to say, it does not take a wise man or a washerwoman to know that 'gryadut peremony' (change is coming). You and I may be neither of those things, but you are our lady."

He waved his hand towards Alexei and beyond, towards the corridor. "And so much more than even the wisest of Russia's mothers. There is deep unrest amongst our people, and it runs across *Leviathan*. This needs addressing. So, I wonder, Tsaritsa, are you the person to do that?" That last was a slight, chauvinistic dig at the classical Russian variety. And though Nikolai had her cornered by that, he also then raised murderous intent with his opposite number.

Ariel turned to him, her rage at this imposition unbridled, her eyes narrowing as she spoke. "Time runs on, gentlemen of the clergy, and so must we."

She said nothing more, and with that, she closed the meeting and, rising, ushered both men from the room.

No response was offered, in a classic narcissist manner. Tsaritsa was shut down when that challenge got too great. And in doing so, I dealt with the immediacy of these 'lesser' men by ignoring both them and their request. Though an onlooker deep in the recesses of her psyche might have spotted the seedlings taking hold in that garden where the only thing nurtured to full fruit was revenge.

Later that evening, the lady entertained again. Sigmund Symonds came to her long after the lights went down when she beckoned. He had come like that, skulking in the shadows, a master of evasion, because that was what she demanded. The enforcer was nothing if not drawn by the brightness of her star. Awed by her simple will to climb to the top of the shit pile. Had the truth been known, Symonds, for all his physical size and verbose bullying, had been much more of a co-dependent type of his whole life. Always number two, never number one, as the saying goes. This pattern was likely established and then journeyed with him out of deepest childhood. That core lack of real leadership—the ability to stand, decide, and deal without reverting to another. But, like many people aboard and historically in the wider world of Russian society, childhood was something about which he, like them, never spoke. And in these latter days, about which nobody ever asked. It seems we each have a companion whispering deeply inside of us, in a voice so well-known as to not be separate from our own. Messages of comfort, words that more often than not get us into trouble, and though he did not yet know it, clearly Sigmund Symonds the enforcer was in big trouble.

Long ago, the big man had lost a wife and a son, too, in the calamity that had claimed so many lives back on Earth. And he would speak not one word about either, nor about his life in London and Istanbul so many years ago. On the surface of his mind, he persuaded himself that he had found love. The disquiet that thought gave him was forced down deep. So many nights he wrestled with his conscience, voicing the fear that he was being used and indeed used up. Many days dawned with him telling his inner voice that was it; he would break free. He blamed himself, and his lady certainly helped him in that sense. The sense that he was, in the end, responsible for what passed between them, not her. He never questioned his lady's moods, swift to change from marble-cold majesty to fiery fury, passionate and yet painfully naïve in bed.

Nonetheless, she touched all of the right circuits inside of him. She was like electricity to Sigmund, and at his core, he only truly felt alive when she had him at her beck and call. Though oftentimes, and more so as the years had drawn on, she could be withdrawn, cruel, seemingly introspective, and disregardful. Oh, had he but known at times when the fey mood took her, how coldly she looked down on him, in her mind, how in those moments she derided the man? How wantonly she would dash him on the rocks of her needs or musts. And yet, it is still likely he would have gone to her. He was in need of service, and she had many needs he could fulfil. And so, though, it was the devil's bargain: for a good number of years now, he had come when she gestured. Departing in the grey early dawn, because that was how she wished it. And no amount of internal lecturing, it seemed, would stop him, because the simple truth was, he was in thrall.

That night, like hundreds that had passed between them, he came at her request. She was quiet, saying little about the events of the day and nothing about the meeting with the two clerics. But even a fool could see she was filled with the rage of a scorned woman. She was told to accept instruction from (defeat at) the hands of those she deemed lesser mortals. Ariel was vindictive, and she knew this about herself, somewhat admiring her ability to take revenge whilst keeping the high ground in the eyes of those that watched from the wings.

Though Symonds did not know it, in one corner of her mind, she was already plotting his demise and planning her own path after. Planning ways to both remove him and, whilst in the act, allow the greater burden of responsibility for all that was about to be made public to pass on to his shoulders. Ariel smiled inside her mind. 'God rest his soul,' a voice said, and the smile turned to a gentle laugh. That said, the lady was also presciently aware that, in the moment, she still had need of him. Ariel still needed that man's voice and urgency to cajole something from the idiots at the lab. The ginger one, whose name she had forgotten every time she had been told, needed pushing, damn him; they all did.

Ariel still had the need for someone at her right hand to keep The Eight in check, and, more particularly, to deal with that irritant Stormbader. The man was a dinosaur, but she knew what it was like to have a Tyrannosaurus on your tail, and so she wanted him taken out of the fray before the sound of his heavy breathing and stomping feet got any closer.

And so, once more, she mechanically went through the motions of making love with her puppet man. Ariel shut her eyes and allowed the whispered invocations close to her ears, the stroking, prying, and prodding into her space, the big bull sweating and spent, lying right up close to her body. The stink of his musk fills her room. Sometime later, she spoke quietly to him, and she shared a warning.

"Sigmund, we are beset; we have enemies all around us," she whispered, and garnered just enough of the bristling man's response to make sure he remained compliant. He and she were against the world; it had worked for her before, so why not once more?

In the dark, the lady heard, "And who are these enemies that beset us?"

"The enemy," said Ariel, tart and now fully in control, "lies within us, Siggy; the enemy lies within you." And so it was that even as she arched her back and feigned the orgasm that a man so desperately needed in order to validate his worth, somewhere deeper in her psyche, she drew up her plans. And let *Leviathan* watch out, because Ariel MP understood that they were coming now to the final crossroads.

10
The Inevitability Syndrome

It was oft said in many corners of that most round and blue world we used to call home that if a thing might come to pass, then in God's or the universe's good time it would come to pass. It was early the next morning. Stormbader had risen before it lit up. Rising early was a part of his life, and, indeed, he didn't really have the architecture to rise late; that was just how he was. Alexei was not a complex character; he liked open and honest people. He liked to see order in all things, and he worked unstintingly at ordering his small corner of the universe. The marshal divided people into good and bad, weak and strong, likeable, and dislikeable, trustworthy and untrustworthy, and that was about it.

Following the lady's sudden and disconcerting announcement the previous day, he had been buttonholed by a pair of what he first considered to have been 'crazy' Russian preachers. But Nikolai, the one who had spoken, had, in fact, seemed smart and honest enough, and Stormbader would have thought that, barring his foolhardy dalliance with religion, he was seemingly a good man. Well, according to his fairly straightforward parameters. The tale he and his sidekick shared with Stormbader smacked slightly of an oversized dose of conjecture for the marshal's usual consumption. Nevertheless, the mention of Symonds had drawn his attention, and, coming straight on the back of the lady's revelations, the soldier was now clear in his mind that much more was afoot than even his cynicism had previously supposed, and more so that the fool Symonds was neck deep in all of it. He had awoken that morning with a headache—the deep and thundering variety, the sort that tablets didn't touch.

That and some vague recollection of disconcerting dreams that had blown away like fluff in the mists of wakefulness, left a sense of woe in their wake. The marshal shook his bear-like head in an effort to shake the sleep and was rewarded with a further dull, sickening slide. He pushed a button on his desk and issued a terse instruction. The voice at the other end assented, and shortly after, two of his better men departed the barracks and began a slow and thorough sweep down below. The marshal was nothing if not a man of his word. That said, he was not absolutely clear on what it was his men were looking for or might find. Shadowy tales of folks disappearing, a couple of images on their scanners, and a couple of names of people not seen for some days.

His marines were not detectives, and there was not a lot going on. Nonetheless, he sent them out, and he had made it clear that they would come back with something if they wanted messy rations that night. Stormbader was not certain that even if they turned upside down every shady joint down below, they would find something that smelled more than the usual reek down there. But they would look, and they would be thorough; he had given his word to that. And anyway, he was certain that if anything did turn up, it would smell of Sigmund Symonds.

Marshal glanced at the small screen that adorned the wall immediately adjacent to his immaculately neat desk. Lady Ariel's face appeared in an animated conversation with a…what was that? Stormbader wondered for a minute and then realised he was looking at a beekeeper. Standing with a mask pulled back and chatted with *Leviathan*'s First Lady, both stood in front of one of the hydroponic gardens. The beekeepers, Alexei knew, doubled as gardeners. Everybody on board *Leviathan* seemed to double as something, and he wondered, therefore, what people imagined he doubled as. Stormbader shrugged and looked back at the screen. The sound was turned down, either muted or broken, like so much of the slowly failing technology on board the whale. Without his reading glasses, he could not quite grab hold of the small text tape that trailed across the bottom of the display.

The old soldier looked long at the face in that small aperture; he concentrated on the smile that was fixed to her face, the one that never budged in public. Whether silently mimicking speech or carefully imitating listening, he was certain that both actions were indeed mimics. Merely, a copy of the actions of warm-blooded mammals from a cold-blooded lizard. He saw the Tsaritsa as a crocodile, one that had adapted and learned the value of such prosaic play. Stormbader looked instead at the lady's eyes; he considered and thought that was where the truth of that one lay. The marshal was a brave man, but should anyone have been watching in that moment, they would have seen him visibly shudder.

He remembered his own warning to the preachers—words that had come to him unbeknownst and unexpectedly.

Unusual for him, but blurted in the moment, terse and urgent, but heartfelt for all that. And as he watched her on screen, his quiet rejoinder to himself was equally stark. The lady was dangerous, a killer, and so, as the pressure of her lies grew and as the weight of truth became a burden, maybe too great to bear. Then she, too, might fall foul of a deceit too complex for even one as artful as her to hide from the masses. But the danger of explosion to wanton death and destruction, he believed, was escalating.

It was like awakening from a twenty-three-year-long dream. And so lately Stormbader had come to believe that he and all the good people of *Leviathan* faced a deadly adversary, one that would stop at nothing to keep her head above water, her hands on the tiller. And, more personally, he believed now that standing on his balding scalp to achieve that would, in fact, simply prove to be a bonus to her. The old soldier ruminated that it was due to the Ariels of this world, of any world, that they had all ended up on this barren rock, spinning slowly and inevitably through the cold, black void.

Turning to scan his quarters, the marshal buttoned the top of his jacket, switched down the lighting to its lowest setting, pressed the handle to exit, and stepped forthrightly out into the day. Though he had shared his whole set of fears and doubts with no one, nonetheless, the marshal was a man of care. He stepped off on his regular path to work, heading towards the barracks two levels down, boots laced efficiently and tightly, shining, and reflecting the plastocrete surroundings. At the end of the short corridor where his quarters were housed, he saluted a squadron guard standing there. Marshal wondered at that.

More than twenty years of guard duty had been based on the ancient prerequisite that he, as the senior officer, might face the danger of some unprecedented attack or assassination. Those decisions all seemed from another life, another time. Nevertheless, today Stormbader was reassured and, after the snappy salute, asked the somewhat younger man if there was anything to report. The soldier looked surprised. Who knew when the last time had been that anyone had asked such a question? Or, indeed, when had there ever been anything to report? "Niet, marshal, quiet, quiet, quiet," he said, without a trace of irony, and watched their leader march confidently off into the morning of another day.

Across the divide, with the upper decks being split into living, working, and commercial, Stormbader headed towards the barracks. Screens were placed, seemingly randomly embedded in the original stone that made up the walls. And it was increasingly the case that, though some seemed to be working, many others were blank. It was, the soldier thought, a sign of the times that the hankering for news in that tiny space had withered to a point where, when a screen went black, nobody really seemed to care. The techs got to them eventually, but there really was no rush, and so more and more were going dark, and longer and longer they stayed that way.

As Stormbader strode across the divide, leaving residential and heading across and down, he saw a number of screen adverts for a vigil. Candles, prayers, and blini pancakes are wallowing in another man's tragedy, that most staple of Russian pastimes. Apparently, this was an event to commemorate, and at that moment he stopped stock still, brought to a halt by sudden recollection and the shock of his own forgetfulness. He remembered a promise he had recently made to Carlos. Master Sergeant Carlos North. Once known to the squadron as 'North by North-West', simply because he was half-English and so not quite one of their own. He was a mercenary, a man who had, though, singularly managed by dedication and utter diligence to work his way into Stormbader's inner circle. A warrior, and yet, for all that, a ruthlessly honest man. But this was a man who was dying of nothing more exotic than cancer.

And a man who had come to him only days before asking if he, Stormbader, would take his boy into barracks, into military care. And so let him work and be around the troops, and that way he can find a life for himself. How could he refuse? The man held fast at Stormbader's back time and again, had covered every shit duty on the roster without sigh or complaint and worked every detail for four years back in the Motherland; and now, twenty-three years on, the *Leviathan*. Even when the man's partner died, he had stood his shifts. And now, in the black middle of the void, this man was to take his leave of life and leave a son behind. Oh, merciful God, Stormbader thought with tight-lipped bitterness. This was the kind of man Alexei liked: one of him made a hundred of the likes of Symonds and his coterie. It appeared as he watched the reel, reminding all of the vigil that others had a liking for Carlos North, too.

This was a last tender farewell to a man who deserved better than the universe seemed to want to give. Who had not been treated with the tenderness his endeavours deserved, and Alexei Stormbader wondered somewhat at that. In that moment, the marshal decided that he, too, would go, and he would show his respects in a more public forum than he was used to. Though ironically, he had been spotted, it was to be held in the gardens of the Agetec Company. Marshals knew only a little about the outfit, wreathed as they were in the secrecy of big budget buy. Sources had told him they dabbled in nanotech, a subject about which he was sceptical. This was despite the understanding that those tiny little bugs had been key in burrowing out and building the rock-space prison they now all lived in.

In fact, he understood how, even now, there were billions upon billions of these little nano-mytes burrowing and clearing new space within the craft's cavernous belly. The microscopic miners are each a little larger than an atom. Self-perpetuating, self-birthing, and repairing, and yet programmable as a group or swarm. As a whole, they added around twenty-five cubic metres a month, about the size of a decent truck back on Earth; well, if there were any trucks left on Earth, he thought. He then briefly considered whether there would be any rock left to burrow and whether the nano-bots might outlive the humans that had programmed them and given them life-feeding on the nuclear protosun until that, too, ran down, and so that was their lot.

Nonetheless, he thought, had not the mad preachers only the previous evening referenced Agetec as being connected with these disappearances and more, with that bastard fool Symonds. Yes, he would go. He would raise a glass with, or at least to, his friend and long-time wingman Carlos. He would eat bliny pancakes, and he would see what he would see, he told himself, striding now with renewed purpose into the day. "It's the not doing anything that lets the fear in," his father's voice whispered, and he smiled.

11
Desire Ask Believe Receive

Hermione caught a reflection of herself and gasped; indeed, she almost fell, and it was only her survival instinct that stopped her from fainting outright. The reflection was on a blanked-out visi-screen, and so it was not with the clarity of a mirror. The woman who looked back at her was not Hermione Zatapec. This was, if Hermione at all, of some other vintage. Her mind whispered, "Hermione Wise, but you weren't wise, were you?" She had found a place to sleep the previous night and had smiled as she drifted away without contest or conflict. She had put her sense of wellness and contentment down to an earlier, quite ethereal meeting with Muriel Cardington, the angelic young girl. But this was something else; this went against nature. And the feelings inside of her, the sensations coruscating around her. "The blood between your legs," her mind suddenly whispered, and as her hand strayed downwards, she realised with even greater shock that she was having a period.

Something that had been so distant in her past as to have been almost beyond memory. Hermione reached into the battered leather case and pulled out a small pack of tissues with a motto writ small, 'Handy in a pinch'. And so, she did what she could to staunch the sudden flow. The lady was crying a little, gentle tears, genuinely lost and confused by what was taking place, and yet, in the same moments, a little ecstatic. When you are older, you will know that sometimes you might, if you are lucky, have a good day. Or, as the years draw on, even a good hour. And this would always mean a brief return to that sense of energy and exuberant, vibrant life that jumps out at you when you are around children and young adults.

This is not to say there are not many other values to being older, but we are, after all, only younger once. To stumble, therefore, upon that in yourself when you have surrendered to those latter years, well, for Hermione Zatapec, it was both terrifying and exhilarating, in a way she could barely grasp, let alone think about or explain. She began to walk around an area down below that was filled with heavy engineering. Thuds and hums increased as the daylight rose once again.

People were milling around, but mostly appeared to be moving towards work or some brief food break before the day went fully live. There is no such purpose for Hermione. Yet she felt purposed in a way that she had not for, "Well, since I don't know when," she told herself, with a firm voice that blew the last of her emotional cobwebs away. But the dilemma of her emotions brought with it a dilemma of purpose. She was curious—no, in fact, desperate—to really understand what was happening to her. Nevertheless, she was also already excited about the prospect of her new self. Shaking off the heavy cloak of age, and who wouldn't be overwhelmed by such a gift? But to investigate brought with it the risk of exposure and the possibility that this thing might be taken away from her.

As she walked, fairly trotting along, so it seemed to her, she spotted on a screen an invitation to attend a vigil. The image came on screen as Carlos North, the veteran officer, recognised the photo as a younger and fitter pictorial of the man she had seen only yesterday beseeching his young son. She thought how much she had hidden from herself; how, in fact, if she actually let her mind do some thinking, she had avoided facing up to her own responsibilities for the death of…

Her mind quieted the thought before it was issued. She walked on, and the train of thought, with irritating elephant-in-the-room persistence, came once more. Had she not tossed him aside, his hopes would have been dashed. Had she not been promised a life of commitment aboard *Leviathan in return?* When did they meet? So long ago, she wondered. In those early weeks of tense solar flight? And more, had she not known exactly what she was doing as she eased him aside, enthused and consumed as she had been in the face of the opportunity to advance, to be 'someone'. The truth, Hermione considered, was that she had loved Jacob mostly and simply for how much he had loved her.

For how much his wonderfully rounded self-had helped enhance her prickly, unfinished self. She saw fragments, like the shiny crystals in the blackest basalt. And as each memory stepped forth and became clearer, without him, she wondered, in fact, whether she would have just remained a tiny speck in a giant universe. Was that not ultimately what she had returned to? Her ego had tried to dispel that thought over and over and over for so many long years now. Once again, she found herself thinking about not thinking, believing that this was all someone else, some other time, and some other place. This, it seemed, was the fog that had dropped over her mind. It didn't matter much though, she told herself; this was a new me, and the clear sightedness that came with her youthful rejoinder was, she decided, long overdue.

"But you cannot bring him back," another voice far back in her mind reminded her bitterly. None of it made any sense. She had no idea who she was or who she should be. But she was filled with a kind of energy that only the elderly can really tell you how much you will miss. The energy that you take for granted in those halcyon younger years. And so, she answered the craven voice of negative ego in her mind and said to herself, "Perhaps not, but I can honour yesterday, and I can live for today."

Her desired purpose and her wisdom, as simple as they were, asked for a purpose. This was a belief she held utterly and absolutely. Though some might have said it was merely a distraction that she sought. Hermione had come to believe that the universe was replete with everything a person might want. That universe would give you bucketloads of whatever it was you craved, whatever it was your deepest Jungian self-decided you deserved. Such a universe did not deal in good or bad, God or the Devil. These were, and always will be, entirely human concepts.

For sure, somewhere out there in that deep inky void, there would be a place that held all good things as bad. A place where perhaps all bad things become good, and so what matters that? No, Hermione believed, as she had for many years, that the universe would reward her with whatever she asked for. And so, she'd best not ask for der'mo (shit), she said to herself grimly. Hermione Zatapec had asked for a purpose that morning, and then, some moments later, was rewarded with an image of that poor boy's father and an itch at the back of her mind as the 'Agetec' logo scrolled across the screen.

The young lady stepped into a nearby washroom and set about making herself decent. She was rocked again, and immediately, with the even greater shock of realising that she looked like a, well, what? In the mid-forties version of herself, of someone else, she was not certain. Time had only ever proceeded in one decaying direction for her until very recently. Forty—that was three decades ago, and her mind had little recollection of how she had shaped up physically back then. God, I wish I had some make-up, she mumbled to herself as she washed and changed into clean under- and over-wear, found folded small and neat, and retrieved from the tan bag.

Shortly after, she exchanged a glass snow globe with a short, middle-aged woman who looked a little lost. But one woman nevertheless seemed delighted to swap the exotic glass bauble for a ration card. One, which provided Hermione sometime later with more steaming noodles and a one-litre carafe of water. These noodles were consumed in a far busier venue than her last meal, but one in which, strangely, this new visceral version of the lady did not feel out of place or at all under threat. She considered this as she ate ravenously and concluded sadly that this was a society thing. In their latter-day society, frailty and age had led naturally to a kind of fear and exclusion zone.

She was reminded of a documentary she had seen on Earth many years before. It had been about the wolf packs in Siberia. It's about how they kept the prime male, even after he was no longer quite prime. But the moment his age and health meant he could not run and could no longer stay on course with the pack, he was expelled with both speed and alarming ferocity. She figured that the problem with humanity—one of very many, she supposed—was that medicine and meddling had kept so many people alive far beyond their prime. The system that had saved them had weakened them, too. Taking them further away from surviving only the fittest of nature's fine balance, she wondered where that balance now placed her.

She had finished eating without event, and, since then, some hours had passed. As she angled her way upwards towards the science and tech district, the lady had, quite literally, a bounce in her step. As the years fell away from her, she found an appreciation of the energy and strength life gave her in a way that she was certain she had not even conceived the first time around. She thought too much about the child, Muriel. She was so bright, and yet malady lay heavy upon her. She thought, too, about the boy: had his name been Remus? She was not certain, but had the old man not referred to him as Remus? Had there been a Romulus, her mind wondered? For the child was not to be abandoned by the cruellest of fates. And she wondered at that, at who had deigned to ask the universe for that.

12
Occam's Razor
Seek the Solution with the Least Number of Assumptions and You Will Discover the Truth

And so it was that, as Alexei Stormbader strode from his daytime offices and, at the same moment, Hermione Zatapec sprang with newfound vigour up the many levels from down below, both headed towards the gardens of Agetec.

Ariel MP, First Lady and leader of that most diverse group of humanity, acquiesced to Symonds's invitation to attend the vigil for herself with officer Carlos North.

As Lyle Cardington held his daughter's frail hand and walked with her, listening with closed ears to her chatter, his own mind far away and dwelt on issues in that other place entirely. But both were heading slowly across the divide to offices that were more home than home to Cardington, similarly to those attending the solemn vigil.

A sizeable number of people were in the small but neat gardens when Hermione arrived—up to one hundred, if she were to place a guess—clumped into groups of two, three, and four. More pleasing, though, to her eyes, as it turned out, was the spread of food. Pancakes specifically, which had become a staple brought from Mother Russia to this faraway void. She smiled and wondered if she had been this obsessed with eating when she was younger; it certainly seemed to be consuming her in the past couple of days, she thought. "But let's be honest, Hermione" her mind's voice piped up, "it's not the food so much as the words 'ugoshchaytes' (help yourself)." And so, she eased across the lawn, case clutching confidently in her newly strong grip. Stride steady and shoulders back, breasts perky and straight back. In that place, who would bat an eyelid at a young, middle-aged woman, perhaps in her late forties, taking a morsel from a table lain exactly for that, and that proved to be the case. As Hermione ate, delving down into a second and third of the small, delicate bliny pancakes, she stood admiring a small, stunted tree of what appeared to be a hardy Japanese origin; then, all of a sudden, she felt a tugging on her coat. She turned, and there, smiling at her, stood none other than Muriel Cardington.

"Hello, Hermione," the girl said, with a beaming smile. "daddy, look, it's Hermione, my friend, that I told you about," Muriel exclaimed.

Cardington grunted, barely an affirmative and released his grip on his daughter's hand in an instant. He seemed to have noted the safe hands of this other adult, and he was gone in that same moment, merging with the growing crowd as he spotted one of his lab technicians, his mind already deeply enmeshed in equations and solutions, and, worse still, in the politics of Sigmund Symonds.

"Well, hello, Muriel," replied Hermione. "Your father seems very busy."

"Oh, he's always like that," Muriel responded. "He doesn't mean it though, Hermione." And once again, the lady was checked by the simple maturity of this young angelic child.

The two then walked around for a minute or two and, after a short time, found a small bench not taken and sat, Muriel with her legs swinging back and forth, as the air smelled of incense. "You look younger!" the girl exclaimed with no artifice.

And Hermione, knowing of nothing to respond with other than the truth, replied, "Yes, I guess I do. I seem to be getting younger and younger," she thought for a few moments and then continued, "If I'm not careful, I'll be your age before I know it!" she smiled.

"OOOH, that would be fun," Muriel replied, laughing gaily.

"Do you know the boy? Remus isn't that his name?" said the older woman.

"No, not really," said Muriel.

"I think I know who he is; there aren't really many of us, are there?" she said this whilst waving her arms vaguely in something that resembled a kind of totting-up gesture.

"My dad said we should come. He said because the boy's father was a brave man, and he was going to die today. Well, I think it was today. Did you come for the pancakes?" she continued with another open and honest laugh.

Hermione spluttered on the last of her pancakes and, laughing herself, replied, "Yes, you might think so." she thought for a moment and then went on,

"No, I saw the boy and his father yesterday for the first time, and, well, you know, they both looked so terribly sad. And so, I wanted to say a prayer to the universe and see if there was anything an old lady like me could do to help."

The child screwed her nose up at that last and simply said, "Old?"

A little time later, "the talker", Alexei Smorzgard of the Russian Orthodox church, entered the gardens. Nikolai Shevchenko was nowhere in sight, but it seemed that this other was to lead the congregation. For such it had become. He began, then, a short service of song and prayer. It appeared that the man, Carlos North, lay gravely ill and close to death, if reports were to be believed. His son was there, though, and an officer of the elite marine guard stood by his side, occasionally whispering, and placing a gentle arm on the younger boy's elbow in a steadying gesture. And just off to the left, hidden somewhat in the shadows, stood Alexei Stormbader. He was the marshal and the most powerful military leader left in that vastly shrunken world of humanity. And should anyone have looked closely at the young boy, features drawn tight, holding together, just in that place full of strangers, with occasional words from the marine at his side. Well, the eagle-eyed perhaps would have been rewarded by spying, clutched tightly in his left hand, with gold gilt glinting from the pages, a small Lutheran Holy Bible.

As a special dispensation and in keeping with the sombre mood, it appeared that someone had arranged to turn down the sunlight in the garden. And so, it appeared to all those present that they stood in the twilight of the day. In that twilight, Symonds quietly came and just as silently eased himself close to Lyle Cardington. Ariel MP came, too, though seen by a few, flanked by her housekeeper and her chief secretary. And yet, for all that, she whispered in like a ghost and seemed not to disturb that space whatsoever.

And so, by the time the preacher began his slow and steady invocation, his sonorous prayer to his God, the God of many of the hundred-plus people that had come to the pretty gardens of Agetec. Well, most of the players in the Game of *Leviathan* stood in that small space. For a few minutes, then, the preacher spoke, his voice slow, and the people, the congregation, becalmed.

The light grew dimmer, and quietly, Muriel whispered to Hermione, "I wish we had candles. It doesn't seem right for that boy to stand in the dark whilst his father is dying."

Hermione looked at the girl and wondered at her empathy and care for someone so young. A flicker of a warm smile crossed her features as she bent over and opened her battered brown case, and from there, she removed a simple brown paper bag from within the bag. "Candles, little one," she said simply. "Pass them out," she continued, holding open the paper bag, which, in turn, held perhaps three dozen small white candles, each no more than three inches high. She then lit a couple, and Muriel quietly lit the other candles in pairs from those first two. Then, walking back and forth quietly and unobtrusively between the various groups, the child handed them out, so that, in only a few minutes, across the garden, a twinkle of light now filled the darkened air.

"That's better," Muriel said, turning and smiling at Hermione, as if she had expected all along that was precisely what the lady had held in her case. Muriel had, of course, held on to a candle, and as a version of Katyusha began to be sung by the elder brethren present, a long-standing melody with deep roots in Russian history, the child spotted her father and, tugging at Hermione's hand, she eased them both towards the scientist Lyle Cardington.

The many candles flickered, and as she drew closer, Hermione Zatapec saw Sigmund Symonds, and in her mind, something went click. Images flashed of dark space, of laboratories, of deep wrenching pain, and at the centre of that cacophony of random flood memories, the man now stood beside her friend Muriel's father and was whispering urgently in his ear. She shuddered involuntarily and stopped abruptly. Muriel, pulled back by her sudden immobility, turned, and looked questioningly.

"You go, child!" Hermione said. And Muriel Cardington, sensing that something was not right but that it was something in the realm of adults, a place where she did not yet dwell, let go of the lady's hand and crossed the divide back to where her father looked down. Cardington smiled briefly and mouthed "Nice candle", all whilst not breaking the bigger man's thrusting whisper into his ear.

Hermione Zatapec, once Hermione Wise. "But you weren't wise, were you?" the voice whispered inevitably. Hermione had, in these latter days, been very much remade for caution. Living down below had sharpened her senses, and no amount of physical changes to her anatomy would take that caution completely out of her nature. So, as the song concluded and the gentle, lilting tones of the preacher thanked God and then introduced those present to another gentle lullaby, Hermione moved carefully amongst those gathered there, easing back towards the garden's edge and also its exit. All the time, the lady was keeping the man that had triggered a cascade of mental half-images in her eyeliner, moving imperceptibly slowly, watching with exhaustive care.

As she approached the exit, she was surprised once again. It had been a good number of years since she had seen Ariel MP, First Lady of The Eight and Tsaritsa of the *Leviathan*, in flesh. The sight of her caused another sharp tug of memory, and she instantly discovered a half-recollection of how a desperate young climber had sought by fair means and foul to make that lady's acquaintance. Her mind rocked at the feelings of needful and eventually fateful questing. Off upwards on the power ladder, round and round the hamster wheel. She recognised Ariel instantly, and, of course, she would have seen her image on hundreds of screens spread across the great craft many hundreds, possibly thousands, of times over the years.

Nonetheless, seeing her here and now in the flesh still came as a shock to Hermione. And the universe does reward the watchful, she considered, as glancing from a woman back to her watchful retreat from that other man, she, and perhaps only her in that small garden, caught sight of the nod and curt smile that passed between the leading lady, hid deep in the recesses of shadow, and the man that had triggered her mind into overdrive.

She left before the close, as quietly as she had come. Respect was given its due, and some hours later that day, Carlos North passed on. The soldier finally left the life he had held onto so tightly those past few weeks, and in military and naval tradition, he would be ejected from the great craft to find his own way to God's kingdom in the days that followed. The boy Remus, who indeed had been his name, had held himself, clutching tightly to the bible in his hand and smiling a wintry and desperate smile at a girl of a similar age as they moved past one another. The only child he saw was present in that awful, tragic place. The preacher Alexei had quietly closed the affair with the words of Revelation 14:13, "And I heard a voice from heaven saying unto me, write. Blessed are the dead that die into the Lord from henceforth: Yea, saith the spirit that they may rest from their labours and their works do follow them."

Stormbader stayed until almost everyone had left. He spotted Ariel, saw the jack monkey Symonds, and deeply felt the pain of a young boy, one whose care had passed somewhat that day to him. Yet, for all that care and concern, a small voice in his mind wondered why the lady had shown up there. Symonds, yes; he was, after all, the *de facto* public face of the company Agetec. But, given what she had shared with him and the other members of The Eight only a day before, he wondered if she did not have one or two more pressing concerns. That, in turn, got him to think about Agetec and her half-said and prophetic words. He remembered Symonds talking urgently to one of the company's scientists, the small gingerbread man. Stormbader tried to put two and two together, but he recognised he still had too many twos.

13
The Cardington Enquiry

To carry fire in one hand and water in the other is a measure of the divine'

"So, who was that lady?" Lyle asked his daughter as they walked hand in hand slowly back from the wake, for he had learned later that was what it had become.

"Daddy, do you know what I miss?" His daughter responded, seemingly ignoring his enquiry. The scientist was used to this with Muriel, as much as he was used to walking with her slowly. They were almost inching their way back in order to ensure she was not too fatigued by the 30 minutes it would take them between quarters and the gardens at Agetec.

"No, Tinkerbell," he said, "what do you miss?"

"Shopping," she replied, simply, sounding ever so slightly sulky.

"Shopping?" he said, raising his eyebrows and sounding surprised. "How can you miss shopping, Muriel? You have never been shopping. Well, I guess you have seen it in the movies," he spoke up, answering his own question in that irritating way adults do.

"I don't know how, but I do miss them. Shop somewhere you can just walk in and buy yourself slices of, well, slices of happiness."

The father looked carefully at his daughter, stopping and gently pulling her to a standstill. "Why, Tink? Are you sad?" said Cardington. "Perhaps I made a mistake, and we should not have gone today?" he observed, with an anxious look creeping across his face.

"No, daddy, you didn't do anything wrong. You're my dad," she continued, as if that were the glue, the rationale. She was a daughter, he was a dad; no room for doubt.

"I'm glad we went. And a lot of those people that were there were not really sad at all, but that boy, whose name was Remus, well, he hasn't got a dad now," she looked up at her father, who had been about to resume their careful walk. And so, he stopped before he had started and focused on his daughter's pained expression once again. "And Hermione told me she heard that he does not have a mum either, like me," she stumbled a little, seemingly still configuring her thoughts.

Her father, slightly misunderstood, jumped in quickly and, crouching down, and gently embracing his daughter before she could say another word, said himself, "You have me, Tinkerbell; you will always have me."

"Yes, I know, daddy. I am very lucky. No, I am not sad for me," she continued, taking, it seemed, a real and compassionate care with her words and perhaps even her thoughts. "But that boy, you know he is out here, and he is all alone."

They had begun walking once again. "And soon he is going to land on a new world; and we," she said, waving her arms to describe the invisible we, "will all be excited, and…" She paused now for some moments, and then ended, "Well, he will still be sad. I wish there was something I could do, that's all."

Lyle Cardington frowned, and his mind did a double, maybe triple, somersault as, in a breath or two, his daughter had shared with him, and in doing so, he opened his mind again to the enormity of the situation he and the other players of games he was vassal to now faced. The human race, or what small morsel of them remained, were alone and in the dark. There was nothing now, and no one, left to save them. Lyle Cardington was on point, and his daughter and sixty thousand other hearts beat to the tune that his science would play in the coming hours and days.

It is perhaps true that humanity finds its greatest advances and triumphs in the moments of its greatest adversity. Cardington would not have been sure of that, but he was certain that his daughter needed him. Not in any way he had ever considered, but now she needed her father to be a hero. She needed him to save everyone, even if she could not understand that clearly herself. He had forgotten, of course, about her friend, the strange, slightly dishevelled, and yes, he could not deny it, rather attractive middle-aged woman. He wondered who she was and how his daughter knew her. Though seen only briefly, the woman seemed somehow different, open, and listening.

Perhaps that explained why he himself had, in fact, listened more, with more care and open ears, on that walk home than, for the longest time, to Muriel's gentle, tinkling voice. In her sharing of stories, she describes the flickering lights of the candles, remembering the sad eyes of the boy, the stern features of the marshal, and the big muscles of the marine that had stood throughout by the side of Remus. Her thoughts and words had darted hither and thither, as is the won't of the young. She had long spoken about their new home and, of course, how she wondered whether they might open some shops when they landed on Tinkerbell. It was odd that her father had picked the very same nickname for her as someone else had for the new world they were going to. This was her frame of reference, her reality, and so she spoke on and on. And so that half an hour, at its end, seemed like many days filled with a bubbling well, a mind of coruscating emotion and energy.

Later, when his daughter and he had broken bread together, another pastime that he had too often sidestepped, he returned to his laboratory. Unencumbered by Muriel, he made the return journey in less than fifteen minutes. Nobody was around as the hours of darkness settled in; indeed, at that hour, people scuttled back to their quarters, or, if they were lucky, perhaps some others' lodgings. Soon enough, they climbed en masse under the covers, fending off the cloying bitter cold, the creeping eternal darkness, and an increasingly godless universe. Humanity had surrendered so much already, brought down to the lowest point in a brief and fiery history of low points. To even try this crazy pilgrimage seemed like an impossible leap of faith; perhaps it was indeed just poetic justice for the misdemeanours of a race.

But Lyle Cardington did not notice the cold, nor did he heed the absence of people, nor did he glance at his watch and wonder at the hour of the day. As he strode down the vaguely sickly green corridor and stepped into his office and small lab area, the overhead lights flickered. It was a time-honoured change from lights up to lights down kicking in. He noticed how musty it smelled in there, then grabbed at his keys, unlocked his desk, and without pause, withdrew the turquoise vial. Its contents continued to shimmer with an otherworldly and ethereal light of their own, soothing, and yet disconcerting in equal measure. Lyle Cardington was in the hands of an imperative.

"I have to get this; I have to," he implored whatever invisible science overlord he deemed had the answer.

He repeated the same invocation several times. And had anyone been watching him, his features reflected bright and blue in the shimmering, aqueous green-blue glow, he would have looked no less than the mad doctor of Mary Shelley's *Frankenstein*. He wrestled late into the night, working, and reworking the numbers, the process, and the mix. The ferocious fire of a shamed parent burned deep inside of him, his mind operating at a level that was all intuition and instinct.

Eventually, many hours later, he returned to quarters, crawling under the covers and up close to his long-suffering girlfriend only bare minutes before lights began for all another day, a fateful day. This was then to be the end, or perhaps the beginning.

In another part of that great *Moby-Dick*, another quite different person wrestled to take hold of the wet and slippery snake that cried out that its name was divinity. Hermione Zatapec, who had once been Hermione Wise but was only recently coming to her wisdom, she believed, had, too, begun to have something of an epiphany. But unlike those eye-watering moments of biblical awakening, hers, it seemed, was a far slower and more gentle progression towards awareness. After the strange events in the garden of remembrance, as her mind now thought of that place, of meeting up once again, and so soon after her first encounter with the child Muriel Cardington. Of the glimmers of recognition that began to trouble her after seeing the girl's father, Lyle Cardington. And that other man, the big, brooding, animated figure.

She had walked away from the solemn affair with an itch in her mind and had begun to scratch at it over and over in the hours that followed. Had she but known that several levels above her head, other people scratched at their itches and that each, in their different ways, sought to uncover the truth. But the truth was seemingly difficult, not easily tamed by the wit or whim of any of those individuals, changing from moment to moment, different in perception from one person to the next. Should they even witness the evident self-same truth, it seems a different thing to register a truth than to register an opinion and then decide that would be good enough. And it is true to say that each of these people lived in entirely separate ego parlours, and each sought a truth not yet evident. In each case, a thing perhaps was able to release them; this, then, was the real deal.

The lady walked now here and now there, with a purpose she could not define and an energy she was ill prepared for. The years had worn her down and, as the years often do, had obliged upon her the gift of patience, with her body at least. Her mind, though, was racing now; she looked often at reflected surfaces and saw without exception that she was growing younger; 'youngering', her mind whispered. This in itself was nothing short of a miracle, she repeatedly reminded herself. She had stopped in the lobby of the 'Showtel'.

In a place where everyone had a bunk, well, except for the poor indigents that populated down below, no such thing as a hotel existed. Yet it had become evident early in the piece that sometimes people needed a change of scenery, a different space to hang their hat. And so, over time, the large cavern, originally set aside to become a restaurant and entertainment venue, had, instead, with the help of a few billion nano-myte rock gobblers, become what everyone now knew as The Showtel. A large, echoing, cavernous space with bars and entertainment, true, but also with many dozen small rooms, each really little more than a bed space set deep in the central heart of the cavernous ballroom-style hall. A home from home for a few hundred lucky souls, who each week could achieve that pretence of a change of scenery in order to try and assuage the cloying feeling, the imprisonment that living on the rock eventually brought to bear on every single passenger on board.

The Showtel had, in fact, just appeared in front of her, and she gazed briefly at a poster for an upcoming show starring 'The Great Bezanto'. But then she had been looking at a reflection, that of a forty-something woman. A young woman with soft auburn hair and a delicately boned face. She was no longer even that surprised at the evolution she seemed to be going through. Hermione had slowly but surely come to the conviction, first, that the brooding, agitated man had been at the heart of the many and repeating black recollections that had seeded her mind the past day or two; and then, and this was perhaps a little more bizarre to her, that the scientist Lyle Cardington, her friend Muriel's father and chief scientist at Agetec, was also a key-holder in the strange turn of tide that beset her.

Part of the issue that Hermione Zatapec wrestled with still, though, was simply that, however bad that black place might appear to her, she found it increasingly difficult to remain immune to the wonderful gift of energy and vibrancy she now found herself dealing with. Quite honestly, she told herself, she felt like a superhero, able to leap tall buildings, had there been any, in a single bound. Restrained as she had been by the chains of being elderly and hard living, this release, increasing and dynamic as it was, was a difficult thing to ignore and a gift she felt thankful for and not rebuked.

But Hermione was also, it seemed, coming to her wisdom one step at a time, as all wisdom should be earned. She thought of the words purported to have been said by the Buddha many centuries before: 'Life is pain, and pain is learning'. And so, if that was 'a truth', then this rollercoaster she found herself aboard belied the truth of her plight. This, in turn, released another raft of whispered memories. A gurney and searing pain, flashing lights cutting green and screaming white. No eyelids, no flesh, no cover—bared. Her insides hung from the outside, and her mind's eye was forced to watch as…as Lyle Cardington cut her and fed her to herself.

She could not tell what was real in her memory and what was the fiction of whatever shroud still lay pulled across so much, but if there was truth in the words of Buddha, then this was where she needed to focus her attention and not ride the crest of some youthful wave. And anyway, a voice whispered deep inside of her, in a place where she had to listen very carefully to hear at all, where will it stop, Hermione Wise…and you weren't wise, were you? And in that hour, the voice sounded less harsh and critical, and if she tuned in and listened as carefully as she might, perhaps she was just a little frightened.

14
Death Does Not Take the Old but the Ripe

The marshal waited until nearly all had departed, and only then he had left the small gathering in honour of his fallen comrade, just moments before its more formal end. He was not a man given to social niceties nor insincere platitudes, and he suspected both might be in the offing. So, the old soldier had stayed immersed in the rearmost shrubbery, nodding once curtly when the preacher caught sight of him. He had, though, taken a couple of minutes, and, stepping quietly up to and behind the shoulder of the boy Remus, he had offered such condolence as he was able. And a more personal reassurance that there was a welcome waiting for him at the marine barracks.

Alexei noted, too, that another small child handing out candles and not recognising it as an unplanned event considered it a particularly dignified touch. He had spied Ariel standing back, similarly hidden deep in the shadows, her henchmen even more deeply buried in the garden's darkness. Though Alexei Stormbader had not sought specifically to disguise his own presence at the wake, nonetheless, he felt a small shiver at the sight of the lady. Upon spying Ariel, he himself moved just a little further into those dark, shadowy recesses under the trees. "Perhaps this is the way it must be for the likes of us," he mused to himself, "hiding and skulking at the end of all things."

He had spied Symonds, too, and the ginger-haired scientist; he did not remember the man's name, but they had crossed paths. This all did little for his good temper, but then he figured they were in the gardens of the corporate carnivores that Symonds ran at the head of, so perhaps the sight of those two was unavoidable. The old man's brain had been working hard, picking, and chewing at the knotted convolutions of the mystery before him. And in that mystery, he was starting to fathom that there was a link of inevitability between those three. Ariel was the invisible architect, and Sigmund Symonds was the get-it-done arraptchik. But the scientist, that had added a new colour and flavour to this cocktail, stirred his mind round and round. He felt increasingly certain, as the day had drawn on, that his men would come back now with something. For if there was something to be known, then they would keep turning over rocks until a light was shone upon them. The old general figured that, armed with that something, alongside his own stoical, steady digging and picking, he would find out. He would uncover whatever dastardly plot was afoot, and perhaps the preacher had been right, too.

Was he in danger? He truly did not know.

The likes of Ariel MP many times on his way up. They were often themselves great leaders in their own way; their capacity for self-regard aside, he acknowledged that whether man or woman, they had the absence of empathy that allowed them to order a man to his death, or many men, and to focus entirely on achieving the win.

Ariel was, he thought, without doubt successful because she was ultimately competitive. Tsaritsa cared not upon whom she trampled to cross that finish line in the first place. He understood that she was a great deal more covert and less ostentatious in the certainty of her own godhood than some others he had known. In years past, he had, when called upon, mastered those others that had crossed him. But now he had begun to have doubts; the lady was wreathed as much in mystery as in power. And just how much of this was smoke and mirrors, the old general had to admit to himself that he did not truly know. What he could not have known was that someone else in that space between mystery and fact had gotten word that Marshal Major-General Alexei Stormbader had men on the field of play and wondered perhaps if he spied glory, and so was about to make a move of his own.

What the older soldier also did not know was that the kind of distinctive people he recognised so clearly had a darker side than that competitive, self-regarding, un-empathic drive he had learned to spot. Such people were driven by fear, a fear of failure, of the loss of regard, and the supply of adulation that in turn gave them the idea of returning to hell their cold, furious hearts had run headlong away from. In the final analysis, this fear was greater even than the will to succeed, simply because it tended the fire under that will. It blinded such a person, and Ariel was just such a person. The simple childlike inability to spy that other people were different and varied at their core meant that the amygdala, the fight or flight mode of the Tsaritsa, was screaming "kill or be killed". The instant danger lurked; real or imagined, it did not matter. Had the soldier thought about that kind of danger, his linear mind would still have looked towards Symonds, and had he done so, then that would have proven his undoing anyway.

Marshal walked away smartly from the garden, his ration-issue boots, the same in every way as those worn by each one of his marine detachments, perfectly cleaned and gleaming under the arc light of evening-time lights down. Those boots scraped and clicked loudly on the echoing floor, his needle-creased marine-issue slacks swishing as he stepped smartly onwards. People came and went. It was a Sunday, and so there were more folk about to and fro from the various religious services held across the great craft, though few paid attention to the soldier. This far forward, the outer hull gravity from the spin was some small way from its ninety-one percent maximum, and the soldier kept walking at a pace. The old man liked the feeling of working his muscles, like the ache that would follow later. This was something he had not attained quite as much as he might have liked in recent times. Of course, he chided himself, he would eventually need to go down the three levels to reach his own residential block.

And as he headed the longer way towards one of the several access staircases, he thought back to those first years on the rock. Those terrifying, skin-of-your-teeth early years, when hope had been high and relief at surviving, nay escaping even, the doom that was back on Earth had seemed quite palpable. In those days, he was not alone in running up and down the many flights of stairs, glistening with well-earned sweat. In a place where well-earned sweat had become, through cold as much as through gravity, a difficult reward to earn. The marshal remembered having learned in second-year officer training that psychopaths do not sweat. The heart rate of a psychopath barely rises under any circumstances. He was told to make his soldiers psychopaths.

At some root level, in those earliest days, he wondered if they were not heading towards group psychopathy. Many of the ship's complements had crafted regimes of improved fitness, improved thinking, and improved self-regard, and control, as he remembered. At times back then, it was almost a procession as dozens ran up and down the sixteen dozen staircases that rose to height, if you could describe the inwards hull as having height. Nevertheless, at the beginning and at the close of each shift, men, and women alike chased steadily up and down the iron staircases, battling the loss of gravity. Running back and forth, grieving not just the loss of loved ones but the loss of their home, the only world any one of them had ever known.

And so that day, in the mid-evening light of a nuclear sun, an old soldier took the long way. Distracted as he was by the thoughts ranging through his mind and the worries that assaulted him from all sides, that soldier critically failed to notice that he was being followed. And that by moving away from the remaining throng of temple-goers, he had effectively signed his own death warrant. Indeed, though, perhaps he had signed that the day he stood up and spoke against Ariel MP.

He had set off that morning filled with anxiety, and caution had been his mentor and his watchword for many decades. Still, a man such as him, in high dudgeon, may be forgiven for missing something once. But then again, a soldier is a different breed, and when soldiers miss things, well, people die.

After a few minutes of walking, keeping up the brisk pace he had set for himself, he effectively marched along an arcing corridor that circumnavigated the outermost inner rock face of what was laughingly called the hull. Flanked to his left by the bare millions of years old rock, a curving wall that ascended visibly up to the next level, perhaps as much as ten metres above the grey-haired man's head. The railing on his other side sat scant centimetres from a grey man-made concrete wall, painted a once-smart, now fading, uniform grey. This was a design mirrored around a sizeable portion of the great whale. *Leviathan* was functional, and so, in greater part, he was not what you might call beautiful. It was a vast and complex beast, and though it was made, or at least tunnelled out, by the artifice of mankind, in large part it existed somehow beyond the dreams of humanity.

Ultimately, it had functioned in many ways, far beyond the whims and hopes of many aboard. They had simply taken a wild stab at the builders, the movers, and the shakers that stood at the very edge of doom. Desperate men and women who had taken a mad swing at bringing some version and some interpretation of Mother Earth's ecology on board. Those men and women had brought cats and dogs, insects, and vermin, plants, and flowers, shrubs, and trees. They had considered that much thought had gone into what might be stored in the asteroid's frozen heart, what might be cultivated and nurtured under a pair of nuclear suns. Yet, somehow, they had forgotten birds, bees and butterflies.

These latter-day Noahs had left behind so much of what made humanity whole, and some amongst them wondered if this was not just the last act of a slow slide to ignominious doom. Those early days, so halcyon in some ways, and yet so filled with the terror of a sudden and violent death for them all in the deep darks of an infinite universe, who might forget to bring all they might need for such a long journey.

Such prosaic anxieties had passed the marshal general. Law and order, or, more properly, the imposition of the laws of man and the acceptance of the reality of the laws of God, had filled his time. His and the time of his men, and for many months. From uplifting the passengers, ultimately all of whom were crew, to settling all of those sixty thousand desperate and disparate people into a pattern of what he had learned to describe as dostoynoye povedeniye (amenable behaviour). The Russians liked discipline, it is said. More than seventy percent of the complement of sixty thousand, when the craft set off on her long voyage, might have called themselves Russian.

And though in the intervening years it may be true that, in fact, a majority of those aboard had come to consider themselves Leviathans. Earth's last wandering tribe, a people that had revelled in the discipline, grew stronger in the unity of purpose on the long and ultimately uneventful voyage, but that had lost something, too. That love of discipline and order showed. Despite being a gruff and utterly serious military man, many aboard recognised and even lauded his achievements. Even from a distance, most loved the marshal. He was pictured as a brave and strong man in the old-fashioned measure. Willing to stand and roar like a grizzled brown bear back at the chaotic universe that each knew would assault them instantly if not for the firm footing of men like Stormbader.

He was, in large numbers, their last bulwark against that chaos. And so, as they grew into a community, his influence was noted as 'to the good of the majority'. Although it did leave in the shadows the simple truth of where humanity trod, murderous intent had always followed closely behind.

Something that had quickly become apparent early in the craft's great journey was that people had enough of the vast communities and the invisibility that had eaten away at the ties of society.

The craft, of course, had no online capabilities; they had been effectively outlawed on Earth for many years previously. Information absorption, overload, and scandalous invisibility within the macro-communities of millions had been rampant. Russia, ironically, had been something of a last enclave; perhaps the cold and the poverty had sought to retain some small family unit. Nonetheless, the global economy, mobile telephony, the simple weight of people in ever larger megacities, had rendered people both invisible and terribly unhappy. The craft *Leviathan* had proven itself an opportunity to re-make and start over. Somewhat ironically, as it turned out, without planning, small groups based on ethnicity, family, geography, and work rosters began to grow. Though around the same time many deemed the journey akin to a prison sentence, it was true that even the Gulag Archipelago comradery existed.

It was therefore the good wishes and the healthy discipline of the majority that Alexei Stormbader, Marshal General of the *Leviathan* marine detachment, was thinking about as he turned into stairwell number sixteen. And that became the last thing that the old soldier ever thought about. He turned onto the landing, glancing up the staircase to the upper level, deep in shadow, where yet another light had gone unrepaired. In that very instant, the silent assassin, spying on his moment, suddenly moved in close. Pulling a spiteful-looking four-inch tempered steel shank from inside the work coverall he was wearing, he buried it brutally and quickly into the soft tissue at the base of the old soldier's neck. It was expertly done—a smooth, even-paced jabbing.

Once, twice, three, and then four times. The soldier did not scream; no words came from him at all. And though blood gouted and pumped copiously and instantly from those sudden death-dealing puncture wounds, flooding outwards in a torrent from the newly opened exits, the old soldier simply remained motionless, standing utterly still for long seconds. He looked, but his eyes were already unseeing, and his mind had already switched off.

The assassin turned and fled, and seconds later, as the man's brain recognised what his body had already figured out, Marshal General Alexei Stormbader of The Eight fell to the ground dead.

15
Better to Be Slapped with the Truth Than Kissed by a Lie

Hermione, after leaving the wake, moved by it, and by her latest encounter with the child Muriel, she had fallen into a deep mental contemplation, a seeming melancholy. This was a thing that had been far outside her conscious countenance for a long time. She walked aimlessly and so ranged far and wide across the craft as the evening grew long into the night. She was energised by her renewed youth and passion; no tiredness took her, and the safety of down below was let fly as that same confidence in herself grew by the hour. Indeed, at a subconscious level, she felt like an athlete—better than at any time she could ever remember. Consciously, she wondered if somehow, she was being given a gift and, at the same time, released from the predations of youthful womanhood that had come with that gift last time around.

So deep in a reverie of thought, of doubt, anxiety, and excitement all rolled together, after a few hours she had ascended to more levels than in very many years and came to one of the more open spaces that was aboard the *Leviathan*. Nearby is the outermost rocky skin of the great craft, a wide open, curving space of approaching three acres. This was a place burrowed to expand on a pocket discovered in the rock by the trusty nanomytes. A place mined and then given over to shrubs, grass, and trees, long since. Perhaps most unique of all was the pair of diametrically opposed, slow-moving, low-gravity waterfalls. A heavy mist hung still in the air around both effluences, and upon closer inspection, it was, in fact, possible to identify that this was not a mist in the earthly sense of the word.

But rather millions and millions of droplets of water, discarded in the lower gravity from the main body of water. And so, with less than optimum assistance, they only find their way slowly to a hard surface to continue their slow trickle.

Had she known of such things, had she been the scientist, Hermione might have looked up the Coriolis effect and many Newtonian and Einsteinian laws to better understand. But the newly youthful lady was in a different space and stood in the dim night-time light, shoes off, squelching her feet on damp grass that grew further from her home world than any ever had. The gravity was indeed lower here; the great craft had been powered spin-ward whilst still in a relatively low polar Earth orbit. Many experts have claimed that the action driven by the two nuclear engines was the moment when they all, some sixty thousands of them, were in the greatest peril.

But they had the multi-million-tonne craft, rock, whale—whatever hybrid thing it had become, they had made it spin on an axis. All of this in spite of the death of the great designer, who many believed had been the last great hope for humanity and who had died scarcely a few months before.

Once moving, simply speaking, in a vacuum, the great rock would continue to spin on the new hypothetical axis that had been created through its centre. So, in miniature, they were able to create a form of minute gravity, whereupon the closer to the outer hull, where the spin was fastest, the slightly less was the gravity effect, and yet an astonishing 91% Earth normal had been achieved deep in the heart of the old rock. This was beyond the predictions and wildest expectations of even the leading technologists.

Hermione Zatapec, though, knew nothing of these matters, and instead she simply felt the usual pushing sickliness deep in her stomach as her body fought and sought to reorient itself once more. She was a creature of down below, and so this new open space was having a significant effect on her bowels and, it seemed to her inner self, her brain, too. The lady had come here before; she was certain of that, though not for a terribly long time. Indeed, so long that she had no real or specific recollection, she was able to latch on to just a feeling, a vague yearning. As she stood there at the entrance, she caught glimpses of white, flashing in and out in the gloom amongst the long grass. She could smell something floral and musky, somehow matching the damp, dark gloom.

Hermione watched for a few minutes, her eyes adjusting to the gloom. Then, after perhaps a minute, with a small chuckle, she realised what the white flashes were. She was watching rabbits, or at least the tail half of rabbits, as they ran about their night-time business with no care for where they washed up or for what they found. So, there was one waterfall running down each side, or, more precisely, each end of the cavernous space. The noise that they made, of cascading, crashing water as each flow hit the rocky, pebbled surface at the base, was glorious—a sound reminiscent of a home from long ago. The younger lady was more than a hundred metres away, and yet even as far away as she stood, that sound was deafening.

Hermione knew, at some level, and remembered enough to understand that, though decoratively beautiful, even this space was created with purpose in mind. Using what gravity there was to wash the water through great carbon and stone filters as a part of the purification process that kept them all alive. Growing an abundance of greenery at the heart of the great rock to scrub as much carbon dioxide as possible where the filters and pumps would otherwise have had to work at their hardest simply to get the damn stuff moving. Indeed, even using the gravity effect and the mass motion, much H_2O still hung in the air, seemingly in the hope of avoiding landing for as long as possible. Hermione knew, though, from personal experience that wind had not been an issue this far up the decks of the *Leviathan*, though whistling and icy as it was all the time in the depths down below.

History told that this space had once been, in effect, a pocket within the great asteroid and had likely been there for many millions of years. It had found a purpose, and in time it had become dubbed 'Waterfall Park'. And over a quarter of a century, Waterfall Park had borne witness to many things, as it became a place for lovers, and for thinkers, for dreamers. And, Hermione Zatapec figured, for rabbits and for sleepless ladies, too.

Each waterfall had an iron railing-clad staircase running up the side, from bottom to the very summit, painted grey on the iron alloy, and the only obvious human symmetry to a place allowed to grow wild. As she gazed upwards, something itched at the back of the lady's mind about that.

Hermione walked towards the nearer of the two cascading falls, wiping droplets from herself as she wandered through the misty cloud. Then, as she drew close, mid-stride, and for no reason could she consciously remember after the event, the newly young woman swivelled away from that nearer fall and headed off to the father of two. Her feet were still bare, and they made a nice, soft thudding sound on the grass. The cold damp and the giving of the turf were an absolute joy after so long thumping around on rock and concrete. Hermione wondered to herself why she had not come here more often—oh, aimless wanderer of so many long days.

After a few more minutes, she approached a staircase and noted sourly that someone had fitted a gate at the base of the stairs. "More damn rules," she mumbled to herself, though she could not hear what she had said as the falls were much louder here. Her mind twisted briefly to a recollection of a story from Sherlock Holmes, the great historical English detective that…Her mind snapped then from thoughts about Reichenbach Falls of Holmesian fame, and she smiled as she noticed that the large, obnoxious-looking padlock was still pinned to the railing, and so the gate, though closed, was, in fact, not locked.

Hermione Zatapec smiled, looked for long moments up into the misty gloom, and then suddenly, without any warning, the lady fell to the ground in a heap. An onlooker would have spied that she had instantly begun sweating profusely, though it was both cold and damp in that place. She was panting and gasping for breath, and between those gasps, a person would not have been able to miss that the woman who had dropped to her knees was sobbing uncontrollably. And her mouth, struggling with all of that, was still trying to form some words, a word. Hermione Zatapec then vomited violently and long. Retching over and over, she fell forward on the ground and then lay still.

After perhaps a minute, still sobbing, now quietly, still gasping, now shallow, short attempts at breath, the pretty, though unadorned, young woman jumped back up onto her haunches and screamed, 'Jacob!' in a tone that tore at the air. For a few short moments, that scream even defeated the noise of the great cascading water. The lady then collapsed back to the ground, unconscious.

So, it was once again that the mind operated in ways far more oblique than even the deepest and most well-researched might have guessed, and Hermione Zatapec, who had not been wise, in that moment, had been introduced to her folly. In the seconds that followed, the magnitude of all that had befallen her and the man that she had loved, too, had proven just too much. So, Hermione, widow of Jacob, lay long on the damp ground, in the mists of a waterfall, in a small park spinning at the outer reaches of an asteroid travelling further from her home than any human had until that point gone.

16

The Muriel Epiphany

You may be gone before we know you, and only God knows why

Muriel had awoken the next morning, the day after attending the wake with her father and all the other high and mighty people of *Leviathan*. The sickness, a cancer of the lymph and bones, as she understood it, had returned in the night with vengeance in mind, it seemed. She had awakened from dreams of dark and evil places that slid with consciousness into uncomfortable hallucinations. Sharp moments of vomiting and a deep, vibrant sense of pain and despair sucked at her very core. That pain and despair were something that she had gotten used to over the long years of her childhood.

Her father was gone, and she could hear the housekeeper, because, to Muriel, that was Susannah's role in the lives of her and her father. She was a pleasant enough woman, but neither Lyle nor Muriel had any great passion for her. Nor, it seemed, did she do it for them. It was a simple and convenient bedroom relationship that had the added benefit of housekeeping. That, and a general detachment between all three, seemed to work as they traipsed their way across the infinite universe. Muriel had once overheard her father describe his relationship with Susannah as the longest 'holiday romance' of all time, just without the holiday…or the romance.

Her room was ice cold; in fact, there was ice literally formed in the rocky corners of the outer-facing wall. Winter had arrived, and it had stayed for twenty-three years. Muriel shivered and buried herself deep under the covers. Her head was swooning as her body went through the throes of rejecting whatever the latest raft of injections had been. It seemed to Muriel that the cancer, itself so adept at changing and re-inventing, had, in the night, concluded that this was the morning for a fresh assault. Lyle Cardington's daughter was a smart adolescent, not just technically, though that was true, but in a more balanced holistic and spiritual sense. This was a sense her father did not appear to possess; lost as he was in the deep well of scientific learning. That part of her had tried over a long period of time to befriend the cancer. The thing that she had been hosting now for most of her young life.

In an effort to get to know the will of that other, to try and understand what was in her that made that other wish to stay, and what it was in her that similarly fired that other. She saw it, in fact, akin to a pack of ravenous and starving dogs, similar to hyenas. Time and time again, she meditated and looked inwards in a child-natural way, wondering at the conflict that went on inside of her. She wondered in her young mind if there was not a way in which they might grow together rather than in opposition. This had caused her repeated issues with her father, though they never argued either one's perspective with volition.

Even more, she had an issue with the various medical consultants she spends nearly as much time with. Muriel Cardington understood that the mechanism that the grown-ups wanted to use to 'treat' her guest was to attack it and hope to kill it. And as much as they discounted her view, could she not understand theirs? She believed that every time they put the chemical concoctions, they came up with inside of her, they were simply firing up the temper of the hounds and declaring war. And she, not them, would pay the price. Muriel was a child and was therefore deemed insufficiently wise to have a place at the table of adult opinion. Though it might indeed relate to her own self and her own life. But whether on Earth or in *Leviathan*, this was nothing new for adults in such situations. To simply ignore and command that they knew best, and in so doing ensure that particular cycles of unique control were neither reviewed nor ever changed.

The child on the skirts of adolescence groaned; on the one hand she felt awfully unwell, and on the other hand she really did not want Susannah fluttering around her with her vague, non-specific 'get some rest, dear' idioms and wisdom. She lay for long minutes, calming her sickness, her heart rate, and her breathing. She had learned long since to make breathing ever so shallow, almost not there, a whisper so as not to wake the angry ogre any further.

Muriel remembered her father reading the fables of Jack, the farmer's boy, and Igor, the giant. She was told a Russian folk tale, though she had no idea what a beanstalk was or if such a thing existed. Nevertheless, her father had told that particular story at her infant bedside over and over. And, with great colour and aplomb, he repeated how the boy Jack crept on silent feet, withheld breath and a calmed heart, past the sleeping giant to the place where the great goose had laid her golden eggs. The story fascinated the infant Muriel, despite the fact that ultimately the giant had awoken, through what her young mind considered the artifice of that goose. The hush upon the boy had become a legend in the mind of Muriel, and so she in turn had learned to mimic that in some parody where her cancer became Igor the Giant, and she became Jack.

Muriel Cardington had been sick for as long as she could remember, and down those long year's stillness had become more than a dream for her; for many long stretches, it was her necessity and her only friend. We are not born with patience; each and every one of us arrives in this life screaming to be seen, to be fed at the breast of our mother, whether that cry is answered or not. We can, though, and must, it seems, learn patience in the face of great hardship or great necessity. Childhood is, for most, the first and greatest hardship. Her father's chief lab assistant, Joshua, was often heard to mutter, "necessity is the mother of invention". So, it was with Muriel; her great hardship had invented and tutored within her the skill of patience. Her father had told her many times that until age three she had been as bouncing as a jumping bean. Those words: she had no idea what that was or whether the jumping bean lived on the beanstalk in Igor's castle. Yet, as children do, somehow Muriel got the message.

So, the story went that after a brief period of illness not being diagnosed, Lyle Cardington, recognising that what was happening was not symptomatic of something short-term, had pushed his daughter to the front of a fairly lengthy queue of geriatrics. Most of those then were suffering the many and varied ailments that came with long incarceration in deep space, mixed with simply getting older. In a short space of time, a battery of tests followed. And though Muriel was a very young child, she still held more than a passing memory of those gaunt and haunted weeks. They were the beginnings of her remembered childhood, and with them came a steady undercurrent of sickness. A sickness that often ran on for weeks or even months at a time.

In every other way, Muriel Cardington was no different than any other child, whether aboard the great ship or of the thousands of generations that had spilled out and grown haphazardly back on Earth. She was an empty vessel waiting to take her fill of lines of wine, whether that be bitter or sweet. Though, conversely, in some other ways she was different, certainly than the Earth-born who had spawned all aboard. She had never seen, never stepped foot on, and never would have seen the planet that gave life to all humankind. The child adolescent was on a path of learning, far from home. So, it was with no real frame of reference to test her sickness against, with which to measure herself, that she simply accepted what was happening inside of her as 'normal', her normal. Muriel's mother had died in childbirth, so she had not known her at all. When Muriel Cardington came into this world screaming, her mother's breast had not been waiting.

As it had turned out, the general absenteeism of her father seemed not as bad as it might be: Muriel had grown older with a quite stoical view of life aboard *Leviathan*. The girl quickly grew used to her physical limitations, both in the lower gravity where building muscle was for all children a challenging task and with the recycling of cancer within her small frame. It soon became apparent to her that whatever the regime of therapy and drugs, this particular cancer was virulent. It came at her again and again, and the periods of respite gained at the cost of medicating her body and sometimes her mind, too, grew shorter and shorter as she grew older. As Muriel Cardington left infancy for a more rounded childhood, she took up the challenge of relating to this other thing that had decided to live inside of her.

A little more than three years ago, the senior surgeon had gone to Lyle Cardington, and they held a council of sorts. Discussing whether it was really fair to keep Muriel on a cross-section of medications that were themselves so harsh as to be damaging her longer-term life prospects every bit as much as the cancer that was eroding her day by day. Cancer, a word derived from Latin, had evolved meaning according to mutated or broken cells or many cells. Whatever its derivation, as the surgeon had explained to Lyle Cardington, it was still beating humankind back on Earth, and the surgeon felt that, despite first-class care, perhaps, in Muriel's case, they needed to take a more palliative view simply for the young girl's well-being. To allow her, by their view of such things, some period of quality of life. Lyle Cardington might have been an absent father; so often the scientist was lost in the hyper-vigilant watch he took on his own complex and twisted version of the universe.

That's the place in which his mind dwelt, and where he might be lost for the longest stretches. Nevertheless, with all his heart, however misunderstood her needs, the father loved his daughter to an absolute full stop. He could not stand to hear this news, or indeed consider even the prospect of 'giving up on her' and had said as much to the surgeon general that he had fought inch by inch to ensure that cure remained the focus. "The longer we have her, the more chance there is we can save her." He had said this over and over, unwilling to budge, firmly pushing back against the remonstration that came like waves onto the shore. That same conversation had repeated itself and gone on for many long weeks until, in the end, the medical task force relented. Acknowledging that, operating as they were, far from their home world, it was true enough that they did not know the full ramifications; neither did they know what existence on board that speck, in universal terms, would in and of itself add to or take away from the girl's chances. And the simple truth had been that in the end, not one person could look the father in the eye and offer no hope, so, with hope alone, they and he continued.

Muriel knew little of this, back then or on this latter morning, as she struggled out of the warmth of her bed to dress quickly and exit the quarters before being spied on by Susannah. Strangely, it was this elongated debate with the surgical team nearly a decade previous that had pushed Lyle Cardington on the first tentative step down the road of gene re-sequencing. A conversation that had got him wondering about cell repair, though he would never identify the cause-and-effect prompt that had taken place.

He had learned in college in Lucerne that cancer had been a word from Latin and had hailed from their word for crab. It had then grown in colloquial parlance as the term for a number of abnormal tumour growths that resembled the swollen legs and claws of a crab on their victims. In turn, at some point during that thousand-year empire, the term had come to mean abnormal growth and then ultimately abnormal cells. This had, back then, all passed as knowledge in a whirlwind of study for the young Cardington. Yet more than two decades later, the scientist had shaken his ginger hair, joined his hands, and cracked his knuckles loudly, and got down to it. And because he did not have another starting line, he started with the crab. That and the question mark in his mind that all medicine had been given over to attacking and killing these 'mutant' cells, and very little if any research had been given over to mending them.

Which, had he known, was to become the quiet whispered mantra of his then-still-infant daughter. This was a crossroads as far as Cardington was concerned. Cells were in four states within all living things at any moment in time: normal, abnormal, dying, or dead. He could not do anything with the last of the four, as much as he could not bring a lifeless rock or a dead tree back to life. But the other three…well, it seemed to him that he needed to keep the normal cells normal for as long as was possible, persuade the abnormal cells to seek a path back along the spectrum towards normality, and invest in the longevity of all cells. It sounded straightforward and not so different than the advice the crew was given every day of their lives for their own health and optimum self-care.

The scientist had a picture in his mind, and had he been asked to formulate it into words or even equations, it is doubtful he could have described what he saw enough for anyone else on board to understand. Perhaps even anyone else that had been alive on that last fateful day back on Earth. Had the technology existed aboard to measure such things, Lyle Cardington's pure IQ was off the chart, possibly in the one hundred and ninety range based on a one hundred population median. What he was able to imagine in his brain's personal paradigm for merged picture, sound, and thought was symmetry. Cardington saw a coalescing of disciplines at a cellular level.

Something that would bring such harmony as to lengthen and improve the simple quality of every single cellular strand that made up the complex web of a human being. He thought it in his mind, and that holistic view, had he but known, was perhaps the clearest indication of all that he and Muriel were father and daughter. Cardington had figured out early on that his daughter Muriel had simply too many 'abnormal' cells, and he could see in his multi-dimensional imaginings how that was affecting her, technically, though perhaps not physically or emotionally. What he did recognise, though, was that the various suites of medications that attacked and killed the cancer cells were without doubt killing his daughter too. This was the ultimate catch, twenty-two.

Similarly, as the scope of his work grew, the scientist was able to visualise the complement of *Leviathan* as they drifted onwards down the long, slow, declining years. They, in turn, had too many dying and dead cells, alongside a complement of abnormal cells distributed among them in increasing numbers. Sixty thousand people on board were all on the wrong side of the Paredo distribution. Either way, whether for his daughter or for them all, it was inescapable that the final outcome was death.

Cardington worked for several years after the ship's take-off for the main crew complement, involved in various functions, but in particular in the management of living things within the ecosystem. With the experience he had gained during his four years in Prague, specifically dealing with reptiles and insects, he was a shoo-in, and he had risen quickly to the top. Simply because he was, though he did not really understand it, the smartest technical person aboard the craft. He had managed cryogenics, genetics, and ecosystems like nursery school time tables, and had little time for the ponderously slow minds of those working around him. His IQ would, in part, for those that might have been measuring metrics, likely be because his mind had an innate ability to read problems with both left and right brain sides simultaneously. This allowed him to be creative as well as logic-driven responses as a merged solution. It was a rare gift, and one that was better for him not knowing or being aware enough to allow his ego to fan that flame.

Looking back towards those years, a more pragmatic individual might have questioned the timing of Sigmund Symonds's entry into the small ginger-haired scientist's world. Perhaps the exact work that man had been doing himself on measuring the IQ and aptitude of those in ascent aboard the great rock. Perhaps such an individual might, too, have questioned the fledgling company, which, only days after the two men had met, had sprung into existence, having been formed literally overnight and called Agetec. The agreeable and listening ear that Symonds had presented to Cardington, the friendship he had allowed, seemingly gently, to flourish. All the while guiding him away from the main crew complement and into a private laboratory.

A laboratory with independent funding and independent support, but where, critically, as the mind of the scientist roved and sought answers, he answered only in the end to Symonds himself. Early in the relationship, the two men had sat long into the night and engaged in a devil's advocate debate surrounding humanity's arrival at and fall from the top table of mammalian life. Indeed, Symonds had recounted the Cro-Magnon split. The move towards meat-eating, which significant sections of the scientific community had heralded as the singular reason for the growth of tripartite thinking and reasoning in the brain. Symonds had pointed out to Cardington that human babies were the least capable mammals in existence at birth. In their current form, a human child at nine months would have died without exception if not for the protection and care of a parent.

Yet each woman generally only carried one infant to term, which suggested a far lower mortality rate or, conversely, a far higher competence rate at birth. Sigmund Symonds 'suggested' that science had proven this was a result of our own meddling. The moment we as a race introduced 'big brains', the babies we carried needed to find the exit before those big brains created big heads, and so those baby mammals became utterly reliant on the protection afforded them by their big-brain parents.

Cardington had heard this debate before, but he bought in, saw the logic, and saw how, in the years since agriculture, humanity had quadrupled the conditions by which they might die. But countering them with an ever greater reliance on medicine and procedures. And at the end of all that, across more than one hundred thousand years, even setting aside the destruction of their home world, humankind still lived only a very few years longer than their distant hunter-gatherer cousins. Cardington saw that, as a race, humanity, whether by accident or design, had changed things with inevitability before. After that night, the scientist set off with avarice to change the future for the better of all, though mostly in the immediate future for the better of his daughter Muriel.

This had become a version of the age-old chicken and egg parlance, dealing with the question that came first: the scientist's ambition or the enforcer's designs? The answer was clear to at least one of those involved. Agetec had grown quickly, with a few side bars and medical balms helping to promote a healthy public image, swanky offices and laboratories in the business district ensuring the proper profile, and the undisclosed yet obvious patronage of Ariel MP similarly ensuring healthy notoriety. Agetec, in turn, had introduced scientists to the qualities and genetics of nematode genes. He had, along the way, discovered a number of things that had allowed his daughter respite in her care. In time, some amongst those medical balms worked through to public consumability, quickly and wondrously reproduced by the team around Cardington. For him, ultimately, as far as he was concerned, each step, each progression, was just there to offer Muriel any semblance of an improved life.

Down long months that had rolled into years, Agetec grew. Lyle Cardington was given full geometry in the imaginings of his deepest scientific brain. Yet somehow, as hard as he tried and as much as he sought a cure for Muriel Cardington, he had failed. This in equal measure meant he had failed in his designs for a life-giving path that his boss and friend Sigmund Symonds had begun by enquiring about and, more latterly by demanding. Any final solution seemed to evade him: still he was not able to save his daughter, nor, though he cared less for them than for her, it seemed, the remainder of those aboard. As days grew into weeks and months into the years, Muriel held on. Lyle became more frantic, and Symonds resigned more. Each one's fate tied to the other; all fates tied to the will and whim of Ariel MP, Tsaritsa of *Leviathan*.

Muriel slowly and carefully dressed herself, pulling on a white overall and a thick quilted jacket. The vomiting had passed for now, but she looked pale and was very weak. She wiped tears from her eyes and then stood for a long minute, gazing blankly at the rock wall of her room. She was deep in thought. Deep, in fact, was in debate with her guest, asking for respite so that she might go her way and explaining that if the grown-ups found her like this, then they would send more of their attack medicines. That was not good for either of them. Whether by virtue of that internal debate, random chance, or some other twist of universal fate, after a few minutes she did feel a little better, and silently she slipped out of the Cardington home.

17
Hate Is a Thing That Destroys Everything Except Itself

The night was full of darkness; there was frost in the corners, and it grew white and encrusted around the room's ducting. It was chilly throughout *Leviathan*, and even at these upper reaches, an icy breeze could be heard whistling its way through the corridors and alleyways. Though people often observed that this icing was an occasional thing and had never become quite a permanent occurrence in the upper reaches, it was still questioned how that might be if they had a steady 'nuclear' input and a steady 'absolute zero' output. It had indeed come to be named a season, though it was quite random amongst a life that was always chill. It was winter now on board the ship, and many lower reaches had a permanent frost. Responding to that most human of instincts, a majority of those on board did their best to hibernate. Many were of Russian origin, and so deep winter in the midst of always winter was not something new. So it was that beyond attending mass and going to work, the vast majority of those on board hunkered down, gazed dejectedly at the ice forming around them, worried at what The Eight were up to, and not telling the likes of them.

Ariel MP, too, was in her quarters, but she was not thinking about these things; though she did shiver, and whether that was the cold or the deeds in her heart, none could tell. The day had been long and difficult, and the rage that sat in her deepest recesses and that she so assiduously hid had scorched her in recent days. Who was there that should challenge her right to be…well, to be right? It was unheard of that some might be investigating her, questioning the judgements and edicts that she issued. Ariel had long suffered from a weakness of object constancy. If you were not with her, then you were against her; if you were not for her there and then you did not exist. Whatever had passed before that moment accounted for nothing, and if you were for something not on Tsaritsa's present wish list, then you were automatically construed as against Ariel MP. Which is to say, you might well be on the receiving end of vitriolic revenge, especially now, when the tide seems to be turning towards a storm.

The truth, never to reveal—the secret that Ariel hid deeper than her anger—was her unrelentingly low opinion of herself. Whilst that lady was very capable of postulating fault onto those around her, in the moments of quiet, when the only excuse she had was herself, a small voice bleated in a tone like a baby lamb, full of need and rejection. That voice was repeating, telling her over and over, "We are not up to this, my dear." And then, when she would not reply, "We are not up to this, my dear, and they will figure us out. The ones who ought to be in charge will come and take the fraudster away." Ariel MP, who was the unelected leader of the free peoples of *Leviathan* and the unelected head of the Council of Eight, the single most powerful person on board that craft, had run in terror from that lamb's bleating for a lifetime.

The lady had spoken earlier that evening with Sigmund and had flatly and coldly refused his support and the company's offer. He had even suggested that she might come to his quarters—something that had not happened since the very earliest days of their then-flourishing connection. The Tsaritsa had said, with hostile finality, 'no'. Then, after a long silence, during which the pesky man had not gone away but rather stayed, hanging at the other end of the radio connection, the lady had gone on to advise him that she needed to work on exactly what she would say on the morrow. When she and not he, nor any of the others of The Eight, were burdened with and intent upon sharing some version of the calamitous news more widely. And she was truly not yet certain what that statement would be.

That night, she did not want an audience for her plans and deeds, and even more, she did not want his air of failure close to her. She considered this and had said as much to him: "You have failed me; you have failed to deliver at all."

She had spoken to him in that manner, and though he had gotten used to her frequent episodes of withdrawal, learning to occupy and refocus himself, and even believing and somehow accepting that she probably had other 'occasional' lovers, nonetheless that last observation had left him reeling. This was punishment, pure and simple, for whatever perceived misdeed Symonds was deemed culpable for. This, too, would allow Ariel to project the focus away from herself in these times of troubling responsibility.

It had left the enforcer feeling as if all the calamities that had befallen them and the failure to resolve them somehow fell squarely on him. He struggled as he had before, manfully and for many years now, and increasingly in the last few years, to square the circle between the warm and fuzzy Ariel that he quietly adored and this vengeful, cold-blooded snake that hissed and spat venom at a moment's notice. The big man considered, in an inspired instant, that she and not he should have been the enforcer, so adept as she was at driving the stake of responsibility deep into another's soul. For her part, across the other side of the great craft from her sometimes lover and long-time wingman, the unofficial leader of sixty thousand souls had come to the conclusion, without too much difficulty at first, that she needed to do something about Symonds.

The buffoon knew too much, perhaps too well. He seemed to her to be increasingly venturing out on his own, sharing ideas with that fool of a scientist. Drawing away from her, which, by its very nature, implied disagreement with her. As a result, this clearly stated to her that he was an enemy and not a friend. Whatever charisma he may have had yesterday, in her mind, was long gone today. Ariel MP did not believe in trust; her religion was in control. The more Symonds had in reality been trying to deliver what she demanded, the more it had begun for her, in her fantasy world, to seem as if he was operating with an independent will. In these heightened times of drama, that made Sigmund an issue of consequence. Tsaritsa resolved to take back control, and, without emotion or doubt entering her mind, she drew her plans against him.

It was a little more than an hour after that terse conversation with her enforcer that a man had come to her, shadowy and indistinct, as such men aren't to be. The man had stood just inside the door to her front office, in the same room where she had met with the two men of God only the previous evening. That man had whispered to Ariel MP, the Tsaritsa, the delicate flower that, as the old wives would say, "could not say boo to a goose". The man had told her in guttural Russian and speakeasy slang down below that it was done. By done, the man had meant to murder most foully, and in the lady's name. She had then brought the man who was the assassin closer and, in hushed tones, had made one further request from him, with the promise of dreams beyond such a man's view of avarice. Ariel's features remained impassive throughout the exchange, though she sneered moments after the killer had left.

Ariel considered how she would relent upon their agreement and bring righteous justice down on that man and his cortege for daring the temerity to kill one of The Eight, and now it seemed the man would kill some other insignificant one too. As an observer sitting in Ariel's world, it seemed she had already, within her mind, disassociated herself from any responsibility for these actions. She had already moved on, like a shark in shallow waters that had fed and had no further concern for the corpse left rotten, bleeding, and bloated. The Tsaritsa had not smiled at the news that the old general was dead; she was a smart woman.

Though cold-blooded, Ariel was change-averse, preferring all the pegs in their holes—the holes that she put them in. Ariel MP spied that there would be difficulty ahead if this did not play out in the letter of her planning. But intrinsically, she was certain it was the right decision, the chosen path for her own greater good, and that, ultimately, she believed was the greater good for all. Had she possessed a greater capacity for self-examination, Ariel would have spied that she had already begun that work of self-excusing and self-justification. Further self-examination would have keenly entreated to her that those very tools, the wiles of the non-empathic, that were the architecture of her character, allowed her to aspire to sit on the highest seat that remained in their diminished world.

Later that same night, she received another visitor into her private anteroom. At the wake of the previous day, her mind was always scheming and looking around the next corner. She had buttonholed the taller of the two religious men, who had described her beauty so prosaically. He might have been a man of God, but Ariel MP recognised that Alexander Smorzgard was also a terrible womaniser, and, widowed as he was, the Tsaritsa knew exactly how to charm someone like him. The preacher came as he was commanded to do, and he spoke with bluff and bluster, and she keenly played to his gallery for close to an hour. Then, using all of the artifice she had learned down the years, Ariel turned the man towards her 'fears and anxiety' about the growing power and reputation of the man, Sigmund Symonds. She provoked a parent in him, despite him never having children, as she portrayed the vulnerable fears of a child and spoke coquettishly about how Symonds was a demon and certainly was not a man of God, and that she believed he might be playing with nature down there at Agetec.

He was the father of a flock and seemed desperate to help, desperate to be rescued. The preacher, Smorzgard, bought the whole package and took the hook and line, too. He would fly away like a good monkey and deliver the same sermon with a few added twists of colour and style to the more intractable Nicholai and other venerable brothers also, exactly as the lady had planned. As the preacher left, he almost collided with her final visitor of the night, and even that had been planned. The preacher walked into the old politico and member of The Eight, Grafton Shevnetski. The preacher was not immune to the status of The Eight, and this simple timing elevated him and his opinion of himself, as he deemed, he had finally arrived in exalted company. Shevnetski, for his part, cared not, simply imagining the religious fool to be the latest in a long line of lovers taken by the Tsaritsa.

He, too, though, had entered her quarters. And with a prior dislike and perhaps even wariness for her enforcer, Sigmund Symonds, the wily old politician was only too pleased to hear her lambast and portend doom for Symonds and all who stood near him. Though that man's heart clearly spelled the danger of accepting what he knew were lies, expediency was a far more immediate and demanding parent. He, too, left with his 'story' intact and ready to regale some time later in that long night.

18
You Cannot Find Happiness in the Same Place You Lost It

Hermione Zatapec lay in a swoon on the damp grass for a long time. She eventually came to it, shivering and uncertain how much time had passed. She walked over to where the water crashed into a deep pool, adjacent to the iron stairs, and looking down, even in that dim light, she saw the reflection of a girl perhaps nineteen or twenty years of age. She did not remember being so beautiful herself at that age and wondered, as a result, what additional devilry this might turn out to be. She was beyond surprised any longer and had accepted that she was on a path of re-treading, at least in a physical sense, the route she had stepped in the other direction for seventy years. When that thought first came to her, a voice in her head carefully suggested that, though she was ageing in reverse, she did not seem to be losing her experience or wisdom.

She had snapped back irritably, "But I wasn't wise, was I?" And for a time, at least, the voice had quieted. Hermione figured, as a seventy-year-old woman standing staring at a teenager staring back, that somehow, for reasons probably too oblique for her to ever completely understand, the blockage, the careful architecture her mind or circumstances had constructed to conceal the whole truth, had finally and irretrievably collapsed. She pondered this as a distraction, as deep inside herself she battled to quell the growing emotions that were forming in her heart. It seemed to her like thunderclouds presaging the storm as they massed on the distant horizon. And as she considered, the image looking back at her spoke once more in her mind.

How old were you when you lost Jacob? She had figured out that she was fifty-six when he had been lost, and she reiterated this last to herself. "When he lost." And she began to feel the raw emotional pain pushing and squeezing past her last boundaries, like the tide running the sea past a child's sand wall defences.

How old were you when you met Jacob Wise? The imperturbable teenage voice continued in her mind.

That had been easy: she was exactly forty-five years old, having been her birthday, though in those latter days, such things were less celebrated than they had been. It turned out to be the best birthday she ever remembered. They met on the lifting craft, a converted US re-usable space shuttle taken out of mothballs and retrofitted with a Soyuz rocket engine. This was to be the patched-up tin crate that would bring them both on board the *Leviathan*. Back then, Hermione suspected that numerous romances had begun in those desperate hours. She remembered the tales of brief, urgent, and passionate love spread like an unkempt forest fire in Moscow and in Leningrad. More than a century ago, whilst Nazi Stormtroopers massed at the gates to the city. And why not? The tall, dark-skinned Indian man had travelled to the launch facility in Baikonur from New Delhi.

A man who had seen such death and carnage as to waylay and break many a lesser soul. Yet still, a man who had been so polite had spoken in such a carefully articulated voice, switching between Russian and English to convey to Hermione the awful world that now pervaded beyond those borders. She, who had never to that point flown further than from her hometown into downtown Moscow and then onto the facility at Baikonur. He was handsome; Hermione had fallen for Jacob the moment she saw him. She was no wallflower herself, though perhaps she was beginning to consider that she was now facing her waning years; whatever, it was real love at first sight. As Jacob lifted the tan satchel, he had carried aboard up into a small storage bin above his head and sat across the aisle, Hermione caught the musky aroma of his scent, the smell of powdered spices and exotic India, a place she could only have dreamt of.

Hermione Zatapec imagined she could smell that scent now, and she swore at herself as it brought cascading sharp recollections following close behind. How she had whispered to the Mexican, the squat little man, 'Diaz Mankato', as she remembered on the name tag, who had been assigned the seat next to 'Jacob D. Wise' on the three-hundred-and-nine-minute ascent, and whom she had contrived to separate from that seat in short order.

Hermione had done little more than flutter her eyelids at the small, tanned man, and he, in response, immediately nodded his head, though it seemed he did not understand a word she had said, and agreed to exchanging seats with her.

So when Jacob returned from a last visit to the restroom before take-off, he found, with absolutely no mask upon her artifice, a chatty, youthful-looking Russian woman sitting next to him and not a short and slightly surly Mexican man with a moustache. Jacob Desire Wise had admitted to himself that this was not an unpleasant turn of events: there was something comely, in a Russian peasant and country girl way, about this lady. She was smart and sassy, and yet she artfully appeared to be painting herself as innocent and beyond reproach. As much as he could read, or at least guess, Jacob figured she was struck by him. Being a man of careful thought, he noted that he, too, was very drawn to her. As she stood there in the dark night-time mist, that last was all speculation in Hermione's mind, but they had talked about that journey many times after. She had opened up about her man in those early months of the voyage, and she had seen how much he loved and wanted to care for her—or, more precisely, with her.

Three hundred and nine minutes: that was the time it took to ascend to the fledgling *Leviathan*, and three hundred and nine was the number of minutes that the two required to fall indisputably in love with each other.

Hermione considered, as she stood staring at her questioning reflection, that it may be that they two, of all the people in the world that they left behind and those thousands that accompanied them on that Star Trek, that Jacob Wise and Hermione Zatapec had been the only two who were truly happy at that precise moment. The newly young lady remembered her feelings and the buzz after the initial screaming Heavy G take-off as they ascended into or beyond the stratosphere; no coffee or sandwiches were being served on that flight. She had been frightened and had felt quite sick. In response, Jacob reached up and, grasping his bag, dragged it into his lap, where it spent much of the next seven years. The tall Indian man had drawn from inside that case a small paperback book, something almost unheard of in the latter-day world in which Hermione had lived. The book had been a copy of Herman Hesse's treatise on the journey to a higher state of being, and in Siddhartha sat much of her Indian companion's spiritual whole.

In Waterfall Park all those years later, she heard his slow, sonorous voice once again, lilting up and down. And as she looked again at her reflection, the echo of that voice reading one particular passage now came back to her as they had ascended from a world filled with storms into heaven and an uncertain future. "But what a path it has been! I have had to experience so much stupidity, so many vices, so much error, so much nausea, disillusionment, and sorrow, just in order to become a child again and begin anew. But it was right that it should be so; my eyes and heart acclaim it." Siddhartha had been speaking to the Ferryman and had learned the wisdom taught by both him and by the water. "How did he know?" Hermione muttered to herself, crying freely, and leaning heavily on the railing simply to stop falling down once again. She saw him, smelled him, and so desperately missed his simple, honest wisdom. "What did I do, Jacob?" she suddenly howled at night. "What did I do?"

After arriving and boarding what was already being dubbed both Moby-Dick and the whale, the two, who had so recently found one another, were instantly separated. People were loading onto the great craft in their hundreds, with three re-usable Soyuz shuttles travelling up every third day, weather permitting. People were tagged for ascent as their talents were deemed required, and so they both found themselves with twenty-four full hours in each and every one of those first few heady, hectic days. Though neither forgot the other, there was barely time to sleep between shifts and to find their way around the great rock. Humankind was operating far beyond the rim of any undertaking it had until that point. One of Hermione's colleagues had laughingly joked that they were like the Egyptians building the pyramids, except they only had a bucket and spade.

On Earth, there had been rumours of death and dictatorship, and as had always been the case with Russians, most met this by bowing their heads, grumbling quietly, and moving on with whatever task had been set for them. Nonetheless, whatever the events below, the other pressure was that they were on the clock. Though things were not going so well back on Earth, and support and tech were increasingly difficult as more people ascended and those left behind had only their own fate to consider, this was all managed against the backdrop of an alarmingly narrow launch window. The window is designed to meet both the optimum nuclear propulsion and the position of the sun and Mars for picking up momentum in the first years after take-off.

An Indian medical and biotech man and a high-functioning middle-aged Russian career climber with a non-specific skillset were too low down the tree at that time to warrant either information or consideration. Somebody back on Earth, likely on a planning committee, had reviewed the personnel rhythm matrix and deemed it acceptable. Optimum and suitable, and few knew what that mix would ever arrive at. Somebody decided it was their time, and as they both laughingly pointed out many weeks later, thank God, they had, after all, been a sixty thousand to one shot.

Hermione then remembered how, much later, when they had found and cemented themselves into something that resembled a relationship, Jacob had shared with her his belief that she would already have forgotten him. His world view had not been so poor of himself; it was more that he was a humble man of working-class New Delhi origins. It was true that, despite great success in the fields of prosthetics and limb re-establishment, he was as close to the leader in his field as any that remained alive, but that was what he had called geek kudos. Jacob was also younger than Hermione by nine years, and though he had felt the electric connection between them both, his emotional brain had simply told him that she was too rich for his blood, or more, that he was too poor for hers.

Jacob Wise had never gone to search for Hermione Zatapec, and she realised, as she stood in that night-time park, that one single fact, which had irked her more than all the man's goodness, had also ultimately ended them, and perhaps killed him, too. So, despite being a first-grade catch, a primary rescuer, and an A-grade advocate for all things Hermione. Despite proposing marriage, the man had still never been forgiven for not chasing her down. Hermione Zatapec had, of course, gleefully agreed to his proposal, and she remembered looking out of a porthole, watching the blue of Earth disappearing slowly into the inky void, and how she had not cared a jot.

That same ship had grown much smaller after nearly a quarter century of incarceration, Hermione considered, as she stood damp and shivering in Waterfall Park. In those first significant weeks, you could still spy the beautiful blue and white pearl of Mother Earth floating serenely on a velvet black backcloth, or so it seemed. The rock had been growing daily, and to Hermione, it had seemed almost a majestic thing—in the face of such tragedy, a crowning achievement for humankind to finally hang their hat on. Things had settled into a pattern; a very different Hermione Zatapek had sought out the tall, dark, handsome Indian man.

And though she had duties that often took twelve to fourteen hours of her day, nevertheless, floor by floor and deck by deck, she worked her way back and forth across the evolving whale. Until, finally, as was so often the case in the movies of old, resigned to the belief that somehow it was just not meant to be, she had come here, to this very park. There had been no iron stairs then ascending next to the twin falling waters, and the grass and shrubs were newly planted and newly removed from Earth's gravity well, clinging on and little more than scrub.

This Hermione, as she looked around in the deepening darkness of night, remembered that another Waterfall Park. She remembered it then as clearly as she remembered her name, and she remembered, too, the moment that Jacob had walked in, his long, slow, languid stride eating up the space between them, a smile twitching at the corners of his mouth as he approached, like he had come simply because he knew that she would be there waiting for him. She, a decade his senior and already a climber in the power set aboard *Leviathan*, stood there like a coy child, unable to speak. "Hello, Hermione," he had said, and she knew then that she had to have him.

The Hermione of those days was a far more needy person; she loved Jacob Wise, but she loved other things, too. Four months later, they were married by the Russian Orthodox Chaplain in a tiny ceremony attended by only two witnesses. Jacob might have been described as a spiritual man, but neither one of them was particularly religious. Yet still, in love and in enchantment, they were, for a time, both moved by the small space given over to the church and the pastor, whose firm intonations had bound them to honourable promises for life. They returned together to the beautiful and tiny chapel; a space hewn into a small recess in the rocky heart of *Leviathan* by nanotechnology that seemed somehow beyond the compass of those gods of old. A simple cave with benches and forever-guttering candles in embrasures all around the room. Cleverly placed coloured glass to resemble the chapels of old in the Motherland. And so, every week, on the eve of the day they married, for nearly three years they returned.

And now, looking back, the old lady rocked back and forth in her teenage frame as she remembered the argument that she now, and only now, acknowledged she had prompted with Jacob all those years before, simply to shift the light of the gas lamp away from her and her own less than creditable actions. Back then, she had climbed a long way in the three intervening years; at least she believed that she had, distracted as she had become by the games of power and persuasion. The lady was smart and had a coterie of supporters and acolytes that fed her adulation, postured, and preened as she sought to climb to the highest eyeries of the developing power structure. Hermione Wise had proven to be adept at turning conversations this way and that. And as she stood there and remembered, often when she shot across Jacob's bows, he would try and debate, and, seeing the failure and confusion of that debate, would simply figure it was easier to accept fault, so he would nod and accept whatever she fired his way.

She had his track, and as a man who saw no value in hiding who he was, he had made no secret of his nature, his warmth, and his generosity. Ultimately, then, she had manufactured a tall tale, as she had increasingly lied in those intervening years. Each lie requires two more, careful study, and then more, and on and on. There came a day when they had not attended their wedding chapel, and he carried the blame. Yet she had caused that, not him, and she had lied terribly to him in spiteful desecration of his loyalty and love for her. She knew he liked that quiet time together each week. Increasingly, the burden of work and life aboard the whale took its toll, and Jacob Wise saw that time together as sacrosanct, a kind of ongoing pledge. And his wife, Hermione Wise, in a moment of spite, had taken it from them both and in the most terrible of circumstances. Then, when she might have somewhat repaired the damage, she was too prideful and too arrogant to ever try and recover, trying to put it back.

"Oh, God," she mouthed in the dark as she saw that vision of herself, what she had become, or, more truthfully, who she had always been, however well she had hidden that from her husband. For three years aboard *Leviathan*, she had won, and in ways never achieved before in her life. First winning over her superstar husband, then climbing the tree, was enough to move them into larger and more opulent quarters. Improved status, upwards social standing, furnishings, and tech that many aboard had no idea had even been part of the complement. As she looked back then, she realised that she had never asked Jacob if this had been what he wanted, and she guessed, looking back, that if indeed she had asked, he would have responded that he was happy to be with her. He was happy that these things made her happy.

And as each new victory had been added, there was just a little less room for them, a little less time for her to think about who she was, what she ought to be responsible for, and where the arc of her choices was taking them. But there's always a little more time for adulation, for the supply to her burgeoning ego. Hermione wondered now if this was all that she had been she sought to question whether Jacob might have done more and said more. But in that dark, cold park, she knew that she had chosen him and sought him out, all those many years before, precisely because, for all his strengths, he would trust her implicitly. And so, he would not question her honour or her motives. She knew now, if not then, that her motive had been in control. For as long as she could remember, she had been frightened by the world, and so young Hermione had designed a pattern buffer that was based on control. As a kid, she used to have a fantasy where she attended the funerals of all of her child friends, her parents, and their dog. She was special; she would outstay them all, stand, and watch each fall to the vagaries of life and age. She shuddered now at the recollection.

So, it had been with her husband: once she had him, she needed to control him; once she had a team under her, fool be he or she that did not abide by her will and whim. That fractured narrative and her own issues with object constancy meant that she always seemed to need a scapegoat. Some fools allow the burden of blame to always be shifted from her. Shit happened, and over the years, as they settled into a pattern, Hermione Wise increasingly brought that shit home and dumped it all over her man. And the one constant about control is that it is an illusion. And so, all these years on, as a sad and lonely woman stood alone in the late hours of night, she saw that picture, that circle of responsibility.

The years had done much for Hermione; she was undoubtedly a different woman, stripped as she had been of the trappings of power, of materialism, of love and kinship, even of her name. It seemed that now she was also being stripped of her life—that slow, inexorable tramp we each make towards our eventual doom. "I am punished, and I deserve all that comes my way," she whispered, in a voice that even were the twin waterways quieted, no one could have heard. She picked up the tan satchel, which had been sitting on the ground at her side and moved steadily towards the iron staircase that rose up beyond her sight. It sat slightly luminous and foreboding in the dark.

This cascade of memories had not just confined themselves to the events surrounding her marriage but also the events that preceded and ultimately led to her brief incarceration and subsequent visit to Agetec. Ah, Agetec, she thought, she was a medical scientist; in fact, as she now believed, a charlatan. A doctor without training or the label, a woman who somehow had a guile enough to ordain herself an unelected guide to those oars in practice and to their need for her acumen. Agetec had been like some halcyon dream. That fledgling, newly birthed organisation had been ripe for a climber like her, crying out for her particular brand of order and organisation.

Hermione was trying hard now not to think about the elephant in the room, but it was simply too big, and she could not avoid it. She folded up and collapsed once again, shaking her head, and whipping tiny droplets from her hair across her face.

"I did not care for him, Jacob," she said angrily to herself. Then instantly they came, memories like hard-falling rain, stinging, and ice cold. The dispassionate sex, Hermione, the smart and sassy climber, was irritated that she and not Jacob seemed to carry all of the burden of their success. She had given her body to a man and told herself she did it to get her name underlined as the next senior business VP at Agetec.

She remembered telling herself, "It was only sex; it was her body!" Then, after how she had demeaned and denied Jacob when he roused himself to question and concern, she projected all of her guilt and shame onto her man.

"Why do you care now? You never even chased me," she had screamed at him in vitriolic rage, tinged with the crimson colour of guilt and shame. "I wanted you, Jacob, and maybe now, maybe now I just don't."

She had cut him deeply, and a sick part of her psyche had been enjoying the attention, however sour its flavour. Hermione Wise had dived in, attacked, and attacked, and, at the end, had just been unable to stop herself. Her voice had escalated, her anger rising higher and higher in the face of her husband's implacable dignity. And so, she had arrived at that place, and she could not, would not, stop now from telling him the ugly and painful truth of her infidelity.

"I think he knew," she mumbled to herself, sobbing once more in the damp, dark park. "I think he just hoped it wasn't so, but he knew." She recognised that for a man like him, there would be no going back. That, on that diminishing rock, where might he go? Where might he start again without the love of his life? She got all of his attention—all the sour, bitter attention that a narcissistic climber could ever hope to feed on. And then, packing a small bag, he looked long at her, kissed her gently on the cheek, said goodbye, and left.

She never saw him alive again, though in the two weeks that intervened, she busied herself and deliberately tried to forget him. She demanded in her mind that he forgive her, fantasising about how he had to understand that she was doing what she had to do to get where she needed to go. Why didn't he understand her needs?

Jacob Desire Wise died in a malfunctioning airlock. He was the best person I ever knew and the smartest to boot. I know now that, sure as eggs is eggs, he ensured that the airlock malfunctioned. And with as much certainty, I ensured that he was left with that choice. Jacob's pain was so great that he just needed to get off. He wasn't made like that, and he could not survive in a world such as the one I had introduced him to. "And now," she spoke to herself, "now it is my turn."

The gate squeaked alarmingly as Hermione opened it, hoisting the bag to lift it over. It screeched slowly back into its frame, appearing not to have been used in some time. She trod tentatively on the first rung. The stairs had flaking paint and were slippery and wet.

"Be careful, dear; you may fall," she said to herself, and laughed harshly. As she climbed the first few steps, she remembered the weeks after Jacob's death: the drinking, the denial, the blame-shifting, and the huge pretence that it didn't matter and that he didn't matter. As those days had grown into weeks, she had collapsed emotionally, and in that breakdown, she had quickly deteriorated physically and spiritually. Her allies, spying on the crash, and none truly being friends, had swiftly departed for safer pastures, and she had gone from high maintenance to high risk. Her fledgling career at Agetec, which, in fact, had amounted to little more than a pair of tentative interviews, was dead in the water, and she ranged around down below from daybreak till night's end, seeking abuse and destructive shaming wherever she might.

Then that night, high on stims and drink, she had attacked a marine; the poor guy had only asked her to move on, and when she had caustically verbally assaulted the officer and he had pointed out she was old enough to be his mother and that she ought to know better, things had gone wrong very quickly. That last had triggered something in her—some vanity about eternal youth—and she had attacked him with glass in hand. Neither he nor her jailers knew about her loss or about Jacob Wise's death. She had made little of it publicly, preferring still to live in denial, avoiding widowhood in favour of going about once more as Hermione Zatapec. She had spent a sobering night in the cells, and they had let her and one other out at what was laughingly called dusk.

The hour was simply a shift change and a downshift of the sun generators to night-time mode. She was still cursing the marines, and in truth, they were glad to be rid of the painfully raw and outspoken woman. So it was that, as she walked away from the prison area, a small set of holding cells next to the squadron barracks, nobody saw as two people grabbed a woman, covered her mouth with a rag containing something nasty that had soon sent her unconscious, and then, bodily lifting her, had carried her away. She remembered coming to. She could still smell the vomit on her clothing from however many nights previously. Hermione had been strapped down.

The younger lady looked over her shoulder and noted that she had already climbed more than twenty feet. Don't fall now, she thought to herself; you might only break a leg. This caused another mental curse, and she wondered in passing if she was letting go of reality, as she realised, she had done all those years before.

They had been testing her, injecting her, or both. She did not know, and though she struggled against the restraints, at some core level, she did not really care. She remembered the room, the bay leaf that had been the symbol chosen for Agetec, the antiseptic smell, and the humming and clicking of machines. Time was lost on her, though she had a sense that she had been in that place for some time, maybe even weeks; her memory faded in and out, and this she knew was not a failure to realise now, simply the condition that they had kept her in then.

She reached the summit of the particular waterfall, around sixty feet up. There was a small gantry and railing that ran all around the rickety platform. This was not an area for the public, but rather for technicians of some discipline or another. In spite of her burgeoning youth, Hermione was seriously out of breath, and so, putting the case down on the gantry, she sat herself on the uppermost step and returned to her musings down memory lane. In fact, it was the spaces between those memories that saved Hermione's life that night.

As she struggled to piece together the events around her kidnapping, trying to make a jigsaw with her eyes closed, more than a decade after the fact, at some point exhaustion had overtaken her, and she had lain down, using the case as a pillow, and fallen into a deep, dream-filled sleep.

19
Hermione's Epiphany

Hermione Zatapec had climbed the long, aged, iron staircase to the top of the falls with some vague notion that she would throw herself from the top. The last three days or so had been a period of incredible change for her: physically, she now resembled a young teenager, and mentally, she had been assaulted by a steady, increasing onrush of memory and recollection of events and incidents in both the nearer and further past. This had all rocked her, and had she been a young teenager, mind perhaps not fully formed, as opposed to a long-lived septuagenarian street urchin from down below, then it is likely that these twin attacks would have led her down that other path. But her mind was tired at the end there, despite her body being young and lithe beyond right or reckoning.

When the amygdala is assaulted, she sat still and deep at the bottom of the myopic pond from which it looks up at the external world. It has little idea whether an assault is real or imagined, but it senses a threat to life, and it has two core responses: fight or flee. This is the old brain, the bit you find in all living things, and the only common ground between warm-blooded vertebrates, mammals, and cold-blooded lizards. However far humanity might have climbed from the sewer, we each have an amygdala, and every one of those rides' shotgun inside of us our whole lives. So, for all Hermione's determination, she could not fight that simple mechanism. That lizard, blinking in the depths of her 'old' brain, looked on and chose instead to flee. You don't get a response mechanism like that without investing in its power to do the job.

It shut her down and sent her brain to sleep when she could no longer contend with the emotional overload she had been placed under. Hermione's old brain made that decision in about one hundredth of a second, and it was fortunate for her that night, and perhaps all humanity, that her young legs had helped her reach the gantry top. The old brain did not care where she, Hermione, was or where she was going, it simply is not that cerebral. Neither would old brain take the time to query what she was planning or considering. For the fight/flight switch to work, you only need to make instant, simple, caution-based life-or-death judgements. And to be willing to act and have the keys to the kingdom at hand, the amygdala is a doubt-free zone. She collapsed, unconscious, at the top of the iron staircase.

Hermione came around sometime later to the face of a swarthy Russian marine corporal. "Miss, are you OK?" he was crouching over her and called loudly and affirmatively down to a comrade, who, it appeared, was still at the staircase's base.

Hermione took the proffered arm and was about to harrumph at the forty-something calling her Miss, when everything came sliding back in. She helped no end by hearing her own voice. She sounded like she was perhaps sixteen years old, in high falsetto tones, as she coughed and replied, "Yes, of course. Why?"

"Now, Miss, you are quite young to be out on your own," continued the marine, helping her gently to her feet with care for the slippery surfaces and small space that they both now occupied. Hermione simply nodded, and they did not speak again until they had both descended the staircase with some care in the half-light. Everything within a dozen feet was made stark by the burning arc of yellow from the torch shining on the ground below. Hermione wondered what the time might be an unusual consideration in her private world. But she had begun in recent hours to recognise that getting younger really was showing little sign of slowing down. And, of course, now she had some inkling of why or what might be, happening to her. Agetec, her mind hissed.

The marine that had helped her down was a squat and heavyset man, but he had friendly eyes, and so Hermione smiled at him, then turned, and greeted his slightly taller and slenderer blond-haired compatriot.

"So, little Miss, I must ask you, why are you here all alone in the dark of night…at Waterfall Park?" It was the heavyset one: he seemed to have rank.

But, of course, he was not speaking to a willowy sixteen- or seventeen-year-old girl, but a streetwise and nail-bitten old lady, who responded tartly, "Officer, I thank you for helping me down the steps, but I was in no danger. I'm not aware that I need to answer you or anyone as to where I choose to take my ease."

Interestingly, if the marine was at all put out, he gave a good impression of not showing it, and he responded quickly and with considerable military courtesy. "Ordinarily, Miss, that would be quite right; but, you see, there has been an incident."

At this, Hermione's senses went to full alert. "An incident?" she replied. "And does that involve me?"

"No, Miss, I am certain it would not, but you see…" The officer hesitated for some moments, but then figured perhaps that the truth would have the desired impact and send this teenage girl scuttling home. "There has been a death; well, we think, actually, a murder."

Up until that second, Hermione Zatapec had been buried deeply in a state of heightened despair, her mind embroiled in events more than a decade ago, but at the mention of murder, she immediately focused on the here and now. And scant seconds later, she retorted, unlike any teenager the marine had ever encountered, "Murder? Who has been murdered? This is *Leviathan*; we had enough of death, of…of murder before we came to this place, this last chance, did we not?" she tailed off, her eyes bore through the face of the marine, and then glanced disdainfully and with equal fire at his lanky and mute companion. It was obvious that they were both stunned by her comments. How might this young girl have had enough of anything, let alone murder and death? She was barely out of childhood. "Tell me what has happened, and be quick about it," Hermione concluded.

Her tone at the end brooked no dissension, and these were simple serving soldiers, both men imbued with recognition of authority. They took orders, and they complied, and so, after a nervous glance and a short moment, "Our chief, the Marshal General Alexei Stormbader, has been found dead." At that point, the marine checked a display on his monitor and then continued, "About three hours ago, on the landing of level A4, the intersect staircase. It's no secret that Miss, an all-points bulletin has been put out asking for witnesses."

There were no cameras, thought Hermione, but the officer answered before she could even consider asking. It seemed that now that he had begun, he would not stop. "There are no cameras, you see, on the stair that intersects. Who would ever need them?"

Hermione had thoughts racing through her head. Had she not seen the marshal at the wake in the gardens at Agetec? She wondered at the toxic mix that seemed to her to be coalescing in her mind. Ariel Tsaritsa, Sigmund Symonds the enforcer, the scientist, Muriel's father, and Marshal Stormbader, the soldier.

She did not know exactly how, but there was some connection between all of these people.

One thing the slow, considering the mind of Hermione had thought, increasingly, as she reflected on her own fractured journey, was how it paralleled the fractured journey of humanity. The increasing narcissism, which she looked back on then as virtually psychotic in her own life, now seemed to her to have been embedded similarly deeply in the psyche of a human race, which, in those latter days of sloth, had increasingly slid into victim-driven, spiteful, blaming narcissism. A control born from switch-and-bait games that ultimately destroyed them all. Essentially, Hermione recognised the macro pattern that validated the micro or individual pattern. She was beginning to understand that altruism is pretty useless if it is not reciprocated: if you just give and give and do not get given to, eventually you will have nothing and someone else will have everything. Whilst she was battling with her own very real demons, this contrary series of thoughts was growing and taking shape in her deeper mind, though she did not yet know why.

The elderly teenager thanked the officers of the marine corps effusively and explained quite ardently that she needed to get home if there were killers about. Hermione had to struggle against their wishes to accompany her, but she refused firmly and politely, and, indeed, these two marines had been out since early the previous morning, turning over stones for their now-dead commanding officer. The man was dead, and he had been their decent and gracious leader for more than a quarter of a century. Once sufficiently reassured that she would take their leave only to get straight back home, they were similarly keen to return to the barracks and find out 'what came next'.

Hermione was regressing; she recognised that; she also recognised there was no sign of this stopping, and she had begun to wonder what that meant for her. Would she die as a crawling, crying infant, no longer able to care for herself? Or perhaps a foetus in some dark, dusty corner of an alley, she thought bitterly. If such was the case, then she needed to get some answers and some help, and both of those needs were becoming increasingly urgent. Hermione thought for long seconds and decided the only place left for those solutions was Agetec.

The waterfalls seemed muted, and the colours of the park were all grey and black at the end of the night's dim light. The mist hung heavy now, and this was no longer a place of recollection. And, despite considering ending her journey only scant hours before, Hermione now felt strangely invigorated and enamoured of the will to survive. What's more, perhaps even to seek some reckoning with those who had cursed her with this twisted cross she bore.

She walked to the same exit by which she had entered, a thirty-foot-high natural cave entrance, and the two marine guards walked with her, all three treading softly on the damp ground, all three silent with their thoughts. The squat marine thought to ask her name and address as they reached the point where it was obvious, they must go separate ways. "Hermione Wise, 2552 level 8 The Burbs." This had been the address she had shared with Jacob in their final days, and so effectively her last home address. She had no idea what would have come of it. Nothing was really 'owned' by anyone aboard, partly because of the recycled nature of their shared lives and partly because, well, how do you own a piece of rock? If any of that information had seemed off to either soldier. It did not show, and so, with a curt nod, they turned and headed back to the barracks.

Hermione Zatapec, the lady who had been Hermione Wise, hoisted a tan briefcase high onto her chest and set off, trying to figure out how to get back to the offices of Agetec. She had made a decision, and so she figured that she needed to find the scientist, Cardington. She was certain now that her time was running out.

20
The Blind Cannot See, the Proud Will Not See

Muriel was dressed quietly, slowly, and patiently: a simple white smock dress covering thick woollen tights and two under layers, enough to battle against the eerie whistling cold. A thick knee-length cardigan over the top of it all is made of wool. A shade of nondescript tan, and that had seen better days; in fact, a relic of her father's wardrobe. She pulled on a tight Russian Ushanka fur hat and knee-length boots (her favourite), and it would have been significantly difficult to recognise who she was under all, unless you were at close quarters or knew her well. That morning, she had avoided giving in to the echoes of adult instruction, and so she had not taken any of the wide-ranging medication that was sitting on a small, wheeled table at one end of her sleeping quarters. This went both ways: it meant no relief for the nausea and the deep sickness that she felt, nor the furnace burning inside of her that she was already sweating out as a fever, and that was quite remorseless, however bitter cold it seemed. But conversely, the medications always left her drowsy and drifting back towards unconsciousness, and this was at least something she could avoid.

Luck favoured her, and about fifty minutes after Muriel Cardington had risen, Susannah could be heard in the shower, singing a merry enough ditty and preparing herself for another day working her shift in the food-harvesting sector. Her job as a crop and recycling tech often meant she came home with a variety of pungent odours on board, and so Muriel knew that the lady she had never deemed to be a mother, or even approaching a parent, was simply another. The lady liked her allotted time and her H_2O shower, so Muriel took the opportunity and slipped out of the front door and into the early morning.

Two miles or so across from the young teen leaving her home filled with fever and more delirium than she quite understood, Ariel MP Tsaritsa was up late into the night. Of course, they had come to her and 'officially' reported the death of Marshal General Alexei Stormbader. She had expressed her deepest sympathy and then manufactured a slightly fearful concern for the well-being of everyone aboard, but not excepting herself. She had also asked that information be released immediately on the internal news feed to ensure that any witnesses or information on what had occurred would be run to the ground quickly.

The lady knew that, if handled right, this was an opportunity, and she had then sat deep into the night and configured a plan and a speech to share her woes and yet to exonerate herself. Alexei is their only and best hope in the days ahead. The only thorn in her side, it seemed to her, might be Symonds. He would know the truth about it, and he might squeal. And so she called him, as the light change to the day shift was barely under way. She had sent him on a spurious fact-finding mission across the other side of *Leviathan* and had then ensured that her shadowy visitor of the previous evening knew exactly where he would be and when. And I also knew that she lady was angry at this individual. She didn't just want him to be removed; she wanted more. Ariel, it seemed, wanted this one to understand the cost of crossing her. She was the boss, and she seemed to be asking that the man die a painful death. Had anyone aboard asked her to explain specifically, and then more, to evidence what Symonds had actually done, almost certainly the lady would have gazed blankly into an inky distance and struggled to come back with anything at all.

As soon as she had been done with the 'dirty work', as her mind viewed these necessary evils and details, she attended her offices. Not the ante room in her private chambers, but a more opulent and business-like area some two floors above. She called ahead, and staff were there waiting with coffee and recording equipment. The lady had notes in front of her, but Ariel had been watching reels of great public speakers since she was a child. From Dylan Thomas and Winston Churchill to Margaret Thatcher and Emma Goldman. Instinctively and fearfully, Tsaritsa recognised she lacked empathy but then considered empathy to be a weakness, a flaw that was not truly real. A falsehood for most. The lady had learned to configure a majority of people just like her, who were only less good at it and less worthy. So, as Ariel did with many things in her life, she learned how to demonstrate empathy and conviction, and the death (murder) of Alexei Stormbader would, for some critical hours, allow the release of the truly bad news to take a modicum of a back seat, to sweat into people's awareness whilst they worried and fretted over the death of the old soldier, and as a result, their own immediate and puny safety concerns.

An hour later, Hermione Zatapec, six floors below the Tsaritsa and, if she was being honest, a little bit lost, came to a halt outside a small general servery. It was in the style of a vendor's outlet, which curiously, in a closed-loop economy such as *Leviathan*, appeared to be boarded up and to have gone out of business. Hermione found this strange; perhaps commerce always won through in the end, she wondered, as she had sat on a kerb, resting up, gathering her wits, and considering in which direction she needed to head. She was still far away from the business district and was just deciding that she needed to make her way to higher levels when she heard a beeping tone that announced an imminent broadcast. Hermione climbed to her fourteen-year-old feet and walked across the main drag to where several people on their way to shift commencement had stopped to view the broadcast.

As a child, she was able to wriggle her way through the older group to the front. She pushed through and came face-to-face with Ariel MP's features. The old-age child squatted on her haunches on the shiny, worn concrete walkway and watched interestingly. The First Lady seemed to be sitting primly, in a fine-cut white business suit, utterly immaculate, with grey lapels softly offsetting her auburn hair, which in turn was just beginning to show a few strands of its own natural grey. Tsaritsa had her hands with fingers splayed and face down on a simple work desk, with a gentle, concerned smile playing across her face. Ariel began to speak, and though Hermione had clambered to the front, she had not especially been listening to the words, rather watching the other lady, and deeply immersed in her own thoughts. Now, though, her ears pricked, and she tuned in more closely at the mention of the marshal.

The First Lady had begun a careful explanation of the previous evening's events, certainly more than had been shared with Hermione by the marines. She looked closely at their unofficial leader's expression, particularly as she spoke about leaving no stone unturned. The teenage veteran from down below marvelled at how Tsaritsa introduced fear for the well-being of all those who watched now. And she recognised how, by the constant re-runs that would follow, the fear would grow exponentially, specifically, and simply by suggesting that nobody was in any danger. It is doubtful until that point if many aboard would have even considered themselves in danger. Watching the screen and the lady's face, the seventy-two-year-old teenager mumbled to herself, "It takes one to know one." And then, "Everything is a performance", as she decided that their leader was sitting up there lying through her teeth. Though she didn't particularly like it, watching Ariel, whom the girl recognised, was akin to watching a re-run version of the Hermione Wise she had so recently been re-introduced to. Her instincts were warning her that much was awry with the lady on the other side of that hard glass screen, and so she watched more closely now.

Ariel was speaking now about Sergio Radzinski, often referred to as *Leviathan*'s father. His name came up less and less often as the long, dark corridors of their journey continued across two decades. But Ariel was not referring to Radzinski as their father; moreover, she was speaking in highly technical language, all ever so carefully constructed, about a series of calculations that had gone wrong and about how they were not yet as close to making landfall on Planet Tinkerbell as they might have hoped. Tsaritsa was alluding to many things and specifying little. All whilst introducing alternative sources of blame, in this case sources that could not defend themselves. The First Lady was clear that the worst case was a very bad case, but that she, Ariel MP, leader of The Eight, and the Tsaritsa of *Leviathan*, had teams working around the clock to broker an ideal and successful solution. Phew!

Hermione noted with sage cynicism that she offered neither specifics on the delayed timescale nor did she offer specifics on these marvellous solutions. The teenager did not mumble this time as she said loudly, "All smoke and mirrors", receiving a number of affirmative grunts from the many others now gathered close around the screen. In her mind, she thought, as she had long ago, about the old proverb concerning Mister Scorpion and the Toad. "It is just her nature," she mused.

Though physically getting younger by the hour, Hermione Zatapec, who had once been Wise, had a sharp and experienced mind, and she could have told Ariel MP in her ivory tower that even with the Stormbader distraction, she had read her audience wrong. For all her artful dancing, the people on board had seemingly had enough. The long years, the daily dose of fear of living so far out on a limb. No turning back, the inky darkness crawling around them, living inside each and every one of them. On that microcosm of home, that rocky outcrop, where the icy cold drifted ceaselessly around every second of every day. The whale had been a fantastic achievement, perhaps even humanity's greatest. But across twenty-three years, it had also become a prison for them all.

Ariel's posturing and her presentation, however slick and well edited, had nonetheless poked a stick into a hornet's nest, and one that had simply been poked enough. As her speech drew to a close and Hermione walked away, the thought in the veteran teenager's mind was how it felt like revolution in the air, "and we Russians do like a revolution," she reminded herself. She stepped smartly away, swinging her case and heading for the nearest access way to the main staircase.

And there, all of a sudden and right in front of her, stopping her dead in her tracks, was Muriel. The Cardington girl looked straight through her, her eyes hollow and burning, filled with fever, and seemingly unseeing. At that very moment, the ill-looking youth dramatically and unceremoniously dropped to the ground in a dead faint. Hermione rushed to Muriel and putting her case on the ground, lifted her and sat her so that she was leaning bodily onto the now only slightly older girl.

After long moments, Muriel began slowly to come around, and Hermione, noticing people moving towards them, waved them away and, turning, looked deep into the other girl's eyes. "Muriel, it's me, Hermione."

Muriel looked back at her, and some small part of her mind seemed to connect with the other, but she was fevered and very ill, and so she did not seem to quite understand who this person was who was only a little older than her. Yet after a moment or two more, she croaked, "Hermione," and then again, "Hermione," and in answer to the question in the other girl's eyes, she whispered in a husky, scratchy voice, "It's cancer…I always had it." She reached inside the smock she was wearing and, with a frail, pale, trembling hand, passed a small booklet to Hermione. It had a stamp on the front that stated simply "The Lymph System". Underneath, hand-written, was a blood type and the child's full name: Muriel Anastasia Cardington. Hermione looked at the book, turned the page, and understood immediately. "I need my father," the ill child said.

And so, without a moment's hesitation, climbing to her feet and never letting go, Hermione Zatapec responded. "Yes, you do, and maybe even more than I do." She lifted Muriel's body, got one arm under her, and then grabbed at the bag. Pulling at the string that hung from one handle, she levered the satchel around her neck, creating a strap of sorts. Like that, they staggered out of that small square and shuffled in the direction of the businesses. On any other day, it is likely that many a soul on their way to a new shift would have stopped and helped two such young children.

But on that day, sixty thousand people, without exception, had something else on their minds, and so the two, though at a snail's pace, continued on their way, crawling little more than one metre at a time. Muriel occasionally tried to speak, managing little more than husky whispers, but enough to show a recognition of who that other was a girl who carried her more manfully than any man. Though Muriel might, even ought to, have been shocked, whether through her illness or simply her child's view of the world, she simply accepted that Hermione was Hermione. Where she found herself, it mattered little whether her carrier was a sixty-year-old woman or a fourteen-year-old child. Hermione was astonished at how the child had gotten to where they had met, and she wondered at that the fact that where she had found her was far from her home.

The two had sat together underneath that home for only two nights previously. Irony is the fate of the thinking mind, Hermione considered, as they struggled slowly along. She had been determined for her own well-being to find Lyle Cardington; now she needed to find the scientist for the lives of two. As she dragged the mortally ill Muriel metre by metre towards the Agetec laboratory, she began to see a picture evolving in her mind. She also began to wonder at the universal symmetry that seemed to be drawing together around her.

Elsewhere in the belly of the whale, Ariel MP sat in an antechamber and battled against gnawing doubt. One voice in her head kept repeating over and over that she was the answer, the route to their salvation, though she did not know what that salvation might be. The voice spoke to her and advised who anyone that stood against her was now committing treason. And that voice would not entertain any consideration other than her inviolated rightness. Yet she was still filled with doubt, shamed by her actions. Though perhaps more because of the fear of revelation, there was a chink inside of her that saw a more desolate road. Strangely, neither thought process held any great desire to solve the pressing issue of sixty thousand people dying a sad and pointless death in the midst of a cold, dark universe. Ariel MP sat in that small room, thinking in circles, for a long time. Then, all of a sudden, waking her almost from her trance, a communicator beeped insistently on the desk next to her.

The First Lady picked it up and answered curtly, and at the other end, she heard, "Madam Tsaritsa, my name is Cardington…"

21
'How Well You Live Makes the Difference, Not How Long'

Two children lay side by side on matching slabs that vaguely, and not in a pleasant way, resembled hospital gurneys. The elder of the two, twelve or thirteen, as an onlooker might have guessed, appeared to be unconscious. She didn't look in great health; she was both terribly pale and equally limp in that damp-cloth kind of way. Indeed, she seemed to be waiting close to the door, the one that no one ever volunteered to step through. And a watcher might have thought that a truly good God would never beckon a child such as her through death's unwelcome portal.

The other child was younger, also female, and perhaps only eight or nine years old, as that same onlooker would have concluded. In contrast to her older gurney mate, this child appeared in the picture of visceral child-enthused good health. Her cheeks were full of colour, and she radiated energy and was vibrant— in a way that was, if you looked at her for too long, quite terrifying. Indeed, it seemed a little like staring at the sun with your eyes uncovered. One might have imagined that this younger girl was in a high dudgeon. She was laid out on that gurney only at the behest of others—adults, elders, and old ones—who had no better mind than to insist that a small child lay down and remain still. Restrained only by the will of those older folk, and in so doing kept away from the playground that by rights would be at the centre of any such child's world. And if so, that thinker would be wrong.

A number of adults stood in various reposes around what was a dimly lit space. The room, a laboratory of sorts, was dull and uninspiring. The place seemed of no value beyond the fact that it enclosed two four-wheel gurney slabs, each with a particular child occupant. The younger of the girls broke what had been a lengthy silence, sitting up, leaning on her elbows, and suddenly speaking.

Though her voice was elfin, high, and clear and small in that dim pressing space, the voice of a child girl of six or seven years, no more, surely. Nonetheless, her words were delivered with an authority that brooked no dissent, certainly not from any of the adults who were at that time present.

Hermione Zatapec, for a time Hermione Wise (and she hadn't been Wise, she thought, smiling to herself), held what she understood might be the only chance left for all that maybe remained of humankind hidden within her tiny body. She was far from certain about passing such a thing on. She was equally uncertain whether it would prove to be a boon or a burden to any of those present. Two children lay in a room, surrounded by a particularly piratical and immoral group of people. She doubted either she or Muriel had ever been surrounded by worse at such close quarters. Hermione is considered for long seconds. Then, as the words formed in her consciousness, in that moment, immediately before it all finally coalesced, she suddenly spied, sat on the floor beside the gurney, lost in the shadows and dark-stained plastocrete of the room, a battered brown case of the type of the life educators favoured that taught the few children aboard *Leviathan*. Finally, in that instant, she had her epiphany.

The seventy-two-years-old Hermione understood it was her time, her final chapter, her grandstand; call it what you might. She understood that, despite her outward appearances, she approached the end of her days. This lady had no wish to live on, to live her life over, a life given to her once again by a curious twist of other men's fate. And if she were honest, even those that remained uncertain, life, she reflected, had always been an uncertain business. Wasn't that what had brought these seven very disparate individuals to this one place? No, she'd had her go, and even were such an opportunity truly to be laid out in front of her, Hermione no longer had any appetite for the game. The young old lady was able to admit to herself finally and honestly that she was tired of life—of this life, of her life. If it was possible, she was even wary of giving what she hoped, in her own small way might be an ounce of redemption, succour, or freedom from pain for those few she encountered.

She had given of herself over and over the past few years, where such might be deserved or, even upon occasion, just come unlooked for. That had been her fate, penance; call it what you would. Her path was to walk for a time in payment of a debt long owed. Such was how the universe worked: you took it and it took it back, in this case, for the actions of a young woman's ego. And as taking had a price, altruism needed reciprocity to be truly effective. Hermione had learned that it was the circle and that it could not be broken. Struggling against that pair of monumental restraints that were free will and other people's free will—two indomitable pillars that sat together alongside the serpent in the rushes that was sometimes called pride and always called ego—well, she had tried. Russians were won't to say, "Your elbow lies close, yet you can't bite it." Hermione realised she had gotten close, but now she was ready to get off. "Come in, number nine; your time is up!" she heard a whisper inside her wise old child's mind.

Her time had come, and whilst it seemed clear to Hermione Zatapec that one path destiny held for humanity might be to shatter the three score years finally and irrevocably and ten myths, now and forever, it was a maybe. Nonetheless, that was a boat of possibility she, and only she, might push from its moorings. But it was one she would just have to miss riding on. The elderly child smiled at the battered carry-all; like her, it, too, was now almost spent. She had lived some seventy-two years and had been given another seventy-two hours on top. That last had not been pre-booked and had not been a part of the package; she understood that she didn't need the overtime.

She spoke, "Children should not be visited by death's cold hand, not in a place where any God might still warm our souls."

Somebody better than I said these words.

"I am dying, but my friend Muriel needs to live here. In fact, I intend to make it imperative for all of you that she does, especially you and Mr. Cardington. You have to give your daughter life."

The elderly child halted, looked around the room almost expectantly, and then continued, "Specifically, you are going to give Muriel one last blood transfusion," pausing again, she smiled at the bemused scientist, refusing just yet to give him the understanding he desperately craved.

Hermione figured he deserved that, at least—perhaps petulant on her part—but some small penance for the crimes that he had committed in the tawdry name of science. But time grew short.

"All of those chemicals, of that scrubbing of her blood, to remove the radiation cancers have run out of, well, shall we just say that it's run out. So, fill her up, Mr Cardington. Fill her with as much of my blood as you can. If you want her to live, if you all want a chance at living, then fill Muriel Cardington with all that my body has left to give."

She paused and then said, "That's what you have to do."

The scientist looked at this small girl, confused and a little in awe. He thought perhaps he recognised her, but he was still having trouble digesting the fact that the girl, a six-year-old infant, was telling him. No, she wasn't telling him…she was instructing him and a room full of adults on what to do. How could that be?

She sounded rational, and that in itself was crazy, and the girl was certainly calmer than he was at that moment. She was not imploring, nor did she sound mad. But then again, she was a child—an infant, barely old enough to enunciate her words.

But to him, this was what took the biscuit. Even more bizarre than all of her utterings were the fact that, in the bare hours she had been in that room, he had been able to find no record of such a child existing anywhere on the ship's passenger log. That three hundred and forty-three was indeed not the sum total of children born since the journey's start. That it was possibly, in fact, three hundred and forty-four, and if that was the case, why not three hundred and forty-five or even four hundred and forty-five? For him just then, that was the craziest of all the crazy stuff that spun around in that dim, dark room.

Hadn't this all started because of the dearth of children, and now everything? He hitched mentally, and then the voice in his head finished the thought…well, it had all gone mad.

Of course, it was not possible; people just did not get on and off of *Leviathan*, especially not six-year-old girls. But even more disconcerting was a child who seemed to burn with a brightness that verged on old-testament revelations.

Not even two hours before, this small, blue-eyed child, who sparkled with the bright knowledge of good and evil in eternal entwine, had walked slowly into his laboratory, carrying his daughter with her—a heavy burden for one so small. Muriel Anastasia Cardington had seemed barely alive then and had been leaning heavily upon this younger one's shoulders. He thought hard and tried now, when it was certainly too late, to remember some details. Perhaps this girl had seemed different then: had she been bigger or older? A little, maybe, he said to himself; he hadn't remembered thinking that there had been such a gulf between Muriel and the other, not then at the first.

Yet in his panic for his daughter's well-being and the turmoil that followed as he stabilised her condition and made the calls that he felt obliged to make, he was no longer certain of anything. Cardington thought momentarily about the monumental effort that the small one must have put into bringing—well, pretty much carrying the deadweight of a bigger girl, his daughter, to that place. And something else suddenly dawned on him: he remembered that she had been carrying, tied around her neck with string, a leather bag. A suitcase, or so it appeared to him, was half her size and yet also hung from that delicate form.

"Hey, girl, who are you? Who are you that instructs me? You can't expect us to do what you say, you're a kid." The voice broke his thoughts, cutting instantly through the uncertainties in Cardington's mind.

That voice, whilst calm enough, emanated command. It was Ariel's silky-smooth voice. Lyle thought that it had probably been a long time since anyone had told Ariel MP what to do. Tsaritsa is an artful political scion and supreme conjuror. The uncrowned leader of *Leviathan*'s community stood back in the shadows and could not be clearly seen by any in that room. That had been her preferred repose-down for so very many years: covert control.

At that other's words, the young girl turned towards the speaker. Looking up from her prone position on the gurney, Hermione squinted and seemed at that lady's commanding tone to make an effort to focus upon her. She gazed at what seemed to be Cardington for a long time, lost, it seemed, in the momentum of her own thoughts. And then, bright as a button, the child Hermione Zatapec continued, because she knew something about Ariel that no one else had guessed. That, beneath the armour and glamour, was simply a child. A frightened little girl was still running, still waiting to be saved. A tiny child in a world of giants, and she spoke to that child.

"Madam Ariel, you have always been, I am thinking, most expert at operating in the shadows, a princess always, in the court of Arthurian kings. Today is not one of those times. I am sorry, Tsaritsa; we have all been wrong for the longest time, and I must bring this out into the light—all of it, everything—and I understand it will hurt. This will seem most difficult for you, but I can help you." She was staring quite belligerently, looking at Ariel and then at each of the room's shadowy occupants in turn. "All of you need to understand this."

She paused and took a couple of quick breaths, shifted into a sitting position, and was swinging her legs off the side of the gurney, as any child her age might. "Once, a lifetime ago, I was, in fact, much alike to the lady Ariel; perhaps not quite the zeal you have, Madam Tsaritsa, to lead, but I knew what it was to compete and to control. Your fear, I think, has been an awful burden to bear, my lady; you have been afraid for the longest time; and yet," she said, waving her arms around the small space. "And yet it has given you all of this."

It was difficult for anyone listening to tell whether the child, of high elfin voice, was being sarcastic or sincere in that moment. The girl's confidence, it appeared, was not wavering one jot. Ariel looked about to speak, and Hermione suddenly said, "SSSHHHHH" in a loud, parenting voice. "I know some things, and though I may be guessing a little in order to link all I know together, I should think that outside of this room there are only one or two people that may verify one way or the other. All the rest of you, well…you're here, so you can decide; in fact, I think you must now decide."

Ariel could not hold herself any longer and suddenly exploded, interrupting the spell as she shot back, "Shut this damn child up, will you, Cardington? I thought when you called that you had something important for me. Not some down below brat with a look-at-me sewer mouth." Ariel sounded both furious and rattled. Indeed, she sounded like a child in a temper. Yet she was afraid, and anyone watching closely might have seen beaded sweat on her forehead. The watcher, had he known the lady at all, would perhaps have wondered when the last time was when she had openly displayed such obvious anxiety. Lyle Cardington was unsure what to do; he still couldn't see the First Lady clearly, and he felt rather than see the edge of fear in her voice. This one had ruled down all these years with an imperturbable calm and an indomitable will. More so, despite her harsh words, Cardington thought he heard underneath the brash tone that the lady was wrestling with something, and that something sounded a little like excitement. Still acting, he wondered, but he was not certain; with people like Ariel MP, you never were.

He managed one short sentence, "Ariel, Madam Tsaritsa, she told me to call you, to bring you here," he said, pointing at Hermione, a look of deep confusion on his face.

Hermione began once more, now direct, avid, and pushy. "Listen, people, cut to the chase. I believe that I know what you know. I recognise that everyone on this million-year-old rock is screwed. Sixty thousand geriatrics, three hundred kids, a leaking fusion reactor, and what? Another hundred, two hundred years from this loneliest of Star Treks? If *Leviathan* gets there at all, well, you're all going to be dead, right?"

Nobody else had been speaking, and yet there was, at the conclusion of those words, a stunned silence that made the previous pervading quiet like a Friday-night party. Nobody appeared to be able to breathe any longer; even Ariel had shut up.

When the marshal died, Symonds was otherwise engaged. Beyond Cardington and the two children, the room was filled by Ariel and her three most trusted cronies—more than half of The Eight that were, in fact, now only seven. So, in fact, the child had been right: the chief decision-makers were indeed all present in that room. It was a reasonable assumption that these would be the people who knew the truth of Mother Russia's scientific miscalculation a quarter century previously.

As one, the thought was racing through them all. How did the girl know this? How could she? Everyone aboard had been talking, and the level of tensions had risen terribly over the past few days; fear was rampant, but till now it had been non-specific for the mass. After Ariel's overdue public speech, there were at least sixty thousand speculations, yet truly only the people in that room had actually known the facts, and of them only Ariel MP, the unadorned queen of the beehive and Tsaritsa of the *Leviathan*, knew everything.

Except, it seemed, for a small child.

Hermione had them; she knew them, and, determined as she was now in her course of action, she continued, still apparently completely unphased.

"How do I know? Well, you might want to thank Lyle Cardington here for that. You see this man," she said, pointing a dainty finger, "he resequenced my genes. Sometime last year, or maybe it was the year before, or, well, you will know. I'm sorry to be vague, but you wiped my mind, Mister Cardington. I think some of you may know something about this. It's taken a while to get it all back, and then, well, then I've had some things of my own to come to terms with."

She faltered, stopped speaking, and took deep breaths. In that instant, Grafton Shevnetski, a bull of a man, once a general in the NKGB and in his mind at least Ariel's closest ally, interrupted. In a gruff tone, he demanded, "Kids, Cardington? You've been testing your damn soup kitchen on bloody children. Christ in the Virgin Mary's arms, man, what's wrong with you?"

Lyle turned scarlet, but before he had any opportunity to reply, the girl, now sitting upright on the gurney, seemingly to ensure undivided attention, spoke in a strident and clear voice spoke once more. "Let me finish. If you do not, Muriel is going to die, and then, well, then so will all of you."

"Not today. I'm not threatening you; how could I?" she said this whilst spreading her arms and smiling. "I am merely a child; others here do threats far better than I ever could." This last was said with particular emphasis. "So now listen to me carefully. Be sure that you all understand that this is how it has to be."

"Mr Cardington did as I said he did. But then, when he did, let us just say I was not the person you see in front of you now. It appears Agetec does have its genius, and if you'll all just let me speak my piece, it seems you all may have your lives, too. Yes, redemption, folks, is just around the corner."

Hermione was in full flow, and all in the room were rapt. "I am…well, I was, at least…an old lady, what, mmm, just three days ago, scratching around down below for a while now, I guess. I used to be a real bitch. Back in the day, I think I might have given any of you a run for your money. But I lost something…someone." You could not miss the wistful glance at the battered case. "And in the long years between, well, it seems I have found something, too."

She paused and looked away for just a few moments; no one noticed as she shivered, for the room was indeed cold.

"That's why you cannot find me on the ship's manifest, Mr Cardington. Look up Hermione Wise, wife of the deceased Jacob Desire Wise, on the advanced team Scarlet Beta. Check your DNA, check whatever you want, and you'll find your match. Mr Cardington, your nasty little experiment might've worked, after all, perhaps a little too well. It seemed, like many things, it just needed a little time." Hermione took a deep breath and swung her legs from the gurney. The lighting caught the pale, waxy skin of a child; no wrinkles or blemishes touched her, and she was as pale as an agate angel.

"I'm guessing that the antigens that you fed me through my bloodstream took some time to figure me out before they bit into my DNA. Then, well, as close as I can guess, and I am merely an expert in the experience, I think I've been losing about a year and an hour these past three days. I don't know if this is an exact science…that's your field."

Everything in the room had stopped; even time, it seemed, stood still, and humankind teetered at one of those pivotal instances that would decide the fate of the race. Cro-Magnon or Neanderthal, dinosaurs or mammals, red or black, heads or tails. The girl breathed and then continued, glancing quickly and urgently, at Muriel.

"You've been bad people, all of you here; you don't need me to tell you that, and maybe the easiest thing for me to do would be to find a quiet corner and wait a few hours, and then, well, then I will die. And that would be quite right, too.

For the majority of my life, I, too, failed to recognise what it is like to be human—to come out of a dream sleep from a life of distractions. It's important to grow beyond the petty constraints of fear and power."

Hermione stopped and took a long look at everybody standing in various reposes around that strange half-lit rocky cavern deep in the bowels of a million-year-old rock, flying across the deep darks of a cold, uncaring universe. Then, for long moments, she looked once more at the pale, shallow-breathing Muriel lying next to her.

"That bit, my time coming, I think, is inevitable, but, and it is a sizeable but, there might be a chance to redeem yourselves here; all of you have an opportunity. Remember who you were, each one of you, before sleep took you and you fell into…" she pointed vaguely around the room. "All of this…rubbish."

"And if you do so, you may have a chance to save yourselves from the dustbin of self-regard and greed, which will otherwise kill you, I can promise you that," she stopped and smiled, the child gulping involuntarily. Hermione was nervous, but despite her being a child, she was nervous with the mind and experiences of a woman of seventy years. So then, hurriedly, she continued attempting to get all of the words out of her whilst the spell remained cast. "Mister Cardington, take my blood; take all of it. I am type O; put it in your daughter; she is type O. I am certain it will make her well, much more so than all those chemicals she has been fed these past months. Then, well, in time, it may make her younger. I don't know for sure, but I've been there, and if it does, as I believe it will do, whatever you gave me will need some time to figure Muriel out, as it needed time to figure me out.

"You see, if it is Muriel, then that becomes the centre of this. More importantly, it will give you that time. A leap of faith, or perhaps simply poetic justice. Either way, I will be dead in an hour or two, so grab this chance. I give you this; it is my gift. Perhaps by working together, you might figure out how to save not just Muriel but all of you, everyone. Because …" And she stared hard at Ariel as she said this last, "There is no empire of one."

Nobody spoke; nobody wanted to speak. The child looked at the scientist, who was glancing between her and his daughter with, to all appearances, something resembling terror writ into his features.

"I don't know if you can figure out the gaps, but you'll need help, Mr Cardington. Whatever you gave me was just a little short of a miracle; certainly amazing, but it didn't take quite as long as it should."

The small, ageing wise girl paused. "It didn't fit, well, right, in my body. It most assuredly reversed the weariness of an old lady, took away my old age, and that is a miracle, Mister Cardington. You went further than anyone ever has before this day. Something that I had carried for many years was lifted from me, and so it made me younger. But it hasn't stopped, you see, and, well, now I understand what is happening, I accept my fate. This is the fate I faced anyway, and I do not wish to cheat fate. I'm about done, and that seems fine to me. Give my blood to your daughter, Master Scientist, and give her the miracle. That is the fate I bequeath to Muriel Cardington. Because she is young and filled with goodness, and so she will carry your hope within her tiny frame. Figure out what you need to do and go do it."

Long minutes had passed, and yet it seemed still no one had breathed. "You'll be a hero; you'll all be heroes," the girl said this with a brief and harsh laugh that echoed momentarily around the room and spoke with a wisdom none in that room had ever aspired to.

"And Muriel Cardington, well, fate will shine its most gracious light upon her…and I would wish only for that and will die as happy as any may when it comes time to switch off the lights."

Hermione shone at the end, then, like some angel blazing at the entrance to God's kingdom. And if a six-year-old could thunder then at the end there, she would have thundered indeed.

"Now remember, you need to work together," she preached. "Joined, not divided, and precious little time remains." She had risen from the gurney and actually wagged her finger at the closely gathered adults.

"If you cannot do this thing, then fate may take Muriel soonest, but fate will soon enough come and take you all. Leave each of you one by one to a withering, slow death in this friendless, cold void. Take this from me and save your daughter save you all." She walked, then, right up close to Lyle Cardington and finished. "My life for hers; do it now…" Her words shook the room.

After a few seconds, there was an urgent, hushed whisper, and Ariel spoke furiously to a communicator. Cardington looked wildly at the girl; he couldn't focus and then realised that tears were streaming down his face. "I'm sorry," he croaked, entirely unable to form the words he owed this girl—this woman, preacher, angel, "for all of it. We, I, was desperate."

The girl smiled, reached out, and grasped his hand. It was so much bigger than hers. There was no bitterness or even pity, just an understanding that made him feel safer than he ever had in his life until that moment.

"I cannot forgive you; you must learn to forgive yourself. I am certain that you can…but only if you save your daughter. Go, do it now."

"How can you know these things?" Cardington mumbled, still, it seemed, trying desperately to rationalise whilst surrounded by the utterly irrational. "Even if I could accept that you are who you say you are, how could you know? You're just a…Ooohh." he trailed off, and the infant Hermione Zatapec smiled, but then, all of a sudden, her smile faltered as she looked across at Muriel and saw how shallow her breathing had become.

"No more questions. Hook me up, Mr Cardington. Or if you can't decide, then don't. It seems fate has placed this squarely in your hands. Mr Cardington's camel is a horse designed by a committee. She's your daughter; Muriel is the most noble and thoroughbred person I have met in all my long years; you must do what you believe is right."

As she spoke, Hermione had climbed back onto the gurney, though not letting go of Cardington's hand, and she managed, with some effort, to drag her battered brown case up beside her. She clicked the flap open and reached her free hand inside. When it was withdrawn, Lyle saw that she was holding an ancient, faded Soviet government blood donor card, of a type he had not seen in maybe forty years. There was an ancient, faded coffee ring imprinted on the front. The handwriting was barely legible, the ink so faded you could no longer tell what colour it might once have been. She handed it to him. Printed more clearly on the front was the name, Hermione Zatapec, and under it, a little more faded but still legible, and 'Russia needs your blood'. The tiny booklet was stiff; it had remained closed, it seemed, for a very long time.

Cardington prised the tiny book open, which seemed to be the girl's wish, and there on the inside flap was printed, 'Blood Type O': the self-same as his daughter's. It was, he supposed, inevitable; today was a day of fate, his mind whispered. He handed the small red book back, looked imploringly once more at the child, and then, catching sight of his daughter and seeing her properly for, it seemed, the first time in so many years, he, too, like the Cowardly Lion in *The Wizard of Oz*, finally found his courage and his resolution. He turned away from his daughter and the child Hermione and, facing the room's other occupants, spoke in a clear, ringing voice, "Ariel, Mr Shevnetski, all of you, mark my words. I find I am in an impossible situation. Though I have done and aided in doing terrible things in the name of science, I did them, I thought, for the greater good. I understand now, here, today, that, in fact, I, we, are more alike to the Nazis that experimented in the concentration camps than the altruist that once, a long time ago, I hoped I might become. *Leviathan* has become our Gulag Archipelago. That is neither a wish nor a hope."

The room's other occupants drew closer as he spoke, one or two with discomfort crossing their features. "But here's the thing, and there's no getting away from it: if she's right, even if there is only a tiny, one percent chance that she's right, then I, we, must do as she says," he stared around at them all belligerently. He dared anyone to contradict him. "I don't care about me anymore, about any of you, any of this, but I have to give my daughter a chance. She's right; if we're that close, I may well be able to get it right in a week, two weeks, a month, or six, but what of that?" he laughed himself at the sincere and ridiculous plight they all now found themselves in. "Especially if we have live blood work. I was not there for Muriel, not enough, and now..." he stopped speaking, tears once more coursing down his cheeks, and the scientist made no attempt at all to wipe them away; that would have meant letting go of Hermione's hand. Whilst it burned so hotly, wrapped in his far greater fist, it appeared she gave him strength—the strength to do what he knew would prove to be the worst thing in his life.

The scientist understood that this was his deal with the devil, his Faustian bargain.

"Finish it, then," Ariel said, and she, too, finally stepped forward into the light. Her voice was quiet, barely more than a whisper.

"This one is about fate, Lyle Cardington; fate is about a lady, and she has decided today. Not you or me, not any of us." Ariel reached out and took Hermione's other hand gently in her own. She looked down into the child's face, beatific, so it seemed, and said simply, "I believe you, little one...Thank you."

The girl Hermione looked up at them all and smiled as she said to the Tsaritsa, "You're welcome. See, it's easy, isn't it?"

Muriel began coughing weakly, her chest hitching alarmingly as she grabbed at breath that was becoming increasingly hard to find. Blood appeared, speckled on the fevered girl's lips. Her father stepped away from the gurneys momentarily, finally letting go of the younger girl's hand, and returned seconds later, dragging an evac trolley, a highly technical medical workbench on wheels that had evidently been parked only a few feet away, deeper in the shadows. He ignored the mutterings that he was aware of at the edge of his hearing. A disagreement seemed to be brewing somewhere among the room's other occupants. Cardington found each movement incredibly difficult; as he reached for the appropriate needle, it was like pushing his whole self through an ocean of treacle. Time seemed to slow to some infinitesimal crawl; he could see the rock-faced outer wall of the room softly merging with the pale green painted plastocrete.

Lyle was about to insert the needle into the arm of Hermione Zatapec when something heavy suddenly slammed into the side of his face. He found himself staring close quarters at the stainless-steel medical bench as he went down. In his mind's eye, this all happened in slow motion. Nonetheless, down he went and landed in a heap. He felt salty, bloody warmth trickling down his throat, and his last thought before darkness took him was how immensely clean the steel implements looked. He faded away to a cacophony of distant shouts.

Symonds did not give in to fear easily. He was a big man who, through many years, had gotten used to intimidating the people around him with his sizeable presence. Yet he had to admit he was afraid; much of that persona had really been bluff and bluster. FOG, as he had learned so many years before, created FOG (fear, obligation, and guilt), and you had them every time in children's games. They were following him; he knew that now. He moved quickly down one rocky plastocrete corridor after another. He didn't know his way around down below quite as well as the rest of the ship, but he had always gotten by. It all looked much the same—just a bit shabbier and a bit dirtier, he figured.

When he first spotted them, he had been for a short while unsure that paranoia wasn't finally catching up with him. But, listening to the voice in his head, he had set off and begun a steady tack and double back, all he kept telling himself in an effort to quell the rising uneasiness that he felt. Most of an hour had passed, and unfortunately, all of the twisting in and out of walkways, sideways, and meandering passageways had done the opposite of what he had hoped.

There was that one strange incident—the meeting with the teen girl. She stopped and stared wide-eyed at Symonds, and he had no idea who she might have been. He was running scared by then and had little time to consider.

Nonetheless, he was both intimidated and elated at the girl when she came and spoke with him. I walked right up to him and handed him that small linen scrap, no more than three inches on a square. She had drawn it from deep inside a big brown leather holdall she had been carrying, hoisted high on her shoulders with string around her neck. Strange, he thought, recollecting the moment once again. He had grunted when she spoke and really not listened to what the girl had said at all; he had deadly danger on his mind, after all.

They were still there—three of them. He did not recognise them; at the distance they kept, that was perhaps not surprising, although he certainly recognised the type. Pack animals and hunters on the scent, eager to take down their prey. He felt sure, though, that he had only recently come to the certainty that they were there at Ariel's request. After all, he was there at Ariel's request, on some fool's errand. He had lately realised how blind he was, how foolish he had been, and how much he had enabled Ariel—well, enabled her to be who she was.

As much as she had programmed Symonds, had he, through his fawning service, programmed her? Though lately he had made a conscious effort to strike out somewhat on his own to prove to the lady he was worthy of her, she still would not have him. She had sent him away and got him far away from the main decks to be killed, it seemed, without care or consideration. Far from witnesses…well, anyone who cared enough to even comment. But worse still for the enforcer far from her, whom he had worshipped down for so many long years. And it only added to his growing disquiet that the woman he had worked alongside so closely appeared to have enforcers that he hadn't learned about, despite nearly twenty years of riding shotgun for the great lady.

At that moment, as he strode into some brief shadow, he fell in his pocket and came upon the scrunched-up linen cloth passing him by the girl. Instinctively, he took it out, and as he was about tossing it, he caught sight of the print on it and unrolled it. And writ there, underneath the faded image of a blue marlin, in clear black print were the words, "But man is not made for defeat; a man can be destroyed, but he cannot be defeated. *Ernest Hemingway.*"

He had been looking for a weapon, and as he fished the small square of linen from his trouser pocket, he had been so startled by those words as to cause long moments of immobility that he found himself thinking. Well, three to one was not insurmountable; they would certainly be armed, and so it was unlikely. But those words, echoing from a century before, had galvanised something inside of him; like the lion in *The Wizard of Oz*, it seemed that the strange child had, with small words, passed by and given a man his courage. Guns were doubtful; the marines kept their stock under tight security; and no other serious projectile weapon had ever surfaced on board, to his knowledge, in twenty-three years, and most especially since the marshal's death.

This seemed like something everyone knew, even hired killers, as he had only recently established there were indeed on board the craft. Well, be that as it may, they would all know that one plasma round through the wrong bulkhead, and they would all be toast. But knives…he felt sure they'd have knives. In fact, he thought that was a given under the circumstances—billy clubs and axes, even. Maybe, if they were real pros, a heat blade or…Stop it, he told himself. This wasn't helping; he needed to get a grip.

It was exceptionally quiet where he now found himself walking, so much so that he heard the fall of his feet slapping on the rock and concrete walkway. He felt as much as he heard the sharp thudding of his heart beating fast in his chest. As to how they would come at him, he understood he would find out soon enough. The big man continued walking, and as he did so, he braced himself for what he believed was to come. Strangely, though, the silence was pervasive, and they were not so far distant any longer. He grew confident that he had no help along the way; neither did they make a sound, or at least no sound that he could hear. His mind spoke up and reminded him that this seemed exactly right for the skillset of a killer, or three.

Three to one is not insurmountable, he told himself once more, with less conviction but still a kind of shaky, strident attempt at belief. "A man may be destroyed, but not defeated" echoed in his deepest brain. OK, but I need a weapon. Probably with that very thought looping around in his subconscious, he had been slowly but surely zigzagging his way across down below, as it turned out towards the area most frequented by the engineers and their coterie of grease monkeys, stuck to them like a cold stick to you in winter.

Well, if there was anything to be had, this was likely to be the place where some heavy iron might be readily available, he supposed. However, in the craft of such limited resources, in actuality, very little was ever left just lying around. The days of Earth's plenty were a memory already distanced by hundreds of millions of miles and nearly a quarter of a century. People were about, but not in great numbers; it wasn't a shifting change, and few minds paid attention to Sigmund Symonds prowling around down below. He considered briefly asking for help, something that went diametrically against his inherent nature. To be honest, he thought to himself, you are hardly going to be popular hereabouts anyway, and to be frank, what are you going to ask for? Nothing has happened, so what would I be asking for help from?

He did spy on one person that stood out amongst the occasional companions in that dark, deep corner of down below. A huge woman, almost his height, and probably not far off his bulk either. He figured her to be an engineer; he would confidently have guessed at 240lbs, looking at her, and not a pound of excess on her. Her fingers and ear tips were blackened; this particular affliction suggested lots of work in a vacuum, and the burn scars were clearly visible around her eyes. Symonds knew that these were a hard and surly bunch of folks, and the few on board were more insular and tighter as a group than these people. They were the few, and yet the ones that kept the *Leviathan* ship-shape and forward moving. Few understood them, and over the long years of their journey, they had grown much more separated from the core of anything resembling the main community.

Sigmund recognised that, whilst he might hope to find a weapon in this district, he was as far away from help as it was possible to get. "Well, that's what I figured out then," he mumbled to himself between tight, quick breaths. He was moving fast now, and he kept walking, but he restrained the urge to run. "Where would you go, fool?"

He didn't recognise the woman, but there was nothing in it other than her size and the fact that she was smiling and singing to herself as she ambled past him along the main walkway. The thing that drew his attention away just momentarily from his pursuers was simply that she appeared to have a pretty flower neatly attached to the front of her coverall. He could not imagine such a thing in down below, or why the wearer was not either working or getting obliterated in some gin and coke (cocaine) dive, as opposed to wandering around, humming, with a flower in her tunic. He also did not know that her timely presence, announced by her smiling, tuneless singing, had caused his pursuers to drop back, just as they were about to close with him. It appeared that, mistakenly hearing the burr of a human voice as the engineer had sung to herself, the three pursuers had imagined for a few moments a conversation between her and Symonds.

Or that they knew one another and that Symonds had been heading that way with purpose. And so, in the moment when he might have been distracted and easy prey, the woman with a flower in her lapel inadvertently, for those moments at least, prevented the enforcer's demise. Though Symonds never knew it, fate gave him a few more critical seconds with that curious twist of circumstance. As she walked gaily past him, Sigmund wondered how much he had begun to miss. Smiling engineers with fresh flowers? Had things moved on so far whilst he had become ever more wrapped up in the affairs of Agetec? Well, no, he corrected himself with the affairs of Ariel. Was he able to admit that he was utterly obsessed with Tsaritsa? He thought that he could, and more, even now, as he closed in on a fate of her choosing, most certainly still his need for succour, of that curious, magical kind that only she had ever really been able to provide him with.

He was still trying to figure some way past these deadly men, and perhaps then some way to win her favour one more time. I think maybe I deserve to die, he thought. He decided that he had lost sight of the big picture, the real big picture, and as he journeyed on, darting from shadow to shadow, his thoughts turned more specifically to the distraction that was Ariel MP, and he struggled with the battle of enabling that had most assuredly led to the demise he now faced. He was walking so fast he might as well have been running, his long legs reaching out, gulping distance in great thudding strides. Sweat now poured from him, and he grunted as breath was exhaled loudly, and he finally began to tire.

As he steadily slipped deeper and deeper into the belly of Jonah's whale, the deepest reaches of down below, he found part of himself again fading to another place, one where he was able to visualise his Tsaritsa clearly, so stark yet majestic and beautiful. He shook his head, and of a sudden it came to him: a recollection of reading Hemingway as a far younger man. He found the reference deep in the pages of the old man's long struggle with the monster of the sea. That was strange, he thought, fate carrying the words from a book he had read perhaps forty years before. Symonds saw Ariel as that giant fish, and he could not deny her the nobility of her purpose. Had she not led them all, and yet was she now not assuredly done for? Her time, too, was up. Certain now that she had hired these thugs to do, well, whatever it was that they were intent on doing, he guessed her patience with him had run out. The thugs, he then surmised, were simply the sharks of Hemingway's tale, coming late to chew at the meat and gristle of the strung corpse. And so, like that old man, he would club and stab at them with a sinewy arm until his last breath was drawn. He was now committed to that path.

In the end, it was not his fault that the age reversion had not succeeded. He had driven the techies on at every step, using means both fair and foul to cajole both maximum resources from a frankly limited supply chain, as well as an astonishing amount of endeavour for what had ultimately proven to be no apparent reward. He believed that no man could have done more to whip a team towards the finish line, but he had learned, too. He thought that, towards the end, the bastard Cardington might just have been keeping something from him, but how could, he be sure? At what point would there have been? They were all knee-deep in the shit by then, but he guessed that was how it went.

She, it seemed, or at least he persuaded himself, believed that he, too, was keeping something back, or that he was just not up to the job any longer. He preferred the former; the latter was just so discarding. Well, it didn't really matter either way; he was on his own, and with some finality, he accepted that he couldn't see a way to get clear. He was the figurehead and the momentum behind Agetec, and he couldn't deny that Agetec had failed.

Though her days were undoubtedly numbered, she would not surrender her power base. Why should she? Though she was as doomed herself as any of them, till then, sink them all. So, for that cycle to circumnavigate to its natural completion, well then, it was logical that someone else needed to take the fall, someone who wouldn't answer back. Perhaps someone who would fit a tale. Who had, upon facing utter despair in the face of certain failure, chosen death over dishonour? He didn't know exactly what the plan, the lie, and the well-enamelled and decorated tale would consist of, but even if he were to beat the odds today, he would overcome the opponents that were, figuratively at least, directly in front of him. She was the power, and he knew then that she had planned against the certainty of this day for a long time. They all cohabitated in an enclosed space from which there was no possible reprieve; in the end, he had nowhere to run, and the only ally he had ever sought had become his chief tormentor in so many ways, and he felt then the certainty of his damnation.

Exhausted now, he moved around a corner, and, finding himself at least briefly out of the direct sight of his pursuers and using the last waning energy, he began to trot, picking up speed as he moved along a longer stretch of the poorly lit plastocrete corridor. A frisson of excitement caused him to shiver as he moved, in part brought on by the fear that was beginning to string out his nerves as he moved closer to a ragged edge, but equally as he remembered how he had been so well paid by Ariel. Of course, the prestige had been a fine thing: chief executive officer was not a title aspired to by many. He guessed that in the corporate power structure that governed *Leviathan*, he had been just about the most powerful individual on the craft outside of her and perhaps the others that remained of The Eight.

Mind you, he countered, playing the devil's advocate for his own mental debate, being of The Eight was not the absolute certainty of the security and privilege it once had been, certainly if the fate of the marshal had been any way by which to judge. But it wasn't the power that he had until so recently held that caused him to shiver, nor was it the ever-pervading cold of a black, sunless universe that crept around inside the whale. No, indeed, and here it was, pure and simple: she had him in thrall; she had captured his heart and his manhood, too. In his mind's eye, he saw her then naked, stunningly beautiful despite her forty and more years. She still had the white, unblemished skin of perfect youth and pert breasts that stood up almost accusingly, like they would never drop. Her texture was like satin to the touch, with just a fuzz of hair covering her mound. Her legs seemed muscled and toned without fat or that repulsive cellulite he hated, and that blotched the mid-life body towards its ruin. She had never done a day's exercise, to his knowledge, and the ninety-one percent gravity should have taken effect long since.

He knew, he had always known, that whatever his qualities and however smart his wingman antics had proven, she never was for someone like him. Simple stock he was by comparison—big, ugly, and brutal—a farm tractor standing next to a Ferrari. And yet, he countered, as he continued swiftly, with her deadly pursuers on her tail, she had taken him into her time and again, across the years of almost two decades. Showing him that whilst she had the outward appearance of a most innocent and coy lady, suffering gently as a victim, the gimcrackery and foolhardiness of so many around her, close to she was a sexual predator, in the end taking and discarding him at her whim, demanding and cajoling both sexual predilections that no other could ever even think to mirror. And here now, no love, no care, simply picking her moment, he had no doubt in order to always ensure her absolute advantage.

Part of him knew that such whoring ought to have diminished her rather than enhanced who she was, but to him, to one who had smelled her musky scent and tasted her sweet, sugary tastes, it could never diminish her. Indeed, he understood that he was so hopelessly overwhelmed by her effect on him that even now, as he ran for his life, he could not bring himself to quite despise her. He supposed that, in spite of what his logical mind had always told him, he had thought for a long time, perhaps, that in some small way she, too, had held a modicum of affection for her enforcer. He wondered as he began to jog a little again, spying a small trickle of water running down the bare rock between the hatchway and the visual screen, noting that he ought to call maintenance on that.

And so, his mind, focused on many things but still wondered, had that belief in some small affection on her part. Had that been what had driven him on, it would've pushed him through greater and greater desperation in his pursuit of the hallowed goal. Yes, to the savings of all, but yes, also to the making of her, the cement in her legacy down all the years yet to come. As he fretted about this, two things impacted in less than a second of each other and so interrupted his train of thought. Firstly, he had come this way in hopes of finding a weapon; he had found none, and that was a bad thing. Secondly, and chasing the first by only a nanosecond or so, they were suddenly in front of Siegfried Symonds.

His stomach turned over with a sickly jolt, and his mind spoke up again for good measure. They're in front of me. How the hell did that happen? He skidded to a halt, panting, bunched his big hands into fists, and tried desperately to push down on the fear that he felt overwhelming him whilst planting his feet firmly where he stood. For it was true that he had dealt out pain many times, and death, too, on more than one occasion, that pesky voice whispered insistently. But the fear countered that this was during his time at the top, or at least during those long years when he scrambled without care or empathy over so many poor souls in order to get to the top. Nevertheless, it had been twenty years or more since he had taken any personal involvement in such events; yes, he had strong-armed, shoved, or even punched one or two.

He was a middleman, and a middle-aged man at that, who spent less time in the gym than he ought and had always relied on size and never on craft, if truth be known. And as he stood there, sucking in breath through panting gasps, hearing the rasping sound of that breathing, focused now on quelling the terror, searching instinctively for the calm that finds a man when he is facing certain death, he realised he was alone, in the dim light of a place far from home, many floors away from anything or anyone that he knew. As they drew closer, he saw that the three that came for him were of the worst kind: younger than him. Flint-hard, razor-sharp, and with that blank-eyed stare that left you in no doubt that you were in all kinds of trouble. There was no fear, no obligation, or guilt here; these people went about their job as professionally as Symonds had gone about his. His foes were now offering neither respite nor apology, the kind of man he would only ever have dreamt of seeking out in a most desperate moment. These people lived on the edge—men who might do what you ask but then equally might do so much more.

"Are you shitting me?" he murmured, looking around, now desperate for a weapon. He noted sourly that his position could not be much worse had he planned it himself. It was dim heading towards dark, with at least two of the six main aisle lights out, probably not repaired due to Agetec's own massive and increasingly disproportionate demands on *Leviathan*'s supply chain. He stood in what his mind quaintly pointed out the French liked to call a cul-de-sac—what he more bluntly thought of as 'a fucking dead end'. This one was found at the bottom of a shallow depression, a natural burr in the rock so far down that it had proven uneconomic to drill out and simply not worthy of the attention of the nanomytes, and so it had just surfaced over. "And this is where you ran us to, you fool," his mind screeched dangerously at him, and he laughed out loud, a strange, flat, cackling laugh. The enforcer had no weapons and not even a decent surface to back himself up against.

A middle-aged man named Sigmund Symonds then spied a heavy steel bulkhead about twenty feet ahead and to one side of his greeting party. He wondered briefly if he could make it up the slope in time to beat the three approaching hardmen. He was uncertain, and in the instant of that uncertainty, he decided to hold his ground; he felt he was mastering his fear. Just…well, that was what he told himself. He did not want to die, and as he stared into the slate-grey, pitiless eyes of the centremost of the three approaching men, he thought that was entirely likely. He was keeping it under control, but he was still searching for that centre, that calm in the eye of the hurricane that his instincts told him lay somewhere just outside his reach. He had never been a man to seek sympathy, and so he would go down fighting.

"What do you want?" he rumbled, trying to mask anxiety with an attempt at brute temper, and as he heard his voice speak, no tremble in the strong bass note, his confidence grew infinitesimally. The middle three assassins held their gaze unblinked as they closed to within a dozen feet. The two winged men, one a slender, black-skinned man, to all appearances fresh from running a marathon across Nigerian mountains in the bleach heat of a blazing summer day, with tight flexing muscles, look ten years Symonds's junior, and though lean, are bare inches shorter. The other man was a brutish, red-headed bull. A Muscovite bar brawler, as might be found in any Moscow-backed alley, and of similar bulk, at least to Symonds himself. They split as they closed in on him and began to flank him on either side.

Sigmund felt no consolation as he realised that he would not have made it to the bulkhead he had spied moments before. This proved scant satisfaction in his current predicament. The middle of the three approaching killers appeared to be of Asian descent, or maybe a little Tibetan, Symonds surmised; it was not easy to be certain in the dim light. Dammit, I'm gonna be killed by Attila the Hun. His mind roared at him. That one, too, was perhaps a decade younger than Sigmund, and, if it were possible, more even than the other two, he looked taut and athletic. More than anything, he appeared unutterably confident in his ability to dish it out and in his ability to kill a man. Attila the Hun seemed to consider the other man's question for a moment, all the while ensuring that all three men were placing Sigmund Symonds in a position from which there would be no escape. He smiled at his victim and, finding his own voice, said in little more than a whisper, "You know."

Then, after a brief pause, during which time he slipped a wicked glinting steel blade out from inside his heavy canvas jacket, "You've done this dance before, eh, mister? Danced on a few, I heard tell." Symonds had no reply, as his complete attention was taken by the nasty-looking death-dealing knife that the other man had taken to swishing gently in arcs as he inched closer. It made a noise as it whisked through the air; the swishing noise was the sound of death. Symonds was aware peripherally that the others were also armed, and so his fullest fears were realised. One man held a heavy-looking steel-headed mallet, which he took to rhythmically thudding against the rock of the wall he skirted. In another, Symonds saw from the corner of his eye and held a mean, single-bladed axe. The axe had a long handle, and the wide-shouldered Muscovite hard man dropped the head of the axe onto the floor and allowed it to drag slowly and menacingly.

They mean to kill you, and his imagination squealed at him quite unnecessarily. Panicky speaks to a recalcitrant son in the voice of his mother, an echo from so long ago as to make him start with surprise. The man knew he had to play for time; when it started, it would all be over really quickly. Where that damn icy calm was, his father spoke up, though of course he could not have known that it was his father's voice he heard had his father not been up and gone in the night when he was barely two years old. And though his mother had lectured him incessantly down the years after that his father was a vagrant and a bad man to the core, still it seemed he had made it here in the end.

He wondered, had that then really been true, or had he just run in the night from the control that his mother exerted? She was like Jupiter's gravity, holding in sway and close orbit all but anything that came within her domain. It had taken her death for him to break free, for Sigmund Symonds to run away, to run straight into her arms. He stopped at that, turned away from his father's voice, turned away from facing that ultimate truth, and turned back to the moment at hand. And finally, with icy detachment, he stared back at his enemies. He thought he might get a lick or two in if he was lucky, but what of that? Then he would go down, and like an ageing bull elephant taken down by the pride of starving young lions, once he was on the ground, they would tear his living body apart, completely oblivious to his screaming.

"Can we deal on this?" he asked, the question an obvious no-go, but maybe giving him a few seconds more. Attila the Hun did not bother to speak; he just shook his head, as if waking from sleep, and settled into a hunter's crouch as he prepared to pounce. Symonds raised his fists boxer-style and, in a last-ditch attempt, turned to the ginger-haired bull, instinctively deciding that his luck might be better away from the knifeman.

"So, what, none of you got the balls to give an old man a fighting chance?" He hoped this might at least appeal to the vanity of the brawler; he looked most like the one who might enjoy a bit of rough and tumble.

The reply was swift. "We aren't being paid to rough you up, skin-kin; be giving you chances, be givin up our pay cheque, you skiv?"

This one held the heavy hammer, and as he spoke, he smacked it menacingly into the open palm of his free hand; it slapped loudly, suddenly sharp, and in the moment. "Don you worry ol man, we gonna hurt you bad, we gonna like it too, you ain't popular, easy genie man, you are all outta the bottle now, an it's time to wipe you," he finished his statement, slipping briefly deep into native down below slang as his excitement began to rise.

Sigmund Symonds spied terror circling him like a flock of buzzards, and so, understanding that his time was done and that he was about to slide over the edge of the panic waterfall, he grabbed every last ounce of whatever he had left and, lunging forward, desperately charged at the red head. In the end, after all the running and debating back and forth in his slowly sliding mind, he had no plan nor any true hope, and so, finally resigned to his fate, he just wanted to get the thing over with. Anything had to be better than the creeping terror growing inside him, along with the complete dismantling of the man and the image of a man he had spent a lifetime building.

And so, he swung both of his massive meat-and-gristle fists towards the redhead's face, like two projectiles, one instantly following the other. He felt an almost instant buzz of satisfaction as one of his big fists connected squarely. At the same moment, Symonds heard from very far away a distant roaring, like the coming of a great storm. He thought about the warriors at Helm's Deep, when the few had held on, and at last, when night had been at its darkest and the horde of the enemy, killed in their droves, had seemed not diminished at all, and then that first sliver of light presaging a new day. A new day brought the great wizard Mithrandir, Gandalf Greyhame, and the men of Erkenbrand and the West. So, at the end of all things, and beyond all hope, the day had yet to be saved. And so, it was with Sigmund Symonds, still hoping, at the end of all things, who had just the merest moment to register that the roaring was him: he was screaming before dying, one last terrible eruption of pent-up emotion before everything went blinding red.

Suddenly, pain assailed him; it was like nothing he had known in his life up to that point. Had he but known it, the bull-man had connected with his temple with a glancing blow with his club hammer, just as Symonds's own monstrous fist had collided with the other man's face. Both blows had affected the other, and as a consequence, instead of the hammer blow killing him outright, as it would have done had it caught him square, and as it was very much meant to, instead the blow glanced off the right side of his head, and Symonds went down moments later like that bull elephant, having taken the hunter's round rather than the lion's teeth. The older man began to lose consciousness as he slammed into the floor hard, the tough plastocrete pushing the air sharply from his lungs. As the enforcer faded away, he wondered at the absence of any more punishment, although he was sure it was coming. But then, curious in that uncertain dark alley of death, he thought he heard a ringing. His head was ringing, but it sounded remarkably like the squawk and buzz of one of *Leviathan*'s transmitters.

"Better get that, it could be the phone," his imagination spoke up, funny till the end. Of course, there were no phones, not on *Leviathan*; it was entirely impossible to fashion a network with the millions of tonnes of rock, iron, and lead, the two fission reactors and their radioactive signals, let alone the spin-ward motion far out in the vacuum of deep space. It was an old-fashioned radio transmitters, and they had proven patchy at best in the great whale—just one more way in which humanity had begun the slow slide back down the bell curve.

Darkness closed on him like a tunnel, scooping him up and removing him from the travails of the moment. Sigmund Symonds slipped away, blood pouring from an open gash in his head, three badly cracked ribs, and a broken collarbone. For certain, he did not hear the conversation between the heads of the three henchmen and one mistress, which then took place. He knew nothing of the momentous events that were taking place twenty or so decks above him as he drifted, deep now out cold and sleeping like a baby.

Nevertheless, through the amazing twists that fate or whatever had provided, the man found his own Helm's Deep. He would indeed wake up and live to see another day. A new day, a day different from any that had gone before.

Lyle Cardington came to; he was groggy and thick-headed. "What's happening?" he drawled, finding himself propped up against a chair. It slowly dawned on him that he was laboratory number four, the place where much of his life had been invested in recent years. Then, as he tried to focus on the other people in the room to cope with the blinding headache that was assaulting him, it all came back to him in an instant, slamming into him like a rocket crash landing—supersonic impact!

"Where are they?" he asked, meaning the girls, still trying to draw his vision together sufficiently to tell who he was sharing the room with. Cardington tried to stand and found that he was falling down again. Then he felt strong arms lifting him, holding him, and helping him rise to an upright position. For a few moments, he rocked with that low blood pressure sensation, but his body finally won that brief skirmish, and his head began to clear. The lab had some visitors, it seemed, new faces that brought no recognition from the scientist, but the girls were not there with them.

"What happened?" he asked urgently, and a voice responded immediately and cut through his haze: it was Ariel. Lyle looked sideways, and there she stood, now flanked by the two largest, meanest-looking personal security men he had ever seen. He thought it might well have been one of those two giants who had stepped behind him and helped him up moments before.

"Zsiobhan Sildar hit you, Lyle. Not all of us, it seems, were in agreement with your plans."

Cardington was shocked. Sildar was one of Ariel's closest allies, and to risk everything like that, he must have felt strongly. He was indeed a desperate man. "What about the girls?" he demanded. "What about Muriel? How much time?"

Ariel was silent for moments longer than she might have been, and as his senses returned, Lyle feared the worst. Damn our future, he thought, and he could see no further than Muriel. But as desperation began to raid his thoughts, Ariel spoke again.

"Calm down and get yourself right, Lyle Cardington; it is done, everything, all done. We called the medic down, as you were out for the count."

"Yes, yes, but Muriel, how is she? Where is she? I need to see her," Lyle interrupted. But then, as he looked into Ariel's face, he stopped in his tracks, astonished by what he saw there. There were tears streaming down Tsaritsa's face. She had always been beautiful; nobody would ever have denied her that. Tragically beautiful, like some princess of a tale a little too perfect for this world of mere mortals, but somehow the grief, the pure naked strength of seeing someone who had always been so indomitable, so inscrutable, so in control of herself. The lady was humanised by those floods of tears in a way she herself might never have discovered without the intervention of two small girls.

Humbled, the scientist reached out and gently took one of Ariel MP's delicate pale hands, and, looking into her tear-filled eyes, he kissed that hand. "My lady, we have all learned today more than we may ever know."

She smiled at him, and the light in her face lifted her up about ninety-nine of one hundred steps in his estimation. "You're crying," he said, stating the obvious.

"She's gone," Ariel responded, smiling a little weaker. "She asked us to do it, told us to, in fact, and we did. I know she wasn't really the child that we saw; she couldn't have been, not really." Ariel paused and silently motioned the two guards away from her side before continuing, "But she's gone, and I didn't really think about that until she did it. I didn't really understand. I've spent my whole life asleep, Lyle Cardington, Master of Science."

Lyle looked back at the woman and saw and understood that, in the face of Hermione's courage and her simple determination to do the right thing, Ariel had seen the light and had received her own moment of enlightenment. An epiphany for all humankind.

"She knew what she was doing, Ariel. She came to us and thanked God for what she did. Now we must make it count, for her, for Muriel, for all of our sakes. Anything less would be an insult to what she gave to us, and I, for one, cannot allow that. You are a great lady, Ariel MP; you have earned the right to lead us all. No more politics, no recriminations; we have all gotten lost, I think, in bitterness, manoeuvring, and manipulation. It has gone on for too long now; we need to find our way past all that. Perhaps we've all been in hibernation deep inside the belly of Moby-Dick."

Moments earlier, the scientist had let go of her hand, but he took it again now, and she did not resist, and he looked at her and spoke with passionate urgency.

"You need to find us a way past this, a way to heal for all of us, to move on from all that has happened up until today, Ariel. Now you must really earn your stripes…Now you must lead us," he paused, but only for a moment, catching his breath before continuing, "And me, well, I need to see my daughter now, and then I need to find out if I am truly the master scientist that you hope." And then, after a pause, "By the way, where is Hermione?" he stopped awkwardly. "Well, her body, where is she now?" he said this last, stumbling a little with the words.

"Hermione lies at peace and is in the room next door to your daughter. Shall we go together? I would like to look in on them both one more time. It's funny, but even though I only knew Hermione Zatapec for the shortest time, I find that I miss her already. I think it must always be that way when you encounter someone who only gives…Your daughter, Muriel has lost a very special friend." Ariel said this last wistfully whilst taking a hold of Lyle Cardington's arm and shooting the security men in front of her.

As they walked slowly out of Laboratory Four, swinging open one of the double doors, Cardington turned and said, "Not Hermione Zatapec, dear Tsaritsa; she was Hermione Wise, and for all our sakes, she was the wisest of us all."

He did not know if the lady heard that last because, at that moment, a man approached from the corridor's other end. They both looked up at a quiet cough from that man, and so it was that the critical trio were re-joined once more. From there, standing perhaps twenty feet distant, was Sigmund Symonds. He appeared to them both dishevelled, and even at that distance, they could both see he was holding a blood-soaked cloth over the right side of his head. He smiled a little carefully at them, and for the man that he had been, Sigmund Symonds approached them both more than a little diffidently, clutching a bandage over his scalp and an arm across his ribcage. Lyle looked at the woman holding tightly onto his arm, saw that her complexion had paled, guessed what might have happened, and thought he understood now who Ariel MP had been urgently speaking with on a small communicator in those last moments before he had been himself knocked unconscious.

In that very same moment of desperate action, after so much desperate inaction, she had, it seemed, chosen to send her chief bulldog to the knacker's yard. But as Cardington glanced between them both, he realised it was unfair. As much as it had taken him, as much as it had taken Ariel, it had needed Sigmund Symonds to bring the circle to completion. And so, for that epiphany right at the end, that moment when Hermione had got them all to finally understand the futility of what they were doing and how they were behaving towards one another, turned them all on their heads. Symonds had been a part of that circle, and the scientist was glad the lady had relented and swallowed the greater part of her narcissistic pride to save the man he knew she loved. Someone who had stood behind her shoulder for many long years. She waved at him and whispered something almost inaudible, which Cardington thought sounded remarkably like 'Thank you, God'. She was moving now towards the big man, with the same urgent fervour he felt about getting to his daughter, reaching out to Symonds with both her arms proffered.

Had she realised that they might need Symonds? Cardington had to admit that he was a talented man who got things done. No, he decided, it was more than that: this woman looked at the wounded man now standing in front of her, clasping tightly together her delicate, tiny hands. This had hurt her grievously; she had learned a whole new kind of pain, and in doing so, had closed the circle in her own world and become someone new upon her path.

Lyle Cardington stepped forward, leaned close to the lady, and whispered in her ear, nudging her closer towards her man. "He loves you, Ariel; he always has; be with him now…I think you have both found your penance."

He peered at her, at both of them, and she shook her head minutely. "I can't, don't you see?"

Cardington replied, and it seemed he had grown large in the events that had passed, "It doesn't matter what you did. Hermione said it: past is past. Care for your man, Lady Ariel; let him forgive you as we must now all forgive."

Ariel half-turned, stared at him for long seconds, and then ushered into a tight embrace with the man she had nearly killed, the man who had stood waiting, not speaking a word. It was her man, and she now realised she loved him right back. As Lyle Cardington turned, he saw through an open door his daughter lying, gently sleeping, and turning back. He caught a final glimpse of the two of them standing awkwardly for long moments holding on, neither one willing to let go. And the scientist did not spy on a passionate embrace; what he saw were two children. Two frightened and angry children who had fought their respective prides to a standstill. He thought that perhaps Hermione Zatapec had been righter than she knew and that maybe they would make it out of this mess, after all.

Much later, when others had retired from the great dramas of the day, when children slept in their beds and adults held on to one another to find solace in the cold and the dark, Lyle Cardington was sitting in his laboratory office. That same darkness surrounded him, broken only by the soft circular glow cast by his small desk lamp. The closing of another day's quiet lay all around him, with only the merest thrum of the *Leviathan*'s generators to keep him company as they, too, continued their bid to protect the lives of sixty thousand disparate souls. They were, perhaps, the last tribe of humanity that they did not know.

The scientist had seen his daughter, Muriel and had begun what he hoped was a long road to fatherly redemption. His daughter had tried to understand what it was that had happened to her; having suffered debilitating cancer for the previous eight years, hospitals and all that went with them were nothing new. But for the longest time, she simply could not grasp where Hermione had gone, and Lyle had realised very early that he would need to work hard in the weeks and months to come in order to fill the huge void that one old, young lady, mother, sister, and daughter had left. The father relished the opportunity, no longer daunted at his daughter's well of love and at her unquenchable passion for life. And that was why he was here now, he reminded himself. He knew in the days to come that he would be battling to reverse-engineer his daughter's new blood and the DNA changes that would result, that he would be finding every moment that he could to spend with her as she recovered and hopefully began coming to terms with all that had happened and all that lay ahead. And Cardington understood that he would play his own pivotal role in the new world that was to be *Leviathan* moving forward; he was, after all, the scientist.

But for now, he had one more thing to do, and he wanted to do that before all of the other chaos ripped him away from this moment.

He pulled up a brown leather bag that he had placed carefully on the floor under his desk some hours before. In the battered brown schoolmaster's case, according to Ariel MP, Miss Hermione held on right until the end, her infant fingers eventually being gently prised off the handles by one of the medics only after she had passed away. Lyle felt nervous; he wondered what might be inside that had demanded so much from both the woman and child. A treasure kept so close, in spite of all that stood in the way, right until the end. He felt like an intruder, as one might feel entering the home of someone only recently deceased, and he supposed that was true.

Hermione had been surviving down below even before she had first been brought to him as a test candidate, and so he guessed that the bag was as close to a home as she had in those later years. Once more, he reminded himself that she really had not been a child at all for the vast majority of the past few years. And, indeed, even at her death, she still had the wisdom, experience, and lifetime of pain invested in a woman who had more than seventy years on her clock. Despite all that, though, ironically, it was a desire to respect the memory of that woman/girl that had driven him to this moment.

So it was that he was weeping softly as his fingers, struggling through the blur of fresh tears, attempted to release the latch. After a minute or so, he succeeded, and, overcoming the butterflies he felt, he gently tugged open the bag. He was not able to see anything distinct as he sought to look inside, and so he reached carefully in and fished around for several moments. He felt like a child with a lucky dip. At first, he thought the bag was empty, but then he heard, at the same moment as felt, the rustle of paper. He carefully removed what turned out to be a single folded piece of paper, a small booklet, and a single aged photograph. He laid the three items out on his desk, checked thoroughly the interior of the case, and found nothing else within it. He did discover, previously unseen in the room's dim light, a set of initials inlaid on the underside of the case's locking flap, and there was imprinted J.D.W.

Lyle wiped his eyes with the back of one hand and turned first to the small booklet. All three items appear to be old. The book, perhaps four inches by two and a half by a bare half-inch thick, turned out to be a copy of *Siddhartha* by Herman Hesse. He opened the book gently and saw it inscribed on the inside of the front cover, *'For my wife, for our journey, with love....Joseph'*. Lyle turned next to the photograph; he had deliberately placed it on his desk, face downwards. It, too, was ancient, of a variety only very rarely seen on board over the past quarter of a century, having long since been superseded by more digital media formats. He saw that on the back of the small photo, perhaps two inches by three, which had yellowed considerably, was faded writing. He could not see the imprint fully, but the script had once upon a time been beautifully written, in what he thought had probably been a blue fountain pen. But that had subsequently faded to an almost invisible pink.

He squinted at it but could only make out the last part of a date scrawled at the end of a two-line entry. 'May 2010'. He turned the snapshot over, and the breath was taken instantly from his lungs as the image of a small girl stared back at him. It was Hermione. From the date, he understood this was, in fact, a snapshot of Hermione Zatapec at perhaps six years old, but it wasn't his Hermione. The clothes and simple hair tied in a ponytail were different from the girl that he had known, and yet the smile, the pretty, simple face, and the intensity in her eyes still shone through nearly seventy years after the snap had been taken. It had knocked him back, seeing her like that, and he suddenly found her more real, more rounded; he felt her tragedy far more than at any moment since he had met her.

The final item that he had placed carefully on the table was an ancient, faded single sheet of what once appeared to have been heavy velour writing paper, a small sheet folded into four. He reached for it and found that his hand was shaking badly. Drawing that hand back, he wondered for long moments what there was left to be afraid about. And so, bolstering himself mentally, after a few more moments, he pushed his hand out once again and gingerly picked up the sheet of paper. He had anticipated that such an old piece of paper would feel dry and brittle, but surprisingly, it had not; instead, it felt heavy, almost oily. He still could not quell the sense of anxiety, and yet he could not put his finger on why. He told himself that the page must contain something pretty darn important for Hermione to have carried it with her for so long.

The plain white sheet was folded into four, and he unravelled it in moments. Inside, he read, in the same beautiful handwriting as had appeared on the reverse of the photograph, the following message: *Hermione. Be good to everyone you meet, and life will pay you back double. Mama.* This was followed by three x's, indicating kisses. Lyle Cardington sat silent and unmoving for a long time after reading the note. Had you been standing outside the circle of light cast by the lamp on his desk, you would not have seen the steady tears that trickled down his cheeks. Although he sat absolutely still, inside his mind was a raging tempest.

He tried to visualise what could possibly have happened to a girl all those years ago. Had she awoken one morning and found a world in which she had no foothold? He could not know what had happened or why she had held on to this simple note all the intervening years. But the fact that the woman had held onto these small tokens for a lifetime suggested some sort of finality. And yet Hermione had grown to maturity, managed to climb up the crap heap, survived the nuclear-ravaged world that they all faced, and thereafter found a place aboard *Leviathan*. Lyle wondered at so many questions they would never have answers to. Hermione Zatapec: What was her story? The scientists wondered whether there was, in fact, anyone left who might tell them.

His mind continued to wander, his thoughts warm against the dark night chill. It had slowly dawned on him that he would probably never know. Whatever modicum of a trail to a woman's roots there might once have been, it would now only exist on a planet that no one aboard *Leviathan* would ever return to. Last but not least, Lyle considered how Hermione Zatapec, née Wise, had, once aboard that great interstellar craft, managed to slide below the waterline, eventually sinking into some other existence down below. Down below, he had never considered it before, but it did have connotations with the Devil's Lair. Hell was, after all, 'down below'. And as if that had not been enough, then subsequently the old lady had been introduced to him. "Be good to who you meet, and life will pay you back double," he hissed quietly to himself. But it seemed all the self-recrimination had drained out of the man of science. Instead, it had slowly blossomed—a determination to honour a human being's memory.

He sat for a longer time, deep in the dark, shadowy recesses of the small space that had been his home. He allowed his eyes to dry, and then, finally, with a wintry smile dancing across his pale features, he rose and, flicking the switch, turned off the desk lamp and, in darkness, left the room.

Epilogue

The headline 'Agetec discovers the secret to eternal life' *appeared yesterday on the front page of the electronic daily download, the public order news sheet available to all on board* Leviathan. *Twenty-four hours later, word has spread quickly that this is no hoax. The news has done much to calm the riots that spread across the craft in the aftermath of Ariel MP's announcement some weeks ago that* Leviathan *remains more than two light years out from Tinkerbell, the planet many had taken to calling Future Earth.*

The article went on to credit Lyle Cardington's team, a biochemist and DNA specialist, with the genetic discovery that many are hailing as a miracle. An Agetec spokesperson stated, 'This discovery will double a healthy human lifespan. Further tremendous benefits, including remedial illness discoveries, have been tested and demonstrated in resultant treatments for wide-ranging conditions.'

And so Agetec has accorded Lyle Cardington the title of 'The Scientist', a man who perhaps has shone a warm light on all mankind after so many dark days.

According to a subsequent statement issued from the laboratories of the biotech firm, a number of people who prefer to remain unnamed have proven absolutely vital to the recent sudden and unanticipated progress.

Volunteers for initial trials will be sought from the beginning of the next thirty days, with public availability planned by the end of the year. A further surprise was the statement that the treatment would be freely available to everyone aboard.

In response to the announcement initiated by the office of Agetec's Sigmund Symonds, Ariel MP made a rare public appearance. During a walk around the below-ground district, she spoke to several groups and made a robust effort to quell the fears of residents there. Tsaritsa was seen with a number of denominational heads as she hailed the news as nothing short of a miracle.

Ariel went on to underline how age-reversion therapy would prove a critical component in devising a new strategy to cope with the extended journey. Whilst some other community leaders responded less enthusiastically, expressing concerns over the effect of messing with the gift of life, Ms MP, as redoubtable and resourceful as ever, deferred to the voice of her 'new' religious council to address these matters of faith.

In other news, a small statue has been unveiled in the uppermost forward viewing gallery at the entrance to Waterfall Park.

A small bronze cast of a satchel, engraved with the message, 'Be good to who you meet, and life will pay you back double.'

THE END

"Out beyond ideas of wrongdoing and rightdoing, there is a field. I'll meet you there.
When the soul lies down in that grass, the world will be too full to talk about."